Make Me Scream

Books by P.J. Mellor

PLEASURE BEACH

GIVE ME MORE

MAKE ME SCREAM

THE COWBOY
(with Vonna Harper, Nelissa Donovan and Nikki Alton)

THE FIREFIGHTER
(with Susan Lyons and Alyssa Brooks)

NAUGHTY, NAUGHTY
(with Melissa MacNeal and Valerie Martinez)

Published by Kensington Publishing Corporation

Make Me Scream

P.J. MELLOR

APHRODISIA

KENSINGTON BOOKS
http://www.kensingtonbooks.com

APHRODISIA BOOKS are published by

Kensington Publishing Corp.
850 Third Avenue
New York, NY 10022

ISBN-13: 978-0-7582-2023-3
ISBN-10: 0-7582-2023-5

First Kensington Trade Paperback Printing: February 2008

10 9 8 7 6 5 4 3 2 1

Printed in the United States of America

To Emily Suzanne Mellor. See you later, baby gator!

As always, special thanks to my wonderful editor, John Scognamiglio—it's taken me a while, but I can now not only pronounce his last name, I can actually spell it!

Thanks, too, to my husband, Michael, for taking on laundry duty while I write. Good job, babe!

And thanks to my martini lunch bunch—you know who you are!—for listening to me whine and helping me brainstorm, even if sometimes it was more like only a drizzle.

1

Hip deep in drug dealers, rogue cops, prostitutes and assorted bad guys, aspiring mystery writer Devon McCloud frowned and tried to recapture his train of thought.

The PI hero of Devon's book had just discovered the lead witness for the crime family hiding naked in his bed.

> *The woman stroked my impressive erection.*
>
> *"Are you going to kick me out?" the buxom blonde asked with a sultry pout.*
>
> *"Something just came up," I replied.*
>
> *"I can help you with that," she whispered, stroking my length.*
>
> *"Put your mouth where your money is," I hissed in a breath when she took my advice. Her mouth closed over me, practically swallowing me whole.*

Okay . . . now what? The flashing cursor on the screen of his laptop mocked him.

Out in the courtyard of the little beachfront apartment community he managed as his day job, voices rumbled. His fellow tenants were starting their nightly celebration early.

Above the laughter and conversations, a deep bark sounded, followed by the shrill voice of his neighbor, Francyne Anderson. Devon's mouth quirked. Petunia, Francyne's one-hundred-and-fifty-pound rottweiler, must be joining the party tonight.

Deliberately shutting out the noise in the courtyard, Devon narrowed his gaze at the flashing cursor.

"C'mon, Mac, be brilliant. What would Trent say?" Trent was the hero of his work-in-progress, *Darkness Becomes Her*. A PI with the prerequisite heart of gold, Trent not only got all the bad guys, he got all the girls.

Devon sighed and rocked back in his desk chair. Maybe that was the problem with finishing the book. Trent had scored approximately every five to seven pages. He, Devon, hadn't been laid in months. Heading way too close to being a year. He didn't have the time, which made him an even more pathetic loser. Who doesn't have time for sex?

Voices rose in the courtyard.

Him, that's who didn't have time for sex. Devon Edward McCloud. With working on his novels by night, writing catalog copy for sex toys by day—which oddly did not help his lack-of-sex problem—while attempting to maintain some sense of normalcy with the rowdy tenants of the Surfside Villas apartment complex, who had the time or energy for sex?

Male laughter vibrated his walls. Opportunity wouldn't hurt either. Of the eight apartments in the old complex, five were occupied by men (six, counting himself), the seventh occupied by a female at least eighty if she was a day. And one vacant unit. Not a lot of opportunity.

He'd just returned to the seedier side of his imagination when a knock sounded on his door. Judging by the lightness of it, his deductive reasoning told him, it was a female knock.

Since Francyne never knocked, it could mean only one thing: someone inquiring about the vacancy.

He growled and saved his work before closing his computer. Obviously the intruder could not tell time. The sign on his door clearly stated office hours. Said hours ended—he glanced at the old school clock on his wall—almost two hours ago.

He threw open his door.

The short, blond woman in a denim miniskirt and yellow tank top hopped back with a squeak.

"Yes?" No point in being polite. Once Blondie got a look at the group sitting around the fire pit in the courtyard, she'd realize this was not the place for her.

She swallowed and licked soft-looking pink lips. "Is—is . . . I mean, are you the manager, the person I need to see about renting an apartment?"

He turned to look meaningfully at the manager sign on his door. "Looks like it, doesn't it?" He tapped the posted hours. "But I'm closed. Office hours don't start again until nine tomorrow morning. Come back then, if you're still interested."

"But I need a place tonight!"

He paused midslam. "Try a motel."

"They're all full. At least, all the close ones." She looked down at her painted toenails peeking out from a pair of ridiculously high-heeled sandals.

He tried not to speculate how short she would be without the heels. He tried not to notice her Barbie-doll build. He also tried not to appreciate the way the firelight from the courtyard played in the silky strands of her blond hair. He failed miserably on all counts.

She looked back up at him, and he forced himself not to break eye contact with her baby blues. She blinked, her long eyelashes creating spidery shadows on her smooth cheeks.

"Please?" Her shiny lower lip gave the faintest of quivers.

"Fine." He spouted off the price of rent, and she nodded. "Don't you want to see it first?"

"No, I'm sure it's fine. The sign said it's furnished?"

He nodded, sure this was a very bad idea but at a loss as to how he could turn her down. Her resulting smile sent a flash of awareness streaking through him. Or . . . did men have hot flashes?

He cleared his throat and stepped back, opening the door wide. "Okay, may as well come on in and get the paperwork out of the way so we can all get some sleep tonight."

"Jamie Cartwright," Blond Barbie said as she stepped in, extending her hand.

A low growl emanated from behind the recliner. "Killer!" he warned, glaring at the pair of glowing eyes visible from below the edge of the chair.

The woman gasped and jumped back, eyes wide, hand at her throat.

Reality dawned. "No! Not me," he explained, pointing to the eyes. "My dog. That's his name. Killer. I'm Devon. Not Killer." He forced a smile. No one would guess he worked with words for a living. He shoved his hand toward her. "Hi."

She took a tentative step forward and allowed him to shake her small hand. "Hi." She looked in his dog's general direction. "What kind of dog is Killer? Is he dangerous?"

"I'll let you be the judge of that." Grinning, he slapped his thigh.

After Devon-not-Killer released her hand, Jamie edged toward the door. Did she really want to rent a place with a killer dog in residence?

At that moment, a ball of white fluff pulled itself out from under the dark leather chair to prance toward them. It looked like it had originally been a Pomeranian before something awful had happened to its face.

Its right eye hung lower than the left, and the poor thing appeared to be missing its bottom jaw. Its pink tongue hung out of its face. Seeing her, it stopped and made a low gurgling growl and then said, "Lark! Lark!"

"He's getting better with his barking," Devon said. "At least now it sounds like he's trying to bark." He squatted and rubbed the dog's shaggy white head. "You're getting better, aren't you, pal?"

In response, Killer raised his nose, tongue lolling down the front of his throat, obviously in doggie-hero worship.

"What happened to his jaw?" she asked Devon-not-Killer.

"He got in a fight. He's lucky all he lost was part of his lower jaw." He grinned and patted the dog's back before straightening. "Also lucky for him, I happened to be passing by the pound the day before they were going to destroy him."

She looked from dog to master. "And you just happened to be strolling past the pound and wondered if they had any dogs they were about to execute?"

He looked sheepish. "Not quite. I'm the one who found him and took him there after the other dog left him for dead. When I found out they were going to put him down, fate intervened and . . ." He shrugged. "Well, I decided I must need a dog." His vivid green gaze met hers. "Do you believe in fate, Jamie?" His voice was low, intimate, sending shivers to her extremities.

She blinked, breaking the spell, and looked around his apartment. "Ah, no, not really."

"Neither did I, but Francyne—that's my neighbor—swears by it. She's made a believer out of me. Well, at least where Killer is concerned, anyway." He shuffled through a pile of papers on an old desk and then waved a fistful of blue ones. "Here's the lease, if you want to read it over."

"Is that necessary?" Being in the same room with Killer was

beginning to affect her allergies. A sinus headache wove its fingers across her forehead and around her eyes. Eyes that were definitely beginning to itch.

"No, it's pretty much standard. First and last month. No real lease time. It's month to month." He gave a bark of laughter. "Francyne suspects it's because the owners plan to sell it to developers and don't want anything standing in their way in case they get an offer."

"Is that what you think, too?" She stepped closer.

He shrugged, trying to ignore her warm, powdery scent. "I dunno. She's lived here for a couple of decades. I've worked here for three years, and it hasn't happened yet."

Jamie took the pen he offered, sneezed and bent over the table to begin filling out and signing the lease.

"Bless you," he muttered, then added a prayer of thanks while he eyed the cleavage revealed when she bent over the table. The firm globes pushing the neckline of her pink sweater to the edge of decency were roughly the size of small cantaloupes and defied gravity. He salivated and resisted the urge to rearrange his enlarging package.

Jamie sensed the manager eyeing her cleavage and resisted the urge to cover up.

"Drop that vibrator!" a heavily Southern-accented female voice shouted. "Stop that damn dog! Petunia! Drop it right now!"

Jamie paused and looked up.

A huge black dog galloped into the apartment, knocking over a small wooden chair and an end table in its wake.

Hot on the dog's heels was a deeply tanned, small woman with snowy white hair. Dressed in a brightly colored muumuu that fluttered around her slight frame, her small feet shod in white socks and sturdy walking shoes, she was a hair's breadth from catching the animal.

"Petunia!" The old lady rounded the couch to head off the

dog who, Jamie now realized, had what appeared to be a purple vibrator in its massive jaws.

The dog faked a left and then darted around the woman.

Before Jamie could form her next coherent thought, the warm feel of fur against her skin registered, followed immediately by a jarring thump as her rear end met the tiled floor beside the dining table.

"Petunia!" Devon grabbed for the dog's collar, missed and ended up tackling and wrestling her to the ground. Panting, he looked over his shoulder at Jamie.

Sitting with her hands braced behind her back, her legs slightly apart, she belatedly realized he could see clear up to her crotch.

"Are you hurt?" he asked.

Numb, she shook her head and tugged on her denim miniskirt then slowly got to her feet.

"Petunia," the older woman said, grasping the big dog's collar and hauling her to her feet. "What am I going to do with you? Give me that! Release!"

She pulled the dripping purple dildo out of the dog's mouth and grimaced. "Oh, yuck. Now you've gone and chewed up another one." She tossed it into a wastebasket overflowing with paper. Magnified blue eyes peered at Jamie through trifocal lenses. "Hello. How you doing? Isn't she just the sweetest thing, Devon?"

Devon mumbled something threatening-sounding. The woman grinned.

"Bless your heart," she said to no one in particular as far as Jamie could tell. "I bet you're here for the job."

"Job?" Devon and Jamie said as one.

"Sexual-aids product tester." With scarcely a breath in between sentences, she continued. "How do you do? I'm Francyne Anderson. I'm the one who put the ad in the paper, but Devon is the one you'll be working with."

2

"Excuse us," Devon said to Jamie. Grasping Francyne's upper arm, he all but dragged the older woman out of his apartment. "Sexual-aids tester?" he asked in a hissing voice once they were on the other side of the door. "An ad? Have you lost your mind?"

"Hey, I'm an old woman! You wouldn't want me to have a heart attack, would you?" Francyne tugged her arm from his grasp. "Darlin', you know I love you like the grandson I never had. But, well, face it, your love life is pitiful. I thought maybe—"

"I can't believe I'm having this conversation with an eighty-year-old woman," he mumbled, forking his fingers through his hair then gripping his skull. "Francyne, I can get my own women!"

"Oh, is that right? And for your information, I'm still seventy-nine. Won't be eighty until fall." Fists on hips, she glared up at him. "About those women you can allegedly get ... well, hotshot, I haven't noticed a harem coming and going from your apartment. In fact, as far as I can tell, until today, Petunia and I have been the only females to come around for nigh onto a year now."

"Thanks for pointing that out. But . . . a sex-aids tester?" He leaned down to look her in the eye. "What were you thinking?"

Francyne sniffed and glared right back. "Maybe that you'd finally get lucky?" Her shoulders slumped. "Hell, I was just trying to help. Face it, I'm old. I can't do justice to product testing like I once could. Guess I thought I could find a replacement and get you a girl in one fell swoop." Glancing coyly up through her lashes, she said, "She's not married, is she?"

"Hmmm?" His active imagination had Blond Barbie stripped naked, spread on his table, helping him test the shipment of new flavored condoms. "Oh. Um, I don't know. I don't think so." Would his knees hold up to climb up onto the table with her? Not that it mattered. The old table probably wouldn't support their combined weight, not to mention any action.

Francyne smacked him on the butt as they walked toward his door. "Go get her, tiger! I'll just collect Petunia, and we'll be on our way." She winked. "You can thank me in the morning."

Jamie scratched and eyed the big black dog and then warily shifted on the hard seat of the old wooden chair. The dog did not even blink. Jamie gauged the distance to the door and realized the dog would be on her before she reached it. She hadn't survived this long, come this far, to end up *Jamie Chow*.

Devon and the old lady, Francyne, stepped back into the apartment.

"Petunia!" Francyne rushed to grasp the rottweiler's collar. "Shame on you, scaring our new neighbor!" She looked at Jamie. "She's really harmless."

"More than harmless," Devon piped in. "She's such a coward, she lets Killer boss her around."

As if to demonstrate, Killer trotted over and proceeded to hump the huge dog.

"Killer! Knock it off!" Devon grabbed his dog and dragged

it away from Petunia. Devon grinned. "He was neutered at the shelter, but he still has high hopes."

Francyne snorted. "He'd also have to be hung like King Kong to get any action from Petunia."

Jamie shifted from foot to foot. Did she really need the apartment that badly? All the frank sexual talk and activities were more than off-putting. Sex—the act, discussions or otherwise—made her uncomfortable.

"Here is a traveler's check for the first and last month's rent," Jaime said, shoving the check at Devon. "I signed the lease. May I have the key?"

"Uh, sure." Devon looked at her like she was the weirdo. "Let me grab it, and I'll walk you over."

She started to tell him it wasn't necessary, then she remembered the men in the courtyard. "Great."

"Petunia and I need to take a walk," Francyne said, "if we want to get back in time for *Matlock*. Nice to meet you, Jamie." She batted her eyes at Devon and flashed a saccharine smile. "Have a great evening, stud muffin."

The men in the courtyard laughed, and Jamie flinched. Lightly grasping her elbow, Devon steered her to the other side, giving the men a wide berth. While she didn't try to pull away from him, her back straightened, and she picked up her pace.

"Here we are." He stuck the key in the door of unit three and jiggled the knob. "You need to fiddle with it a little, but the key works. After you live here a while, it'll loosen up." At her stare, he babbled on. "I lived here before I was the manager. It's been vacant for a while, but it should still be clean." He swung open the door, reaching in to flip the light switch.

Jamie peeked around Devon's shoulder and scanned the small living room now bathed in the weak light of an ancient-looking floor lamp.

"It's . . . orange," she said. Orange and yellow shag carpeting covered the floor, proving her grandmother's theory that ugly never wears out.

The couch, with its cannonball-wooden-post arms, had plaid upholstery comprised of orange, yellow and lime green bright enough to make your eyes bleed. Next to the saggy couch was a spindly looking end table made of what appeared to be genuine imitation wood. How it held the massive glass lamp with the light-up orange base was a natural phenomenon. The wall behind the furniture was painted a bright orange, too. At least, she thought it was. It could have been reflected from the upholstery.

"And here's the dining area," Devon said, hurrying to flip the switch illuminating a yellow and orange daisy swag lamp dangling precariously over a once white formed plastic table. Stained yellow and orange cushions on the plastic barrel chairs completed the ensemble. Shiny bright yellow and orange large daisy wallpaper covered the end wall.

"I feel like I should say groovy, for some reason." Jamie walked farther into the apartment and peeked into the tiny kitchen. "Are those brown appliances?"

"Um, I think they're called Coppertone."

Biting back a smile, she turned to him. "The owners have never updated?" No wonder the rent was so reasonable.

He stuffed his hands into the front pockets of his jean shorts and rocked back on the heels of his clunky sandals. "Oh, sure, they did. I think it was in 1972." A lopsided grin transformed his face from scruffy to kind of cute. "I told you, we think they're planning to sell the complex."

She nodded and pushed open a door next to the kitchen. At least the bathroom was clean. Small and brilliantly yellow, but clean. "Well, this should wake me up in the mornings."

"Yep, it sure did me, I know." He motioned toward the bathtub. "I left the shower massage. It still works," he added.

"Thanks." She pointed to another door next to the bathroom. "Is that the bedroom?" At his nod, she pushed the door open.

"It's a new mattress."

She gazed at the big bed that practically filled the small room, intensely aware of the heat coming from the man behind her.

Okay, big guy, strip down and let's take this baby for a test drive. She blinked, heat suffusing her cheeks. Where on earth had that thought come from? They'd just met. Sex was bad enough with someone she knew.

"You'll need to get some sheets," he said, close to her ear.

Startled, not to mention horrified, she jumped back, eyes wide. "I don't think so!" Did she have the word *slut* across her forehead?

Devon looked at her like he thought she'd lost her mind and then shrugged. "Whatever. I personally like to sleep on a mattress pad and sheets as opposed to a bare mattress."

Jamie did a mental head slap. *Duh. Get your mind out of the gutter.* "Of course. I knew what you meant." She licked her lips and took a deep breath. "I don't have a car yet. Would you happen to have an extra mattress pad and a set of sheets I could borrow for a couple of days? Just until I can get to a store," she hurried to assure him when his eyes widened.

He nodded. "Sure. I could even spare a blanket. It gets kind of cold at night, especially if you leave the windows open, with the breeze off the Gulf."

"Thanks."

He glanced around. "If you tell me where your stuff is, I can help you carry it in."

She looked at her feet for a second and then met his gaze. "All I have is a small suitcase. I left it outside your door. I hope that's okay. No one will bother it, will they?" To her knowledge, the men in the courtyard had barely acknowledged her existence, but that didn't mean they could be trusted.

"No. It's safe." He shifted his weight from foot to foot. "I'll go get it while you finish looking around."

Practically tripping over his own feet, he didn't breathe until he closed the door behind him.

Following her around the small apartment, watching the sway of her sweet little ass, his shorts had shrunk two sizes. When she'd licked her lips, his respiration changed. Then when she'd puffed out her chest, he thought for sure she'd fall out of the low-cut neckline. That's when he knew he had to get out of there.

He adjusted his shorts and took the long way back to his door in order to get his body to calm down. After months of abstinence, it was primed and ready for action.

Jamie was the first woman in a long time his dick had been even remotely happy to see. He sure as hell didn't want to scare her away.

Jamie opened a vanity door and looked under the sink in her new bathroom. Maybe Devon would also loan her a couple of towels. She frowned. And soap. And shampoo.

Allowing her legs to push out in front of her, she sat back against the open bathroom door. She'd been in such a rush to escape Fred, she'd taken off without much more than the clothes on her back.

Thoughts of Fred sent a shiver through her. Money was getting low. If he found her again, she wasn't sure how much farther she could run.

"Don't borrow trouble," she whispered. She had no reason to think Fred would find her. He wasn't that smart. The last two times were just dumb luck. She hoped.

Her thoughts strayed to Devon. He had a nice smile, an open, friendly face. Of course, he could stand a shave. But he was still kind of cute, in a frumpy kind of way. He seemed harmless enough. And she could sure use a friend.

* * *

Jamie's suitcase felt almost empty. Tamping down the urge to unzip it and see what was inside, Devon strolled toward the group of men at the fire pit.

Dropping the small suitcase by the center fountain, he plopped down on a vacant wrought-iron chair and stretched his legs toward the fire.

"Hey," he said to the group.

They mumbled their greetings.

"So who's the blond chick?" Drew from unit two asked, stretching to look past Devon as if he might find Jamie hiding behind the chair.

The others quieted, waiting for Devon to answer.

"Jamie," Devon answered. "Jamie Cartwright. And before you ask, no, I don't know much more than that, and, no, she is not interested in being shown around. Keep away from her until she at least gets settled in. Remember what happened with Alexis."

3

"Aw, shit, Dev, you make it sound like we gang-raped her or something." Chris scowled and flipped his long ponytail over his shoulder and then crossed his arms over his tanned chest. He referred to himself as a dancer, but Devon knew a stripper when he saw one—male or female.

"I'm not the one who got in the shower with her," Drew pointed out then glared at Chris. "I still can't believe you did that."

"So I read the signals wrong," Chris groused. "Sue me."

"You're lucky she didn't have your ass thrown in jail!" Drew shot back.

Todd, the newest resident—until now—shifted and glanced around. Todd worked with Chris and had already gained a bigger reputation with the ladies. He snickered and crossed one bare foot over his waxed leg. "Dude, what were you thinking?"

Chris took a swig from his longneck beer before answering. "Her pussy was practically dripping for me. Why do you think she was squirming on my lap? Plus," he said, pointing the beer-bottle neck at the crowd around the fire, "she had her hot little hand in my pants not fifteen minutes before she went to her apartment to shower. Any one of you sons of bitches would have done the same thing. You're just pissed because she chose me."

"That's not what she told me when she came in to break the lease." Devon, along with the others, had seen the foreplay in the courtyard and had the same interpretation as Chris. But Alexis told an entirely different story. Not wanting to get in serious shit with the management company—or worse—he'd gladly refunded her deposit and waved good-bye.

He glanced at his watch and wondered if he'd given Jamie enough time. Immediate memories of her straining sweater had the fabric of his shorts doing the same. *Down, boy.*

"But all that's history," Devon said with a smile, glancing around. "My point is you need to play it cool with Jamie. We don't want another woman to run screaming from the complex. I mean, who knows if this one would run straight to the police."

The men shifted in uncomfortable silence, and Devon heaved an inward sigh of relief.

He wasn't ugly, but he also wasn't stupid. Compared to most of the specimens gathered around the fire pit, he would come up lacking. He'd had a view of Chris's package when he crossed his legs. He absolutely did not want to be compared and come up lacking—in any area.

"Leaving already?" Chris asked when Devon stood and retrieved the suitcase.

"Hell, no," Devon answered, wracking his brain for a reason not to return. "I'll be back in a few. I need to drop off the suitcase. Need more beer? I can make a beer run after I do this."

The men voiced their approval, and he nodded, then turned toward Jamie's door.

He knocked and waited, his overactive imagination playing out a scene he craved with every cell in his body.

Jamie would open the door, dressed in nothing but one of the old yellow towels and a smile. He'd kick the door shut just as she dropped the towel, her nipples puckered and hard on her firm breasts.

"I've been waiting for you all my life," she'd say in her little sex-kitten voice as she walked to him and rubbed her nipples across his bare chest. Her hand would close around his erection.

He wondered when he'd undressed, but since it was his daydream, he went with it and pulled her into his arms.

"Devon? Are you okay?" Jamie stood in the open doorway, fully clothed, a puzzled look on her face. Her gaze dropped to his obvious erection, made all the more obvious by his death grip on his shorts. "What are you doing?"

Did he detect horror in her voice? Damn straight, he did. Of course she was horrified to open her door to find her apartment manager fondling himself. Hell, *he* was horrified.

"Ah . . ." *Think, McCloud, think!* What would Trent do? He'd whip out a smart-ass reply, that's what. "Um, I read once if it moves, fondle it." He grimaced. Smooth, real smooth.

Her eyes widened. "Excuse me?"

"Ha. Ha. Just kidding." His smile felt as if it might fracture his cheeks, but he'd be damned if he'd retreat. She hadn't slammed the door or screamed. That had to mean something.

She just stood looking up at him, making his mouth water with the view he had down her cleavage.

In his mind, she was naked again. This time she stood beneath the daisy light, the shadows playing peekaboo with her close-shaved pussy. She placed one stiletto-clad foot up on the chair, exposing her moist lips. He briefly wondered when she'd put on high heels, but since he was lost in his sexual imagination, he put it out of his mind.

She reached between her spread legs and flicked a tiny gold ring.

His penis tried to escape his shorts the hard way—through his zipper. Oh, my God, she had a pierced pussy. The little gold labia ring sparkled in the dim light.

"What did you say about a ring?" She closed the door behind him, once again fully clothed. Damn. "I didn't bring any jewelry, so if you found a ring, it's not mine."

"Oh. Ah, okay." He glanced around the living room. "Where would you like me to put it—the suitcase. I'm talking about the suitcase. Where would you like me to put the suitcase?"

She walked closer and peered into his eyes. "Devon, are you sure you're okay? You're kind of flushed." Her cool hand singed his forehead. "And, no offense, but you're kind of babbling."

She was close enough to kiss. The lightbulb from the daisy lamp did marvelous things to her skin.

He wanted to lick it. Lick her. All over.

Great. Now he was babbling to himself, too.

Would she freak if he pulled her into his arms and tried to kiss her?

"No," she said and stepped back. "I wouldn't freak, but I don't want you to try it."

Shit. He must have said it out loud.

"Yes, you did."

Damn! He did it again.

She eased the suitcase from his fist. "Thanks for bringing my suitcase. I think it's time for you to leave."

He swallowed, the feel of his Adam's apple dragging down his throat like a tennis ball. "I'm sorry," he said in a low voice. "I don't usually act like this. You're just so cute and, well, hot, and it was all I could think of when I looked at you standing there. I mean—"

"Oh, for goodness' sake!" She grabbed the front of his shirt and pulled him flush against her awe-inspiring chest. "Just kiss me and get it over with so we can both get some sleep!"

Get it over with? Did she really think one kiss would do it and they would go on their merry way?

He gazed down into her big blue eyes. No. Fucking. Way. If he kissed her—and he fully intended to do so—it was going to be a kiss to remember. Legendary. A kiss to curl her toes. Hell, it may even be a kiss to make her come in her pretty little silk panties.

He damned well was going to give it his best shot.

His stomach clenched, his palms sweated. He fumbled in the pocket of his shorts until he found what he sought.

Sssst! The calming mint of his breath spray gave him the burst of freshness and courage he needed.

Against his chest, Jamie's breasts jiggled with her laugh.

"Don't laugh, woman," he said in the sternest voice he could muster. "Good oral hygiene is important."

Her smile faltered. "In that case, give me a blast." She opened her mouth, the sight of her pink tongue and inner cheeks making her seem vulnerable.

After spraying her delectable mouth, he set the dispenser on the table and pulled her back into his arms.

"Ready?"

A slow smile curved her lips. "Yes, I think I am."

A breath away from her mouth, he traced her lips with the tip of his tongue, encouraged by the way her breath hitched. Her lip gloss tasted faintly sweet. He closed his teeth on her plump lower lip and held it gently while he ran his tongue back and forth across it.

She pressed closer, her breasts flattened against his chest, her breathing becoming shallow.

He released her lip and made full contact, rubbing his mouth against hers. As he'd hoped, she opened for him.

Sweet. She tasted as sweet as she looked. And refreshingly minty. Oh, wait, that was the breath spray.

A sound escaped from deep in her throat, and he deepened the kiss.

Behind his zipper, his cock did a desperate dance. He tried to put some distance between it and Jamie's abdomen, but her hands at his hips stopped his effort.

Something warm and delicious blossomed within Jamie. Wow. Devon certainly knew how to kiss. Her bones felt liquid. She had to lock her knees if she wanted to remain upright. And she did. Fred had made her wary. She wasn't about to fall into bed with the first guy who turned her on. Been there, done that.

The kiss went on, drugging her with its passion, seducing her with its promise. Mild surprise registered when Devon cupped her bottom and pulled her closer.

She should stop, break the kiss. But it had been so long since she'd felt anything even remotely close to desire or passion, and it felt so good, so right. Okay, she was selfish. She was using Devon.

She wasn't ready for the kiss to end.

He pulled her closer, blurring her thoughts with the feel of his erection pushing against her, making her moist, needy.

She squirmed against him, blindly seeking what his hardness offered. Would it be so bad to take a chance?

Devon slid his left hand around and down to the edge of Jamie's short skirt, encouraged when she did nothing to stop him.

The smooth silkiness of her thigh made him weak in the knees. Up, up, up his hand inched. He paused to play with the incredible softness of her inner thigh, drawing patterns on her flesh.

She shifted, giving him greater access.

At the edge of her damp panty, he traced the leg opening with the tip of his finger, holding his breath in anticipation of her shoving him away.

Instead, she widened her stance. His cock leaped for joy. Maybe his dry spell was finally coming to an end.

He dipped his finger beneath the elastic and probed her wet heat.

Someone groaned. Maybe him.

Her hot hand gripped his wrist. But instead of pulling his hand away, she pushed it deeper between her legs, along her velvety folds.

She whimpered, pressing down on his hand.

After playing with her slick folds a moment, he inserted his fingertip.

Jamie went wild, coming down on his hand until his entire finger was deeply embedded, then riding him. Hard.

Her excitement was palpable. His hips began a rhythmic arching between his arm and Jamie's leg, his penis begging for more.

Her back arched, her breath caught. Internal muscles clenched, drawing his finger deeper still while her moisture drenched his hand.

Before he could assimilate her actions, much less drop his pants and bury himself in her, she pulled away from him, straightening her skirt, eyes wide.

"I'm sorry!" Her voice was breathy, like a woman who'd just climaxed. Which she had. Splendidly. "Please. Don't say anything. Just go. I'm so embarrassed!"

Resisting the need to rearrange himself, Devon strode to the door, not stopping until he stood on the other side.

4

Still in mourning for his nonexistent sex life, Devon made the beer run.

The party around the pit was getting rowdy. Grant, the mysterious guy from upstairs, was in Devon's chair with a girl when he returned with the beer.

"This is Mindy," Grant said as Devon walked up. Their eyes met. "Did we take your seat?" He stood, lifting Mindy high in his arms, treating everyone to a view of her smooth little ass and the strip of fabric separating the firm globes.

Which was probably exactly what Grant had planned, Devon thought, when Grant casually tweaked Mindy's nipple through her cropped-off tank top, eliciting a giggle.

She, obviously, was not the shy type.

Grant strolled to a chair in the darkened corner behind the fire and sat down.

Devon took a draw from his beer, watching over the bottle as Grant reached beneath his date's skirt and pulled off her thong.

Devon glanced around at the other tenants who were engrossed in conversation. He had no idea what they were talking about because their voices were just a murmur, drowned out by the blood roaring in his ears. No one seemed to notice the little sex show going on in the corner.

Although he told himself not to look, Devon's gaze kept drifting over to the couple.

While Devon's attention had shifted, Grant had removed Mindy's top. It was almost like Grant wanted an audience, the way he had her stretched out over his lap, legs spread while he played with her pussy and leaned over her shoulder to suck her obviously augmented tits.

Beneath Devon's shorts, his cock twitched against his zipper, wanting to come out and play.

Grant stretched Mindy's nipple, clenched in his teeth, when he looked up and across the fire, directly at Devon.

Grant's teeth showed white in the semidarkness. He smiled, never relinquishing the nipple, then shifted, spreading his date wider as though giving a better view.

The obliging Mindy arched sideways, encouraging Grant to take her nipple deeper into his mouth while he spread her legs to rest on each arm of the patio chair. Her nether lips parted, exposing her shining cherry-red folds. He reached around her to grasp her gaping lips in both hands and pull them so far apart Devon wondered if Grant was hurting her.

Evidently not, since her giggles drifted over the conversation.

Devon watched with rapt attention as Grant manipulated Mindy's genitals, rubbing, pulling, flicking and finally slapping. To Devon's fascinated surprise, the girl only whispered things to Grant, spreading her legs impossibly wider and occasionally giggling.

She slid off his lap. Devon noticed sometime during their sex play that Grant had released his erection from his basketball shorts. Mindy straddled his legs, bent almost double in order to take him in her mouth. While she went down on him, Grant some-how managed to reach through her legs and play with her clit.

Although turned on by his latent foray into voyeurism, Devon wondered how she could bend like that.

He must have looked away because when he looked back he saw that Mindy had climbed back onto Grant's lap. She now faced forward, her breasts jiggling slightly with each thrust of Grant's hips. Grant pushed on her back, causing her to practi-cally lay on her stomach on his legs, her breasts hanging over his knees while he continued to pound into her.

Todd walked across Devon's line of vision, talking in low tones to Grant.

Mindy did something, but Todd was in the way, so Devon couldn't see.

Damn. Reality hit Devon.

As the manager, he should put a stop to it. If the other ten-ants saw what was going on, they gave no indication. Francyne was holed up in her apartment, no doubt dozing in front of the TV by now. But what about Jamie? If she was embarrassed by what they'd done behind closed doors, what would she think about what was going on in the courtyard?

From her front window, Jamie peeked through the curtain to watch the group of men by the fire. Her gaze kept drifting back to Devon. Firelight bathed him in a warm, intimate glow. Though definitely not the most handsome man at the gather-ing, he was easily the most fascinating.

She watched the play of light on his face as he lifted his beer bottle, the ripple of his throat when he swallowed. What was it about him that called to her?

And what held his attention so thoroughly?

She edged closer to the side of the window. *What on earth . . . oh, my!*

Beyond the fire, a man and woman were clearly having sex. Darn. Another guy walked up, blocking her view.

Dropping the curtain, she leaned against the wall and fanned her face and then put her hand over her mouth to stifle the giggle.

She lifted the curtain for another peek. The guy blocking her sure had a great butt, she'd give him that. Under normal circumstances, she'd have enjoyed the view. But right now, he was spoiling hers.

Thoughts of herself in a similar position as the woman in the courtyard shot heat through her, tingling her nerve endings. Fanning away the blush, she tried to conjure up the scene in her mind. But the only man she could imagine doing such intimate things with—and enjoying them so much—was, strangely, Devon. And that was, well, dumb.

She snuck another peek. Would Devon be turned on from what he saw? Would he want to come back to finish what they'd started? More importantly, did she want him to?

She ran her hands over her chest and pushed up her new, impressive cleavage. Would her ex-boyfriend, Fred, or anyone for that matter, even recognize her now?

The image of a stranger stared back at her from the old mirror on the back of the door. She was still in there somewhere. She had to hide for just a while longer.

Flipping on the bathroom light, she leaned close to the mirror to inspect her hair for dark roots. The last highlight job had taken care of most of them, but if she looked close, she could see tiny traces of her once auburn hair.

She pulled her makeup kit from her shoulder bag and rummaged until she found her contact case. The blue contacts folded into the case until she squirted the disinfectant into the little pods and closed the lids. The little bar of soap would have to do for now. She dried her face on the threadbare washcloth she'd found under the sink and then stared at the mirror.

Pale green eyes stared back at her.

"Now you look more like you," she told her reflection. Turning on her heel, she strode to the bedroom and pulled a nightshirt from her suitcase and then reached into her bra and pulled out the flesh-colored gel sacks, tossing them into their storage box.

It itched where the latex had rested against her breasts, so she hopped into the shower. She could always drip dry. A laugh escaped her. Heck, she could even sleep in the nude now if she wanted to. No one was around to stop her.

Humming, she lathered with the little sliver of soap and rinsed off.

Through the haze of steam, she exited the bathroom only to walk naked into a hard chest.

She screamed and staggered back. Strong hands shot out to steady her.

"I'm sorry!" Devon's voice sounded strangled. "I knocked. When no one answered, I let myself in to leave the sheets and towels, with the pillows and stuff." He pointed to a pile of linens on the bed. "Then I heard the shower and thought I'd reach in and leave a towel for you to dry off on." He shrugged and swallowed. "Then . . . there you were. Are." His gaze did a slow track down her nude body. At least, she thought it did. Without glasses or contacts, it was kind of hard to tell. Wait. Naked. She was naked.

Belated modesty washed over her, and she hopped behind the partially open bathroom door. "That still gave you no right to come into my apartment, *my* apartment, uninvited!"

"I know. I'm sorry. I guess I wasn't thinking." He turned his back. "If you want to dry off and get dressed, I won't look."

"Darn right you won't look! Get out of here!"

"I—I can't. I need to talk to you about something. It can't

wait." Pause. "After you get dressed, I can help you make the bed while we talk."

Shoot. If he stuck around, he'd see her. The real her. She looked longingly at the bed.

"Turn off the light." Maybe if they made the bed in the dark, he wouldn't notice the discrepancy in her appearance.

"Why? It would make putting on the sheets kind of difficult."

"Um, I don't like to be seen without my makeup."

He sighed. "You may not believe this, but I really don't care about your makeup. Jamie, I'm tired, and I still have a lot of work to do tonight. I know you must be tired, too. Just throw on some clothes and come out here so we can get your bed made. Then I'll leave and you can get some sleep. I promise," he added.

When she didn't answer, he ran his hands through his hair in a gesture she was already coming to recognize and said, "Fine. Stay there. I'll make the bed, and you can come out after I leave."

The soft, squishy feeling came back to her. No one had ever been that nice to her.

Memories of his kiss and her subsequent orgasm ran through her mind. Could she set aside her inhibitions and just let nature take its course? Men had one-night stands all the time. Also a lot of women. Unfortunately not her. But she could . . . couldn't she?

Devon told his semierection to behave and flipped the top sheet onto the bed.

The bedroom plunged into darkness.

He reached back for the light switch and encountered a feminine hand.

"Keep it off," she commanded in a husky whisper.

"Why?" He swallowed around the lump of anticipation in his throat. If he was misinterpreting her intentions again, he'd have no choice but to go home and whack off. Maybe he should find some new ways to use the plethora of sex toys he'd accumulated over the years.

Her hand closed over the bulge in his shorts, and he bit back a surprised yelp. Barely.

"Ah, Jamie?" A trickle of sweat ran down his cheek. If she kept stroking him like that, he'd come in his pants.

Her hands shoved at his clothing until he stood naked. The blackout shade he'd installed when he lived there made it impossible to see anything, but he knew she was naked, too. Naked was a good thing.

He turned off his mind to all the reasons why he shouldn't take her up on what she was offering.

Her breasts branded his chest. Well, maybe closer to his upper abs, since she was short.

She hopped into his arms, pushing her arms against the top of his shoulders, her moist center pressed against him, aligning his mouth to her breast.

"Suck it," she commanded.

If he did as she ordered, he would lose any control. He could live with that.

He drew her pebbled nipple into his mouth and frowned against the fragrant skin. Something was different.

He staggered toward the window.

"What are you doing?" There was no mistaking the panic in her voice.

"Call me old-fashioned, but I like to see what I put in my mouth." He reached for the shade.

Her hand gripped his arm. "Stop! Don't you want to, *you know*?"

"Of course I want to *you know*." He reached, stretching for the cord. "I'll just put the shade up enough to let in a little light. I want to see your beautiful breasts."

The amount of light coming in through the six-inch opening

barely illuminated anything, but at least it became obvious he was holding a woman.

"Just because we do this, it doesn't mean anything, you know." Her voice was coming in little pants while he suckled her.

"Right," he said against her skin and then dropped her to bounce on the clean sheets. He grabbed her legs and put them around his hips. "Not a thing. Maybe you should think of baseball."

He plunged into her wet heat, biting back a curse at the rightness, the ecstasy of it.

Jamie, however, screamed.

5

"Yeah, baby, that's right, scream for me," he said against her ear. Hot damn. He'd never been with a screamer.

She screamed again. He must be better than he thought. Practicing alone must have paid off.

"Get away from me." She shoved on his shoulders until their connection was severed and she scurried across the mattress, dragging the sheet to cover her. "He's out there!" She pointed toward the window.

"Who?"

She scooted to the edge of the bed, taking the sheet with her. Raising one shaking hand, she pointed and said in a tremulous voice, "Fred. I'd know his beady little eyes anywhere. He was looking in the window at us!" Then she promptly fell off the edge of the mattress with a teeth-rattling thump.

Devon peered over the edge of the bed, sympathy taking the place of sexual urgency. "Who is Fred, and why is he peeping in your window?"

Instead of answering, she struggled to stand, battling the sheet until she got her feet under her.

Under normal circumstances, he'd have enjoyed the view or even thought up a way to recapture the mood. After one look at her terrified face, though, normal went out the window.

"Nice dive, by the way," he said, hoping to lighten the mood. "I'd give it a seven-point-five. You need to work on your form." He wiggled his eyebrows and said in his best Groucho imitation, "Or I could work on your form, if you'd rather."

She turned, her lips tightly compressed, and stared at him.

"Feel free to laugh." He reclined on the stack of pillows he'd tossed on the bed when he'd thought he was getting lucky. "I know you want to." He motioned with his hand. "Go ahead. I'm used to women laughing at me in the bedroom. I've even, in some weird, perverse way, come to expect and even enjoy it."

She smiled and sat on the edge of the mattress. "Right. Do they point when they laugh?"

"Okay, that's enough, woman. Let's not get insulting here." Smiling, he took her hand and drew light circles on her palm. "Want to tell me about this Fred?"

For a moment, he thought she might and felt an urge to tell her he was kidding, he didn't really want to hear about another guy. Lucky for him, the moment passed when she shook her head.

She reached beside the bed and tossed his pants and boxers to him.

"It's late," she said, turning her back while he pulled on his clothes.

"You're right." He gathered her into his arms and softly brushed her lips with his. "Stop begging, I can't sleep with you tonight," he said with a grin and then kissed the tip of her nose. "I have work to do anyway, so it's just as well. Let's call it a night."

He stepped back, his arms falling to his sides. "But if you play your cards right, I may just cut you a break and let you have your way with me next time."

She laughed. "I'll have to remember that. Next time."

He nodded and stepped out of the room. No point in bringing up the lease at that moment. "Good night. Make sure you lock the door behind me."

And he was gone.

Damn, he hated being a nice guy.

Whoever had been outside Jamie's window most likely was long gone, but he walked to the side of her unit just to make sure.

Petunia sat on her haunches just below the window ledge, a forlorn look on her grizzled face.

"You do realize," he said to the big dog, scratching her ear, "you just put a major hitch in my previously nonexistent sex life."

"That's because you're standing around talking to animals, you ninny. Don't go blaming my precious Petunia." Francyne walked up and swatted his butt and then deftly attached a leash to Petunia's collar. "Bad girl! I've been looking all over for you." Shoving her glasses up on her thin nose, she looked at Devon. "Shot down again, huh?" She shook her head. "And I had such high hopes for this one, pumpkin."

"Well, if you'd keep your animal under control so she wouldn't peep into windows, I might be able to change my luck," he said and then immediately felt guilty for snapping at her. "I'm sorry. It's been a long day. In fact, I'm going home. Night."

Devon walked past the crowd in the courtyard, not stopping until he gained the relative safety of his apartment.

He leaned against the closed door, allowing his eyes to adjust to the darkness.

Killer pranced over to welcome him home, leaving a trail of drool.

"Hey, big guy, you hungry?" Devon walked to the cupboard and surveyed the dinner selection. Cooking, his usual comfort activity, held no appeal. "I'm thinking I might fix myself a Hungry Man dinner." He pulled out two jars of baby food. "How about beef stew with an apple-crisp chaser?" The dog sneezed and shook his head, scattering little droplets of doggy spit. "Okay, beef stew it is. And an excellent choice, monsieur. Have I mentioned what a discriminating palate you have, big guy?"

After their late dinner, Killer snoozed under the chair while Devon stared at the flashing cursor on his laptop. Trent's PI adventures held no appeal for him. If he had to write another sex scene for the hapless detective, he just might puke.

He switched files and brought up the catalog copy he was working on for Midnight Fantasies, one of three sex-toy manufacturers who bought his product pitches. The last item he'd described was the Float Like a Butterfly, Sting Like a Bee combination nipple clamp and personal waterproof vibrator. He absently rubbed his still tender nipple.

According to the technical jargon, the apparatus could be used by either sex. He picked up the innocuous-looking blob of lime-green, sparkling soft gel shaped like a bee with an unusually large wing span and flicked the little red stinger. Glancing at the spec sheet, he pushed the bee's nose, activating the "stinger," touching it with the tip of his index finger. A not unpleasant buzz of low voltage current warmed the tip of his finger.

"Wonder where you'd use that," he mused and then activated the fluttering wings, holding the bee close to his bare chest. The wings vibrating against his nipples shot an unexpected surge of arousal to his extremities.

A guilty glance at the chair confirmed that Killer was still lost in dreamland. Slowly, in an effort not to disturb the dog, Devon stood and let his shorts and boxers fall to the floor with a soft plop. Killer twitched but resumed snoring.

Devon looked down at his erection casting a shadow across

his keyboard. No doubt about it, something had to be done or he'd never get any work done tonight. He thought of Jamie, frustrated to see his cock grow and swell at just the memory of his time with her. Whacking off would be faster, but he needed to do research for the catalog anyway, so why not.

Slowly moving the fluttering wings down his abs, he watched his penis twitch with anticipation. The gel wings lapped at the length of his cock, reminding him of the eager tongue of a lover. A dry tongue.

He grabbed his glass of iced tea and fluttered the wings in the cold liquid before putting them back on his now iron-hard shaft.

"Aahh!" He shuddered and resisted the urge to close his eyes and savor the feeling of the cool wet gel gently slapping the sensitive skin. Research. It was research, and he needed to make mental if not physical notes.

The gel wings lapping at his engorged head had his hips pumping in a lazy rhythm, the old leather desk chair creaking with each thrust.

He noted that the wings felt especially erotic on his clenched balls. His excitement ratcheted up another notch.

Gripping his erection, he pumped, slowly at first and then gaining momentum. The wings continued their sensual torture. He found it added to his excitement to allow them to flutter against the head of his cock while his other hand continued to pump.

The pre-climax built, tightening the muscles progressively up the backs of his legs. Too soon. He wanted to fantasize a little longer about his new neighbor.

Slackening his grip, he fumbled with the bee to push the button that would halt the fluttering wings.

A searing jolt of electricity shot into the tip of his penis, streaking clear up to his belly button. He screamed and contracted with the pain filling his abdomen.

Wrong button.

6

Jamie tossed and turned on the softly worn sheets, tangling her feet in them. She kicked them away and flopped to her stomach, punching the pillow into submission.

Visions of Devon standing naked in her bedroom, moonlight combining with the light from the courtyard spilling in to bathe his naked sex in a warm glow. His hard, erect, naked sex. Hard and erect and pulsing for her.

She shifted in a failed attempt to ease the ache between her legs.

She'd blown it. Totally ruined the moment by freaking out. But she'd been so sure she'd seen something at the window. Something with eyes. Fred had immediately flashed into her mind, but now that she'd had a chance to calm down she wasn't as sure of what she'd seen.

Fred may not have found her or been the one peeking in her window, but she didn't fool herself. If he wasn't around, he would be soon. He always found her.

A glance at the still partially open shade confirmed that no one was at the window. She should get up and let it down, just in case. But to do that required more energy than she had at the moment.

She flopped onto her back and watched the faint shadows on the ceiling, the lazy rotation of the ceiling fan. One night. All she needed was one full night's sleep. Sleep uninterrupted by the man who haunted her days and now invaded her nights.

Her mind went to Devon, and the constriction in her chest eased. Her muscles relaxed. She smiled. Who would have guessed that under the frumpiness was a body of a god? Her hands covered her breasts, absently rubbing the hardened nipples through her threadbare University of Michigan nightshirt. It had felt so good, so right, when he'd sucked them. She gave the hard buds a little tweak, moving her legs restlessly on the sheet.

What would Devon think of her body, her real body? She's seen the way his eyes had practically bugged out of his head when he'd eyed her cleavage. Yet he hadn't seemed to notice the disparity in size when he'd held and suckled her.

She ran her hand under the nightshirt and massaged her aching breasts. Ever so slowly, she dragged her hands down her rib cage, past the indention of her waist, over the flair of her hips. She traced a line over her thighs and up, up until her fingertips brushed her intimate moisture. Tightening her stomach muscles, she raised to look at her genitals in the shadowed light and then ran her fingertip over the petal-soft, ultrasensitive skin she'd exfoliated that morning.

Relaxing against the pillow, she dipped her fingertip into her moisture and then spread it with lazy motions over her labia, imagining Devon's tongue tracing the same path. The thought made her squirm, made her hips want to buck off the sheets in an age-old plea for sexual appeasement.

Ache. She ached for him. Planting her heels on the mattress, she spread her legs. The coolness from the fan bathed her heated center. It wasn't enough. Reaching between her legs, she cupped her sex and ground the heel of her hand against her mons. Instead of subsiding, the ache grew stronger. Hand still cupped, she lightly slapped at the ache. A pleasant twinge zinged up into her womb. Another slap brought her to the brink of . . . what? An orgasm? She had to find out.

Dipping her finger again, she swirled her juices over her heated skin, her heart rate increasing with each stroke of fingertip to smooth, hot skin. Two more stinging slaps, each one a bit harder, and she was gasping, panting, yearning for release.

Desperate, she plunged her finger deep. Her inner muscles clamped around her finger, the plump walls hot and slick with her excitement. It wasn't enough. She couldn't divorce the sensation of something filling her from the knowledge of what she felt like inside.

With a frustrated groan, she rolled onto her stomach, rubbing against the sheet in an effort to find release. Instead, her frustration mounted.

She stuck her hand beneath her, flicking her distended labia, rubbing her swollen nub, the pressure of her knuckles against the springs of the mattress taking away some of the awareness of exactly where her hand was and what it was doing. Maybe if she squeezed her eyes shut tight and focused on the feeling of her most private area being petted and teased. . . .

Her knees came up, pushing her bare bottom toward the breeze from the ceiling fan. She imagined Devon blowing gently on her wet folds while he manipulated and played with her femininity. Her back jerked. Her hand rubbed harder and faster, occasionally slapping and then petting the stinging flesh.

In her mind's eye, she saw Devon on his knees behind her, doing all those wondrous things to her, his hot penis thumping against her butt, kissing her vagina.

And she was there.

With a sound that was half groan, half animal mating call, her back arched as her climax raced through her. Tiny shards of electricity zipped through her veins to tingle her nipples, teasing them into hard buds. Every muscle in her body vibrated with the charge shooting through her to all her extremities. She wouldn't have been surprised to see sparks shooting from her nipples.

With a final gasp, she fell back onto the mattress, eyes shut, savoring the little aftershocks of pleasure.

Devon's entire body vibrated. Weak, he gathered the strength to pull up his boxers and shorts, then dropped back into his chair.

After a moment, he typed: *WARNING! Do not confuse the vibrator button with the stinger operation button.*

Killer made a little whimper in his sleep, and Devon smiled as he watched the dog chasing something in his dreams.

Devon rearranged his still semihard, tingling dick to a more comfortable position and frowned. Had Jamie not freaked, they could have soothed the ache filling his groin, impeding his creative thoughts.

He picked up the Float Like a Butterfly, Sting Like a Bee personal device and turned it over in his hand. The gel was soft, almost pliant, still warm from his body heat, he supposed. Idly flicking one wing with his index finger, he compared it to the feel of a woman's labia. Of course, a labia was firmer, tighter . . . unless in the midst of arousal.

Immediately his thoughts zipped to Jamie and how her labia had felt in the precious few moments he'd been able to touch it. Hot. Soft. Wet and lush.

His cock stirred at the memory. Eyes still trained on the wing, he unzipped in order to relax enough to spur creativity. Within seconds, the engorged head peeked through the flap in his boxers. He ignored it, intent on coming up with something clever and positive to say about the product in his hand.

He turned off the desk lamp, its click echoing in the quiet apartment. In the distance, the rumble of male voices continued. In the soft light from his laptop screen, the bee took on an ethereal glow.

How would lovers use this for mutual satisfaction?

A vision of Jamie, her bare bottom sitting right where his laptop had been, gorgeous legs spread wide for his viewing pleasure, came to him. She smiled down at him and they both looked at her moist cherry folds. He stroked them with the wing of the bee. Gentle at first, he increased the tempo and pressure.

Bathed in moonlight, she leaned back on her hands, elbows locked, the puckered nipples of her impressive rack jutting toward him.

He stood, replacing the busy bee wings with his equally busy fingers while he fluttered her distended nipples with the device.

She moaned. Maybe it was him.

His eager cock nudged her ass. She scooted forward for easier access, her smooth legs going around his hips, pulling him into her wet heat.

He sucked one breast hard, the wings still gently slapping her other breast. Her wetness pulled him deeper. His hips bucked, increasing in intensity. He switched nipples and moved the bee. Her hot breath fanned his ear. Faster. Harder. Deeper.

Deeper?

It was his fantasy, so why not? His hips pumped faster, driving hard into her welcoming body.

Inspiration struck. Dragging his hands down her smooth legs, he placed her bare feet on his shoulders, spreading her for deeper thrusts. Muscles tightened in his legs. Too soon. He didn't want to come without her. He fumbled for the bee. He must have dropped it in the heat of passion. Got it. The wings gently slapped his balls as he positioned the device so it would propel Jamie over the edge to free-fall with him and pushed the button as his release rushed toward him.

Pain shot from his dick to his balls and squeezed. His lungs seized. He may have lost consciousness for a second or two.

When he came to, he was half lying across the keyboard of his laptop, his pants around his ankles. Humiliation washed over him. Something nudged him. Hot breath fanned his ear.

"Lark?" Killer stood on his hind legs, straining to see what was going on.

Devon regarded his keyboard and said a silent prayer he hadn't ruined his computer. Will, his computer guru, would never let him live it down.

Killer tilted his head, regarding his master. "Lark?"

"Don't ask."

7

Sun peeking through the partially opened blinds warmed Jamie's bare bottom. On the edge of wakefulness, she smiled against the soft fabric of the sheet. Today was the beginning of the rest of her life, and, for a change, optimism stroked her along with the warm sunshine.

As soon as she showered and dressed, she would explore the neighborhood and find a place to eat breakfast. After that, a serious shopping trip was in order. She couldn't rely on Devon's generosity forever. Plus, she needed to buy groceries.

By the time she'd showered and dressed, she was sweaty again. The window air conditioner in the bedroom hummed, chugging along, but the air had taken on a definite warmth and humidity by the time she walked into the living room. The gel from the bust enhancers was already sticking to the undersides of her breasts. She blinked her unnaturally blue eyes at the reflection in the scratched mirror, still surprised at the transformation.

Her bottle tan was beginning to fade and show a few uneven streaks on her arms and legs. Darn. The self-tanner was expensive. Hiking the skirt up to her hip, she surveyed as far down the back of her leg as she could. Maybe she'd be better off investing in a bathing suit and working on her tan by the pool.

Despite the pep talk Devon had given himself during his shower, he stepped to the side of Jamie's door and peeked through the front window. It wasn't like he was window peeping. He was just being considerate. He didn't want to knock and wake her up.

His mouth went dry, the breath mint he'd just popped in sticking to his tongue.

Jamie stood, with one shapely leg lifted, her bare foot resting on the chair. She hiked up the skirt of her flowered halter dress and bent over, giving him a bird's-eye view of her smooth ass cheek.

He stepped aside and rapped on her door and then took a deep breath and swallowed. The breath mint karate-chopped his Adam's apple, causing him to double over, wheezing and choking in an effort to dislodge the thing.

At that moment, Jamie opened her door.

Through the tears blurring his vision, he could see her tanned feet, pink toenails glistening in the morning sunshine, trim ankles, shapely calves, the edge of her dress.

"Devon!" The bare feet moved closer. Now he could see the flowers on the skirt of her sundress. "Are you all right? Should I call someone?"

He shook his head and wheezed and then went into a coughing fit again.

She grasped his arm and tugged him into her apartment and then leaned in to look closer, so close he could have licked the upper swell of her tanned cleavage. Was it his imagination or could he see the dark edge of a nipple? Was she tan all over? It had been too dark in the bedroom last night to tell.

"Devon?"

The concern on her face brought instant remorse. He nodded and tried to swallow around the hard lump of minty freshness in his throat. "I'm fine," he finally managed to croak out.

At an even six feet, he considered himself average height, but looking down at Jamie he felt like a giant.

"Damn, you're short." Not exactly a great conversation opener, but it popped into his mind and fell out of his mouth before he had a chance to censor. It seemed to be happening a lot lately. He blamed his long work hours but wondered if it was really a by-product of being alone.

If Jamie was offended, she didn't show it. She flashed a white grin. "It depends what you call short. I'm almost five feet, but I guess, to some people, that would be vertically challenged."

Her smile was contagious. He stood, grinning down at her. "You look nice. Going somewhere?"

"Thanks." She smoothed her hand down the skirt of her dress. "I need to do some grocery shopping. And buy some sheets and stuff so I can return yours."

"Want some company?"

She glanced up. "You don't have to work today?"

"I work every day. And most nights. But I can ask Francyne to keep an eye on the office while I'm gone. I could use a break."

After Jamie got her purse and shoes and locked the door, they walked to the front of the complex.

She stopped and inhaled the salty breeze. "How do you ever get any work done, living right here on the beach?" She closed her eyes and tilted her head back to the sun.

"I suppose, after a while, it's like living in any other picturesque place. You sort of become immune to it." He glanced out across the white sandy beach and watched the white-capped waves breaking on the wet sand, leaving a gray shadow on its perfection. How long had it been since he'd even looked at the beach, much less walked along it?

He pulled a pair of Ray-Bans from his Hawaiian-shirt pocket and slid them on. "I'm a writer, and I've been concentrating so hard on my book, along with my other jobs, I haven't had time to get out much."

"Really?" Her amazing blue eyes were wide when she turned to him. "What do you write?"

"I'm a mystery writer. Right now, I'm working on a series of books featuring the same private detective."

Her gasp sent shivers down his spine. Clasping her hands together, she looked at him with what could only be described as awe. "Where can I buy them? This is so exciting! I've never known a real writer before!"

Damn, he hated it when people said stuff like that. "Ah, well, they're not out yet." Maybe never will be if he didn't ever finish them. Or even one, for that matter. Then there was the lack-of-agent thing and actually submitting the finished manuscript to an editor.

Amazingly her animation didn't dim. "Great! Then I can be the first to read it! You'll let me read it before you send it out, won't you?"

Would he? He'd never shared his work. He looked down at her smiling face and then lower to where the sun shone on her exposed cleavage and salivated. If her reading his manuscript got him closer to that, it was no contest. "Sure. If you really want to."

Fairly skipping with happiness, she took his hand in hers. "Oh, great! I can't wait!"

They walked, hand in hand for a while, along the boardwalk.

"Are we heading in the right direction?" Jamie scrunched up her nose, her hand shielding her eyes, and looked toward the first cluster of stores.

"Yeah, there's a linen outlet up ahead and a little mom-and-pop grocery store at the end of the block." He squeezed her hand a little, more than pleased to see her smile widen and feel her return the squeeze. "I thought, if you were hungry, we might have lunch after we hit the linen place and then go to the grocery store."

"Okay."

He could tell she wasn't really paying attention to him. Instead she kept looking out over the beach, checking out every guy who walked past. He ground his teeth. When she almost stopped to stare at a tall guy who Rollerbladed down the walk, he could stand it no more.

"Jamie? Are you expecting someone? Looking for someone?" Maybe she was just wasting time with him while she waited for a boyfriend.

"Hmmm?" She turned back to look at him. "No. Why?"

"Well, you seem to be looking for someone."

"No." She shrugged, her tan skin sparkling with a fine sheen of perspiration. "Just taking in the sights."

Taking in the sights. Right. He'd like to take in some sights himself. Sights like Jamie naked and glistening in the sun.

They walked past the ice-cream parlor, and he pictured Jamie, still naked, sitting on the table, her legs spread wide, bare feet on the bench on either side of his hips. He'd take his big scoop of ice cream and drag it along her pussy, then lean and lick it off. He swallowed a groan at the thought of how her sweetness would taste, mingled with the melting temptation of the ice cream.

"We can stop, you know." Jamie's voice broke through his daydream. "If you really want some ice cream. We can always eat lunch later."

"What makes you think I want ice cream?" Oh, Lord, please don't let him have said anything embarrassing.

"Well, the way you looked at the ice-cream shop and the little moan you did as we walked by." She shrugged, and he held his breath when her cleavage threatened to make an escape over the edge of her plunging neckline.

To his disappointment, she hooked her thumbs under the edge of the bodice and tugged it back up.

"Do you want to get some ice cream?" she asked again.

"No, not unless you do." He wasn't sure he could live through the experience of watching her eat ice cream and not ache to fulfill his fantasy. "I'm not a big ice-cream eater," he lied.

"Then let's go on to the linen place."

He'd never had so much fun buying sheets and towels. He and Jamie tried out small appliances, ate several samples, smelled every candle and still managed to fill their cart with bedding and towels.

"I still think you should have bought that flavored massage oil," Jamie said while they waited in line. "It smelled great. Maybe you could have used it for inspiration in your book."

Inspiration. She had no idea, standing there in her skimpy fuck-me sundress with all her luscious skin right there to tempt him, what it was he needed for inspiration.

She inspired him. Inspired him to do things he'd never thought about doing. Well, okay, maybe he'd thought about doing them, but never had he had a face to put on his dream girl. Until now. He knew exactly what he'd do with the pineapple-flavored oil.

He'd take the bright, tropical-print comforter she bought and lay her back on it in the cart. She wouldn't have on any panties, for easier access. He'd stroke the sweet oil between her legs and then lick it away until she was writhing, begging him to fuck her, right there in the twenty-items-or-less lane. He wondered if they could do it on the moving conveyer belt without injury.

"Devon!" Jamie's voice broke into his fantasy. "Cut it out. You're pushing the cart into me."

"Oh! Sorry." At least she didn't realize how he'd pushed the cart. *Get a grip, Mac. You don't want to be banned from the shopping center.* "You ready for lunch?"

"Why don't we take all this stuff back to the apartment first so we won't have so much to carry."

Devon insisted on carrying all the bags. She held on to his elbow to guide him since his view was obstructed. Where she touched him burned, but she refused to break contact.

All through the store, she'd fantasized about them being married and that they were buying stuff for their apartment. She'd caught a couple of girls eyeing Devon and glared at them, warning them off. For some reason, it felt like he was hers.

Maybe because he was safe. Or seemed to be. He wasn't breathtakingly handsome. But sometimes . . . sometimes she caught a flash of such pure sex appeal it took her breath away. At those times she knew, beyond a shadow of a doubt, if he shaved and cleaned up, dressed up a bit, he would be devastating. Literally oozing sex appeal, she'd have to lock him up to keep the women away. Hmmm . . . locking Devon up definitely had potential.

It was at that moment she had an epiphany: she wanted to make love with Devon. No, not something so innocuous. She wanted hot, raging, no-holds-barred sex with him.

Unfortunately she had no clue as to how to bring that dream to reality. Not without sounding like a total slut anyway.

A tall man walking along the beach several yards from them caught her attention. Fred? Her heart stumbled and then resumed its pace when she realized it was just her imagination.

"Hey! Hey!" Devon lagged back, shifting his load of white plastic shopping bags. "Wasn't that the apartments we just passed?"

She glanced over her shoulder at the faded tile roof. "Oops.

Sorry. I guess I wasn't paying attention. I was just enjoying the breeze and the sights and sounds." She directed him into the courtyard with its terra-cotta tile and colorful tiled fountain. For not the first time, she thought the Spanish hacienda style was very cozy and appealing. "The sign says there's a pool. I thought it would be in the courtyard. Where is it?"

He walked into her apartment as soon as she opened the door and dumped the packages onto the sofa. Rubbing his back, he said, "It's out back. It was supposed to be in front of the complex, according to Francyne, but the builder dug the foundation too close to the easement. Guess no one noticed until after the foundation had been poured."

"Too bad. A pool with an ocean view would have been really cool." She picked up the linens. "Which way is the laundry room? I want to wash and dry these before I put them on the bed."

"Ah." He nodded. "I wondered why you bought detergent and softener at the bed place when it's cheaper at the market." He dug in his pocket and brought out a bundle of tokens. "And you're in luck. The washers and driers don't use money. We had a problem with kids breaking in and looting the machines. We use these little pink jobs now." He held up the one-inch-by-two-inch plastic card the machines took instead of coins. "As a renting ploy, we even stopped selling them. So tenants can use the facility for free."

"Why use anything? Why not just make the washers and driers work with the punch of a button?" She picked up the fabric softener and detergent bottles.

"Because anyone could walk in off the street and use them if we did that, and before you know it the machines would need replacing."

She nodded. "Good point. Lead the way. I want to get a couple of loads going and then go to lunch. I'm starving!"

* * *

The laundry room was empty, so while Jamie made use of the washers, Devon went and picked up sandwiches at the corner deli.

A sack in his teeth and a drink in each hand, he was trying to figure out how to open the door or get Jamie's attention when her laughter floated through the fragrant air coming through the vents in the door.

Giving up, he set the drinks down and turned the knob.

Just as he'd suspected, she was not alone. Chris and Drew flanked her like two waxed pit bulls, their laser-whitened smiles dazzling in their tanned faces.

The good news was that everyone remained fully clothed. The bad news was the fact that the men were there at all. Since when did they do their own laundry?

Reaching back out for the drinks, he stepped into the open door. "Hey, look who's here." He glanced meaningfully around at the empty washers. "Where's your laundry?"

Chris's smile widened, if that was possible. "No laundry. We saw Jamie come in here and thought we'd mosey over and introduce ourselves. Keep her company while she does her laundry."

Devon just stared. He knew exactly what those two had on their minds and it wasn't getting to know Jamie, unless you counted in the biblical sense.

The men pushed away from the washers.

"We were on our way to the gym," Drew said, edging toward the door. "It was nice meeting you, Jamie. See you around."

"Yeah. See you around," Chris echoed, and they left.

"Is there a problem with me talking to them?" Jamie asked when he handed her a sandwich and her drink. "Is there something I should know?"

Was there? Slowly he shook his head, took a bite of his roast-beef sandwich and swallowed before answering. "No, they're okay. I was just worried they might scare you. They can be kind of intimidating, especially together."

She swallowed a bite of sandwich and grinned. "You're telling me. The testosterone level was getting a bit high in here."

They chuckled and continued eating their lunch in companionable silence.

Jamie shifted on the vibrating washer and realized it was a poor choice of a place to sit. The vibrations were doing absolutely sinful things to her genitalia. It didn't help to have Devon sitting there, oblivious to her state, reading a sports magazine. Would he help her relieve her need if she asked him? Would she dare ask?

Devon hid behind an old magazine and tried to regulate his breathing. From his vantage point, he could see clear up Jamie's dress to her upper thigh. It didn't take much of an imagination to know what lay beyond.

And Devon had a great imagination.

8

Jamie crunched an ice cube and watched Devon. So immersed in his magazine, he hadn't so much as looked her way in a good twenty minutes.

She dug another piece of ice from her cup and glanced his way. Did she dare? What if he saw what she did?

The thought of Devon watching her pleasure herself fueled her excitement. Instead of putting the ice in her mouth, she shifted on the vibrating washer and slid the cool wetness up her leg until she reached the crotch of her panties.

Another quick glance confirmed he was oblivious. She closed her eyes and pulled aside her panty leg, slipping the ice along her aching folds. Up, down, around the spot that yearned for more. The ice quickly melted against her heat. She dug in the cup for another piece and quickly returned to stroke her heated genitals until her lips and petals were numb to the touch.

It wasn't enough.

Devon clutched the magazine in a death grip. Sweat trickled down his forehead, stinging his eyes. A drip rolled down his nose, hanging from the tip like a trapeze artist before plopping with a splat onto the slick page. He watched the gray spot enlarge and wondered how much longer he could pretend to be so engrossed in the magazine he did not notice Jamie doing unspeakably erotic things with the leftover ice.

When she released a shuddering sigh, he almost screamed from pent-up tension.

Averting his eyes, he threw the magazine down on the blue plastic chair and jumped up.

"I, um, I'll go get a laundry basket so you can carry everything back to your apartment in one trip." He tripped on the leg of the chair, hitting the doorjamb with a painful thud, but straightened immediately and staggered out the door, rubbing his forehead as he made his way back home.

His toe bumped something warm when he stepped into his apartment. Had he not grabbed the snack bar counter, he'd have done a face-plant onto the tile.

Petunia blinked sleepy eyes at him.

"Damnit, dog! Why do you have to sleep right in front of my door?" Now that he thought about it, what was she doing in his apartment in the first place?

At that moment, Francyne turned her head from the couch. "You're out of beer."

"No, there were three this morning." He leafed through the mail on the counter.

"That's what I said. You're out of beer." She lifted the longneck in her hand. "This here is the last one." She tipped the bottle up and drained it and then belched. "Now you're officially out."

He grinned and tossed all but an official-looking envelope into the trash. "Why don't you pick up some when you walk Petunia?"

"I don't go to liquor stores." She lowered her voice. "Perverts hang out there, you know." Leaning back, she resumed her TV viewing. "Besides, I'm watching my soaps."

"What's wrong with your TV?"

"Someone forgot to pay my cable bill."

"That would be you."

"No need for name calling." She flicked off the remote and stood. "It's a good thing I came over. We had three calls about the sexual-aids tester position while you were gone. I told them the position had been filled. Also called the paper and told them to stop running my ad." She looked at him over the rim of her glasses. "You should be thanking me. And you didn't lock your door again. Anyone could have walked right in."

He raised his eyebrow and made a show of looking at her. "Looks like anyone did."

"Hush up. It's a good thing I was here. You had a visitor."

"Oh, yeah? Who?"

"Don't know his name, but he was a big fella." She raised on tiptoe to hold her hand in demonstration. "And he seemed awfully interested in Jamie."

Pausing in his reach for a bottle of water, his stomach clenched. Was this the guy she was watching for? "That so? What did you tell him?"

"Nothing. He had shifty eyes. Never trust a person with shifty eyes."

"Francyne—"

"I'm getting to it. Anyway, he didn't come right out and ask if Jamie lived here. Instead, he kept looking around, like he was casing the place. Then he asked if there were a lot of pretty girls who lived here."

"What did you say?"

"What do you think I said? I asked him what he'd call me."

"And?"

"You probably don't want to know what he said. Anyway,

then he asked if any pretty girls had moved in here lately. I said no, that our tenants were mostly men." She paused and pushed her glasses up on her bony nose. "Come to think of it, he didn't seem too happy with that answer. Then he says, in a real mean, sort of threatening tone, 'You mean to tell me no pretty, short woman with dark hair and light green eyes has been here,' and I said that's exactly what I'm saying and if you have a problem with that I suggest you take it up with the manager when he gets back from teaching his karate class."

"Karate? I don't even know karate, much less teach it." Damn, he hoped Francyne hadn't pissed off some Neanderthal who could come back to rip his arm off and beat him with it.

"Oh, relax," she said, waving her hand. "I also told him you had a black belt and were in special services."

"What!" The woman was going to get him killed.

"Hey, it worked, sunshine, don't worry. He left, and I doubt he'll be back. I think I scared him pretty good."

"I hope so." He tried not to shudder at the thought of some goon returning to pound on him. "But if he was looking for a short woman with dark hair and green eyes, what made you think he was looking for Jamie? She's blonde and blue-eyed."

Francyne shrugged and nudged Petunia up. "I don't know. Just a feeling I had, I guess." She snapped the leash on the dog. "Killer had to be restrained while he was here, and Petunia didn't like him either. That's what tipped me off. My daddy always said not to trust anyone an animal doesn't like." She opened the door and paused. "Where is Jamie? I thought you told me you'd be gone until tonight."

She's masturbating on the washer in the laundry room. Of course he couldn't tell Francyne that. "She's still doing laundry. I came back to pick up a laundry basket for her. We forgot to buy one this afternoon."

"Well, you'd better get back to her. Them machines always make me horny." Francyne chuckled and left.

"Way too much information!" he yelled as the door shut.

He hoped she hadn't ruined doing laundry for him.

Jamie fanned her sweating face and chest with the magazine Devon had been reading and eyed the washer. Who knew it could be such a seductive appliance? Sitting on it during the spin cycle gave a whole new meaning to being wrung out. She easily came three times after Devon's hasty exit.

The laundry room may be her new favorite place.

Devon stepped through the door, carrying a big blue plastic laundry basket.

"Is everything done?" He placed the basket on the bright yellow folding counter that ran the length of the laundry room.

She shook her head. "No, the driers still have about half an hour." She patted the chair next to her. "May as well have a seat. Or did you have other things to do? If you do," she hurried on, "that's fine. I can fold everything and carry it back to my place and make my bed by myself."

"Are you kidding?" He slumped down in the chair next to her and crossed a tan ankle over his knee. "And miss all the excitement?" He grinned. "Besides, after spending most of the day helping you pick everything out, I'm kind of looking forward to seeing how it will look."

He shifted, the action causing the leg of his khaki cargo shorts to hike up. Dang. Devon had sexy legs.

Her gaze traveled from his flip-flop-clad tanned feet up legs that were only lightly furred with soft-looking, dark hair. The tour stopped midthigh, spoiled by the leg of his shorts. Darn.

"Your shorts got a little dirty today. I don't mind sharing my supplies, if you want to throw them in for a quick wash and dry." At his widened gaze, she hurried on. "It's not like you'd be naked or anything. I mean, face it, most bathing suits reveal more than, um, men's underwear." Boxers or briefs? It had been difficult to tell in the dark. She'd been wondering since the first time she saw him. Another one of her weird little mind games. In reality, she'd only found out, up close and personal, with about three or four guys in her entire life. Still, it was always fun to try to guess.

"That's okay." He looked at her like he was worried she might attack him or something and shifted away a little. "I probably have at least ten pair of shorts just like these. All clean, so it's no problem."

"Is it your manager's uniform or something?"

He laughed, and she felt the warmth speed through her body.

"Francyne would say it is. She's always accusing me of dressing like the Crocodile Hunter." He glanced down at his shorts. "I always enjoyed watching him. Still can't believe he's gone."

"I know," she said softly.

They sat in silence for a while, watching the digital timer on the driers count down.

"So when are you going to let me read one of your books?"

"Right now, there's only one available to read."

"Are the others with your agent or publisher?"

Damn, he hated to lie. "Ah, something like that. So, Jamie, what do you do?"

What did she do? Nothing for the last year and a half, unless running from Fred could be considered a career. It felt more like a lifetime sentence.

She licked her lips, stalling for time. "Well, until a couple of years ago, I taught kindergarten."

"Really? Wow. I sure never had a kindergarten teacher who looked like you." His smile flashed white in the dwindling light from the window.

"Thanks." Damn, she hated playing the dumb blonde. She plastered on a pleased smile as though she hadn't heard that line a million times. Although, in truth, her students had not had a teacher who looked like her either. At least, not the way she looked now.

"So, what happened during the last couple of years?"

"Well . . . I was in a, um, less than healthy relationship."

"But it's over now, right?"

"Oh, yeah. It's definitely over. At least, as far as I'm concerned." Her shoulders slumped. "Unfortunately he doesn't seem to think so."

Alert, Devon sat up straighter. Maybe Francyne was right and the Neanderthal really had been looking for Jamie. "Has he been . . . bothering you?"

An unladylike snort escaped. "Oh, yeah, you could definitely say that."

"Does he live around here?" Just what he needed. He had finally met someone he thought was a nice girl and she had issues.

"No! At least, I hope not." She glanced nervously around the empty room as if expecting her ex to pop out of one of the driers. "I think I finally lost him in Tallahassee." She leaned closer, bringing with her the sexy scent of fabric softener. Pretty pathetic when fabric softener turned him on. "That's why I haven't been working as a teacher." Her words brought him back to their conversation. "I've been trying to get away from Fred."

"Fred? Him again? What does ole Fred do, that he can travel around making your life miserable?"

"He's rich. Independently wealthy."

Of course he was. Just his luck, the first girl to interest him in ages not only had baggage, the baggage had deep pockets. Meanwhile, if he didn't get free rent by managing the Surfside Villas, he'd have to make the choice between living indoors and eating.

Suffering for your art sucked.

9

"Jamie, we don't have to talk about this if it upsets you."
Please. Shut. Up.

"Hmmm?" She looked up from folding a pillowcase.

"You don't have to talk about Fred. I understand." How
could he be getting hard just from watching her hands while
she folded? Must be all the stroking she was doing. *Damn, the
wrinkles are out, for cripes' sake.*

"I don't mind talking about him."

Great. Discreetly arranging his package, he sat down, folding his hands in his lap. "You don't?"

"Devon, you have to understand how totally I am over him.
He has severe anger issues, and when his temper is riled, he's
mean as a snake."

"Did he hurt you physically?" Men who abused women
were pond scum.

"No, but not because he didn't think about it. I was just too
quick. When I realized how seriously deranged he could get, I
left. But he followed me. That's why I had to keep moving for
the last couple of years." Her shoulders slumped, drawing his

attention to her cleavage. "I'm just tired of constantly looking over my shoulder and having to relocate. I'm hoping I out-smarted him this time." She smiled and stacked the clean laundry in the basket. "I'm originally from Colorado, and I always talked about going back when we were together. When I started moving around, I realized I was heading in that general direction. I'm hoping he thinks that's where I went. Maybe when he doesn't find me, he'll give up."

He thought of the man Francyne talked with and decided not to mention the old lady's hunch.

Taking the basket from her, he held open the door and then followed her across the courtyard. "If you're not too tired, I thought maybe we could have dinner at my place."

"You cook, too? I love to cook. Baking is my specialty." Her face fell. "I should have picked up some pans and groceries. I could have brought dessert."

"Next time," he promised, setting her basket inside her door when she opened it. "I made a decadence cake the other day that will still be good."

"Decadence cake?"

"You never heard of a chocolate decadence cake? It's devil's food with fudge marbled through it. Very rich and moist. Gooey fudge frosting, and then I go one step beyond by adding whipped cream and a drizzle of hot fudge right before I serve it."

"Stop!" She placed her hand on her flat stomach. "I think I just gained five pounds from talking about it! What time should I come over? I saw a shop on the corner, would you like me to bring anything? How about wine?"

"Wine would be good, but I have some, so don't bother unless you just want to go out. How about in an hour or so?"

"No bother." Her teeth flashed in the shadows when she smiled. "See you in an hour." She went up on her toes and brushed a kiss across his cheek, setting off sparks to travel up to the tops of his ears.

* * *

Jamie twirled in front of the mirror at the resale shop around the corner from her apartment. The blond hair and deep tan no longer shocked her, and the yellow tank dress she had on looked fabulous with her new coloring. A glance at the price tag had her chewing on her lower lip. Though not pricey, the dress would easily pay for a week of groceries.

"That dress was made for you, doll," Shirl, the salesperson of questionable gender, said in her/his deep, gravelly voice. "You should buy it."

Without waiting for a reply, Shirl resumed flipping the pages of a tattered issue of *Vogue*.

"I should, shouldn't I?" Jamie turned and glanced at her back in the mirror, enjoying the way the yellow brought out the tan on her skin and the way the neckline dipped scandalously low. "But . . . I just don't know."

"Didn't you see the sale sign in the window?"

"What sale sign?"

They walked to the plateglass storefront and looked at the signless window.

"Damn kids," Shirl said. "Must've snatched it. Anyway, today is Tuesday. It's half off of half off day."

"Really?" What luck. She did some quick tabulations. The dress still would set her back more than she really should spend.

"And it's also, ah, blond-hair day. You get an additional thirty percent."

"But I'm not really a blonde," she confided.

"That's okay." Shirl patted the voluminous pile of red hair he/she sported. "I'm not really a redhead either. So what's your name, doll?"

"Jamie. But I—"

"Listen up, Jamie." Shirl looked around the deserted store. "Tell you what I'm gonna do. For today only, for the next five minutes, I'm giving a special Jamie discount. An additional fifteen percent. You look totally hot in that dress. You know it. I know it. Whoever you're dolling up for will know it, too. So what do you say?"

"Sold!"

Devon stirred the rapidly thickening sauce and shot a worried glance at the clock. He should have waited to add the sherry. Jamie said she'd be there in an hour. That was one hour and fifteen minutes ago. If she didn't get here soon, he couldn't guarantee the quality of the Shrimp Newburg. As for the pastry cups he'd planned to serve it over . . . well, even Killer wouldn't want them in a few minutes.

A knock on his door brought a wave of relief that surprised him. Tapping his wooden spoon on the edge of the pot, he quickly covered it and set the spoon on the trivet before going to the door.

What he saw there was worth the wait.

The sunset gilded Jamie's shoulder-length hair and made her tanned skin glow like burnished gold. The warm, sunny yellow of the minidress she wore had him salivating, eager to peel it off.

But that would have to wait. If he didn't serve the food immediately, he may as well pitch it.

"I didn't know what you were making, so I brought a Lambrusco and a white," she said with a smile, holding up two wine bottles. "Mmm. Something smells great!"

"You like it? It's a new aftershave I got at Christmas—oh!" He grinned at her. "You meant the food, I guess." He pretended to wince when she cuffed his arm. "It's Shrimp Newburg. I consider it one of my specialties."

"I don't think I've ever tasted it." She wandered into the living room, shoved a pile of magazines to the side and sat down on the sofa.

"It's a lot like Lobster Newburg, only made with salad

shrimp. And I add a few other things to give it a kick. It's just about ready." He went back into the kitchen and took the pastry puffs out of the oven.

She nodded and watched Devon walk into his kitchen. He was so cute in his *Kiss the Cook* apron. And she fully intended to kiss the cook before the night was through.

Nervous, she picked up a wrapped square from the candy dish on the scarred end table and frowned. What was that? It looked like one of those thin red licorice strings she used to love as a kid, rolled into a circle. Must be leftover from Halloween or something. She ripped open the cellophane packet and popped the treat in her mouth.

Wow. It must be really old. The cherry taste she'd been expecting was a bit off, kind of dusty tasting. She chewed a little more. Man, the licorice was rubbery.

"All set!" Devon's voice caught her attention. "Ready to eat?"

She quickly swallowed the licorice bite, trying not to gag. Embarrassment heated her cheek at Devon's look of outrage. Maybe he was particularly territorial of his candy.

"What the hell did you do?" He set the basket of something down on the table, which she now noticed was set with a light linen tablecloth and mismatched plates.

"I-I'm sorry! I didn't think you'd mind if I had a piece of licorice. I—"

"Licorice!" He roared with laughter. "Li-lic-licorice!" He wiped tears from his eyes and snickered again before speaking. "Jamie, that wasn't licorice." Another snicker.

"It wasn't?" Whatever it was had formed a wad in her stomach. "What was it?"

"Was it in that bowl?" He pointed, and she nodded. "It was a condom."

"A condom!" Her face could quite possibly burst into flames at any moment. "Who keeps condoms in a candy dish?"

"I do. I write for a few sex-toy manufacturers, for their catalogs. They send me all kinds of samples so I can see what they look like, what they feel like. How they taste." He burst out laughing again. "H-how did it taste, by the way?"

She giggled. "Rubbery."

10

"Should I try to throw it up?" That would really make it a fun date.

"I think you'll be okay." He held the chair out for her. "You're still hungry, aren't you?"

With a grimace, she sat down. "Very funny. Yes, I'm starved! That's why I ate the, ah, thing in the first place."

The cherry dust taste made her stomach revolt practically before the words left her mouth.

Gagging, she held her hand over her mouth and looked frantically around the apartment.

Eyes wide, he pointed, and she ran, barely closing the bathroom door before losing the battle. The condom hit the water of the toilet with an echoing plop. What little lunch she'd had left soon followed.

Weak, she leaned against the counter and turned on the cold water. After splashing her face, she rinsed her mouth and then helped herself to a fingerful of toothpaste from the tube on the counter.

A light tap sounded on the door, followed by Devon's concerned voice. "Are you okay? Do you think you should see a doctor?"

She took her time refolding and hanging the towel, then opened the door. "Thanks. I'm fine. Just incredibly embarrassed."

"I'm sorry. I should have known better than to leave stuff like that lying around."

"Um, do you have a lot of need for . . . um, those things?" Maybe she should have stayed home. The guy didn't look like some sex fiend, but you just never knew about stuff like that. "I should probably go now."

"Wait. You haven't even had dinner yet." He held up his hand when she began to protest. "I can't eat it all, and Killer is allergic to shellfish. C'mon. You would be doing me a favor."

"You have a dog who's allergic to shellfish?"

He shrugged. "No, not really, but it sounded good, didn't it?"

"Well, I guess I could at least eat and help you clean up."

"Thanks." He motioned her to sit and went back into the kitchen only to reappear a moment later with a steaming serving dish. From a basket on the table, he placed a little pastry bowl on each of their plates and then ladled the thick coral-colored sauce over it.

He stomach gurgled its anticipation. "Mmm," she said, hoping to cover the rumble of her stomach. "That smells wonderful!"

"Thanks, I hope you like it."

She took a cautious bite of the sauce and had to hold back a moan of ecstasy. The delicate flavor of the shrimp blended with other flavors on her tongue to make her taste buds sit up and take notice. "Are those mushrooms?"

He nodded. "Is there a problem?"

Swallowing, she shook her head. "No, it's fine. I just wondered." She cautiously swallowed her bite. Man, she hated mushrooms. Always had. It was like swallowing slime.

"Are you sure you're okay?" Devon poured her another glass of wine after she gulped down the first one.

"Yes." She smiled her brightest smile. "This really is delicious. I've made Lobster Newburg before, but this has a different flavor to it, besides the fact that it was made with shrimp."

"I use a little extra spice to give it more kick."

Sweat broke out along her upper lip and forehead. She wouldn't be surprised if her cheeks were heat flushed. She drank her wine in three swallows. "Delicious. Really unique."

He nodded, his smile transforming his features from cute to devilishly handsome. "Cayenne. About four times the amount called for, plus seafood cocktail sauce. And about twice the amount of cooking sherry, just to kick it up another notch."

"Well, you certainly did that." She set her glass down.

His opinion of Jamie had ratcheted up while watching her devour her meal. It was great to find a woman who liked to eat and had a healthy appetite.

Killer chose that moment to crawl out from under the chair and yawn while he stretched. The dog spared little more than a glance at their company before coming over to sit next to Devon's chair.

"Not tonight, sport, we have a guest." Devon looked over at Jamie, who was watching Killer with a strained look on her face. "He's harmless, Jamie. Really. He just likes to be included, and shrimp is one of his weaknesses. I usually give him any leftovers." He shrugged. "I guess I spoil him, but he has had such a hard time eating."

Her heart tugged at the expression on Devon's face. What a guy, to be worried about hurting a dog's feelings.

"I totally understand. It's just that I'm allergic to most dogs. . . ."

"From what I've been told, Pomeranians are hypoallergenic. Killer shouldn't bother you."

"You know, come to think of it, I had a reaction the first day, but I seem to be okay now."

"I bet it was Petunia, Francyne's dog, not Killer, that was getting to you." Noting her empty plate, he rose, clearing the dishes. "Save room for dessert?"

"Absolutely. Do you need some help?"

"Nope. All under control," he called from the kitchen.

He returned to set a piece of chocolate sin, if she ever saw it, in front of her. Topped with a satiny dollop of whipped cream that was sectioned by drizzles of hot fudge cascading to be soaked up by the dark chocolate cake, the scent alone probably caused weight gain.

"This looks positively decadent," she said once he'd sat down and picked up his fork. She took a tentative bite and had to force back a moan as the moist cake melted in her mouth, the combination of rich whipped cream and warm, smooth fudge topping sliding down her throat with the smoothness of an experienced lover's caress.

The taste was so purely seductive, an image of him painting her body with the dessert and licking it all off flashed through her mind. Her nipples hardened to needy peaks. She swallowed and pushed away from the table.

"That was delicious. Here, let me clean up, since you cooked."

He leaped to his feet. "No, not necessary. You're my guest, after all. I can take care of them later. Would you like a cup of coffee? I have some made."

"That would be great, thank you."

"Have a seat. Let me feed the beast and I'll bring it right out."

She wandered over to the bookshelf and took in the vast array of books. Her host certainly had eclectic taste in reading material.

She trailed her hand along the sofa table, only somewhat surprised to find it dust free.

The plaid sofa was old, but the burgundy, navy and green colors were still vivid. The cushions gave to hold her in a comfy hug. It wasn't hard to imagine snuggling up on the couch to read or watch a movie.

"Here you go. I hope you like flavored coffee. This is from the shop down the beach. Amaretto toffee." He handed her a mug and grinned. "I added the whipped cream."

The smooth sweetness of the coffee warmed her mouth and throat. "Mmm," she said, licking away her whipped-cream mustache. "This is so good! You're going to make me fat."

The way his gaze swept her body caused a wave of heat to follow.

"I doubt that," he said, his voice low and intimate.

She resisted the urge to scoot over when he sat down as close to her as possible without sitting in her lap. Should she move? Ignore the tingling where their hips touched? Rip his clothes off and jump his bones?

Heat streaked up her chest and neck to settle in her cheeks. The tops of her ears felt as if they might burst into flames. She'd never considered herself a sexual being. Never really been all that interested in sex, to be honest. Yet, since moving into her apartment, she'd been able to think of almost nothing else. Maybe she was becoming a latent sex fiend.

Devon kicked at something, and she looked down. "What's that? A doggy toy?"

Now *his* cheeks colored. "No. Besides writing novels, I write catalog copy. For sex-toy companies, remember? The manufacturer sends samples, and I sort of, um, test the stuff and then write the descriptions."

She picked up a handful of condoms from the candy dish next to the lamp. "Right. I forgot."

He nodded.

"What did you kick under the couch?"

In reply, he reached down and brought up a bright red dildo. "This model is called Red Hot and Ready. It not only vibrates, it glows in the dark and has a warming feature."

"Wow. Warming? How do you turn it on?"

He reached around her and turned off the light, his arm brushing her already aching nipples. "It shows up better with the light off. See the little darker red button by the base? Push it."

She did, and the button changed from red to green.

"As it warms," he explained, "the color changes from green to blue."

She ran her hand up and down the shiny length, trying to decide if she was imagining already feeling the phallus warm.

A glance at Devon told her the dildo wasn't the only thing hot in the apartment.

11

Devon watched Jamie stroke the vibrator and shifted position on the sofa cushion in an attempt to gain some distance. He really wanted to rip the stupid thing out of her hands and tell her to try the real thing.

Well, not quite. What he really wanted to do was play with her and the vibrator until she was as hot for him as he was for her and then toss the appliance aside and show her what a real flesh-and-blood penis could do.

He thought of his lackluster love life. Maybe she'd prefer the gigantic rubber penis to the real thing, come to think of it.

After all, why would someone as hot as Jamie want anything to do with a geek like him?

Then again, her nipples were practically poking holes through the top of her skimpy little dress. Maybe she found him at least marginally attractive.

Hell, at this point, he'd be ridiculously grateful for a mercy fuck.

"Devon?" Jamie's words brought him back to the scene playing out on his couch. "Are you okay? If you're tired, we don't have to talk anymore. I can go on home so you can get some rest or work or . . . well, whatever you need to do."

"I enjoy the company. Working all day and most of the nights, you get to where you look forward to doing other things."

I want, I need, to do you. But, of course, he kept that thought to himself. But what if he had said it? What would she do? How would she react?

His mind's eye saw her eyes widen, heat suffuse her cheeks. She'd wiggle a little, obvious in her arousal. They might kiss, and she would rest her hand trustingly on his bulging fly, massaging his erection in time to the cadence of their tongues.

Sometime during the kiss, she would unbutton her sexy little yellow dress, allowing her perfect breasts to escape, begging him to play with her nipples.

Of course, he'd comply. It wouldn't do to make a lady beg.

He smiled, imagining taking the succulent morsel into his mouth, sucking greedily while he slid his hand beneath her skirt. She would be pantyless. And wet.

She'd part her legs, inviting a closer inspection. But when he would slide to his knees before her, she'd say, "Wait. Use this." And hand him the Red Hot and Ready model with the instant-heat feature.

He'd watch while he pleasured her moist lips with the tip of the vibrator, feeling the warmth heat his palm, before he'd slide the bulbous tip into her cherry-red opening, making her gasp with the sensation. Carefully, oh, so carefully, he'd slip it deeper and deeper until—

"Devon!" Jamie's voice sliced through his fantasy, filleting the scene before his inner eye. "Are you sure you're okay? You look kind of, well, odd. And you're mumbling." She narrowed her eyes and leaned closer, giving him a delightful view down the front of her gaping bodice. "You can tell me. You were thinking about your book, weren't you?"

Swallowing, he nodded. "Sorry about that." He cleared his throat. "Now, where were we?"

She hesitated. She should probably go, but the truth was she was so turned on by holding the rapidly warming vibrator, she would probably walk funny if she tried to get up. It had been so long since she'd had sex. . . .

Of course, sex with Fred had been, for the most part, unappealing. When you allow someone access to your body because you're afraid to say no, the arousal isn't there. She glanced at Devon. But Devon was different. He was nice, polite. Nonthreatening.

"What do you think about get-acquainted sex?" As soon as the words left her mouth, she wanted to sink through the cushions and slink back to her apartment. She closed her eyes, mortification washing through her. "Forget I said that. I don't know what I was thinking. I—"

"I think it's a great idea," Devon broke in. "An excellent one, in fact." He drew the tip of one finger along the neckline of her dress, leaving a blazing trail of need. "I don't know why I didn't think of it myself."

"Maybe because you weren't all that interested." She started to get up, but he took her wrist in his hand, pulling her back to sit and her hand to his erection, straining the zipper of his shorts.

"Does that feel like I'm not interested?" He smiled and leaned to brush his lips across hers. "Now . . . I think we have on too many clothes." He glanced at the vibrator, still clutched in her other hand. "Or . . . would you like to play a little first?"

Until that point, she'd thought sex was just that, sex. Now, glancing down at the shining object in her hand, a whole world of possibilities and alternatives dawned on her.

"Could we? I think I like the idea of sex play." Heat suffused her cheeks. "Well, I think I'd like it anyway." She peeked through her lashes. "What do we do first?"

His heart squeezed, and he had to make a real effort to speak through the lump in his throat. Never in his life had a woman looked at him like he was the master of his domain. And hers.

He liked it.

"Anything you want, darlin', anything at all." He reached out and slipped the buttons on the bodice of her dress open until he had an unobstructed view of her lace bra and impressive cleavage. His mouth salivated with the thought of tasting her sweet nipples.

"Um, let's not start there, okay?" She clutched at the dress, yanking it together until she could shove the buttons back through their holes. At his confused look, she smiled and offered, "How about a demonstration of this?" She held up the Red Hot and Ready, shoving it in his direction.

"Sure." He took it from her and turned it in his hand a few times, recalling the spec sheet. "Well, you already know it's a vibrator." She nodded. "And it not only glows, it's got a self-heating feature for added stimulation." He suppressed a smile when he noticed her breathing had gone shallow.

"There are many things you could do with it, I suppose, either alone or with someone else." He flicked open the buttons on her dress again and flipped the activation switch on the vibrator. "For instance, you can stimulate yourself or someone else like this." He held the tip of the vibrating phallus to the beaded tip of her breast, letting her feel the vibration through the lace.

She whimpered.

"It would feel better against your skin." He reached for the front closure of her bra.

"No!" She jackknifed to a full sitting position and once again jerked her bodice closed. "I mean, where else could you use it?"

Devon raised his eyebrows.

"Well," she stammered, her cheeks heating, "besides the obvious place, of course."

"It works great with massage oil." He reached back to the table and grabbed a little bottle with a red label. "Relax, okay? I won't hurt you, and I'll stop anytime you tell me to, just say the word."

He poured a little puddle into his palm and rolled the vibrator head across it a few times; then he leaned down to slide her sandals from her feet.

The warm, oiled vibration on the arch of her feet set off wondrous sensations to travel up her legs to tingle the tips of her hardened nipples. Miraculously, it even seemed to vibrate her labia, milking it of moisture.

She tried not to squirm on the couch. Suddenly, for the first time since she learned what sex was, she wanted it. All of it. After years of ignorant abstinence, she was shocked to find she wanted to wallow in her newfound sexuality. And who better to initiate her than the kind and gentle man diligently vibrating the bottom of her arches with such a fierce look of concentration?

Slowly, he traveled up her leg, pausing to allow her to feel the vibration on the sensitive skin behind each knee. The sensation almost had her climaxing in her new panties.

Panting now, she lolled back against the arm of the sofa, a pile of boneless need.

"You like that, I take it?" He chuckled at her weak nod. "What else do you think you might like?"

In answer, she spread her legs, vaguely aware she should probably take off her panties but too weak from arousal to make the effort.

"Not yet, sweet thing, not yet." He reached to the other side of the couch and stuck the still vibrating tip into a pot of some kind. "This is raspberry flavored. It's actually pretty good. Here, taste it." He probed her mouth with the vibrating tip.

The distinctive smell of ripe raspberries wafted to her, and she obediently opened her mouth.

Against her teeth, the soft silicone of the vibrator buzzed, the warmth of it melting the delicious raspberry gel onto her tongue. On sensual overload, she sucked and licked the dildo clean and then ran her tongue over her flavored lips.

"I want to suck you," he said in a strangled voice. "I want to smear flavored gel all over your tits and lick and suck until it's all gone." He reached for her bra closure. "Will you let me suck you?"

"Later." She grasped her bodice to prevent him from exposing her falsies. "Let's play some more."

A devilish grin curved his mouth, transforming him from cute to hunk status. "Whatever the lady wants."

He pushed the tight short skirt of her dress up past her waist. Before she realized what he intended, he took a dollop of flavored gel and plopped it smack dab in the center of the crotch of her new yellow cotton panties. Next he smeared it around a bit.

His teeth flashed white in the dimness.

When had he turned off the dining room light? The apartment was now lit by only a dim light from the kitchen.

Her thoughts short-circuited when he closed his mouth over the cotton covering her mound and began sucking.

If she'd thought her bones were in danger of dissolving before, she hadn't seen anything yet. With a mewl, she spread her legs more and watched the top of his dark head while he pleasured her. Even through the fabric, the sensation was euphoric. Her eyes widened in surprise as a wave of pleasure washed over her.

She'd never climaxed with a partner before and found that the stimulation exceeded her wildest dreams. What must it be like to come while having sex?

Devon drew her attention back by tracing the line of her now damp panties with the head of the buzzing phallus. Close, ever closer to the center that ached for appeasement.

He paused again to roll the head in gel, and she thought about shoving his hand back to the business at hand, but a part of her waited. Wondering what would come next. Or who.

His teeth nipped her swollen folds as he gripped her panties in his mouth and tugged them from her body.

Shocked and so turned on she was speechless, she raised her hips to accommodate his action. He held her hips down, the pads of his thumb doing miraculous things to her while he bent to finish stripping the underwear from her body.

Before she could protest the coldness, he was back, the warm dildo vibrating at the door to her desire. He drew circles around and around her opening, the slick, warm head of the vibrator teasing her, before finally—finally!—dipping the tip into her weeping flesh.

On sensory overload, she bucked her hips, sending the buzzing warmth deep inside where it was met with orgasm number two.

Weak and somewhat disoriented, she opened her eyes to see Devon tearing at his clothing. "Wait," she managed to whisper.

He must have heard her because he stopped and looked down at her, his eyes hot and wild.

"My turn," she said. She had to take some kind of control. Another experience like she'd just had and she would be putty in his hands. She never again intended to let a man have control over her. And, after the last two rock-her-world orgasms, she also never intended to be celibate again either.

And Devon was the perfect man to introduce her to the hotter side of her sexuality.

She sat up, her dress still bunched at her waist, pleased to see his Adam's apple bob when he swallowed while still staring at her moist lips. Surprisingly it didn't embarrass her. In fact, the knowledge that Devon lusted after her was very empowering.

She tugged the waistband of his cargo shorts from his hands and pulled them down to his feet. His serviceable cotton boxers followed.

Watching him watch her, she took the vibrator firmly in her hand and plunged it deeply into her body, arching at the delicious sensation that immediately followed. But no time to delay right now.

Slowly, ever so slowly, she withdrew the dildo, performing little inflammatory circles on the way out until she was circling her opening with the warm, wet tip.

Immediately she reached out, grasping his firm buttocks, and drew him close, circling the purple head of his engorged penis with the tip of the red vibrator.

He closed his eyes and shivered. His hips convulsed, pumping against the device, flopping it one way and then the other.

She stifled a giggle at the thought of dueling penises and gripped the base of his shaft, her little finger rubbing and circling his sack like she'd read about in a magazine at the grocery store.

From the vibrations in his thighs, she assumed he liked what she was doing. Did she dare take it up a notch?

Keeping the dildo at work battling Devon's penis, she dipped her finger into the little pot, now on the coffee table in front of her, and quickly bathed Devon's engorged tip, all the while stimulating him with the vibrator.

In one movement, she tossed the vibrator down and closed her mouth over him. She swirled her tongue around and around, like she'd done with the vibrator, careful to keep her teeth sheathed. Encouraged by his moan, she sucked him more deeply into her mouth, all the while stroking his testicles while keeping a firm grip on his shaft.

Her jaw began to ache, but the delicious tingling between her legs kept her sucking, wondering what would happen next.

She didn't have to wait long.

12

Every muscle in Devon's body vibrated with need. A deep, primal need to mate. To plunge his throbbing cock to the hilt in the soft, wet warmth of the woman kneeling before him.

Where had he set the damn condoms? He glanced frantically around for the candy dish he'd moved after Jamie's mistake. Instead of laughing again, the thought of Jamie swallowing a condom had him impossibly harder.

Something brushed Jamie's back. Hot breath bathed her skin. Her blood ran cold.

What was she thinking? Had Fred found her? Was he watching right now?

"Lark, lark!"

She released her suction and looked at Devon's dog.

Making eye contact, the dog ran to the window, barking all the way, and then ran to the door and back to the window.

She stood, fumbling with her clothes. "I need to go. I'm sorry. Thanks for dinner."

"Wait!" Devon stumbled after her, tugging up his pants along the way. "Killer probably just needs to go out. He gets anxious about it if he waits too long. Just let me take him out and then we can—"

"No, we can't. This was a mistake, Devon. I'm not ready for, well, anything right now."

"But I—"

"I can't. I'm sorry. Bye!"

He stood, barefoot, and watched until Jamie closed the door of her apartment. Next to his feet, Killer pranced, all but crossing his legs.

"Oh, all right. Let me grab my flip-flops and we'll go." Stepping back inside, he slipped on the shoes and a shirt and took the leash from the hook by the door. "I want you to know you really messed up my date. I was this close." He held up his hand as if the dog would know what he was talking about. "This close to ending my losing streak. Your little bladder couldn't have held on for another twenty minutes?"

In answer, the dog trotted to the edge of the building and lifted his leg on a flowery bush.

"Guess not, huh?" He bent and rubbed the furry white head, scratching the pointed ears. "It's okay. Probably wasn't my best timing anyway. She has a lot going on in her life right now. She doesn't need to add me to the mix."

But, damn, it would have been fun.

"I thought you had a hot date." Francyne's voice carried in the night air.

They watched their dogs sniff each other.

"Yeah, it ended kind of early. Killer needed attention, and Jamie was tired." He clipped the reeling leash onto the line to allow Killer to run ahead of him.

Francyne fell into step beside him as they headed out onto the beach.

"My second husband and I used to love to walk on the beach," Francyne said a while later as they walked. "I still do. Guess that's why I stayed here."

"I didn't know you were married, Francyne."

She nodded, still looking out across the breaking waves. "Oh, yeah. Eight times. I'm a big fan of marriage. I just can't seem to sustain it for the long haul." She bent and picked up a shell, dusting it off before putting it in her pocket. "That's why I gave up after I lost my eighth husband."

"When did he die?'

"Die? He's not dead. Least, as far as I know. I said I lost him. We went on a cruise, and he didn't come back with me. Took up with some bimbo he met at one of those all-night buffets."

"I'm sorry. That must have been a shock."

"Aw." She waved her hand negligently while she spoke. "Not really. Truth be told, he was getting kind of boring. Good riddance."

"Well, you must not have thought so initially. You married him."

"Yeah, well, a lot of women get excited over nothing, and then they marry them. Petunia! Put that down!" She stalked to the big dog and pulled a clump of seaweed from her jaws. "That stuff is nasty. If you're so damn hungry, why didn't you finish your food? So," Francyne said when she was once more close enough to speak, "how did the 'product testing' go tonight?"

"It's just now ten o'clock. How do you think it went?"

"Dang, boy, you need to get some moves if you expect to be a player."

"Thanks for reminding me, Francyne." He ran his hand through his hair and stared out at the water. "I thought every-thing was going great; then the dog butted in and in seconds it all fell apart. I dunno. Maybe I'm jinxed."

They turned back toward the complex, their dogs trotting along beside them. "No, pumpkin, you're not jinxed. You're just out of practice. Don't worry. It's like riding a bike." She tugged her dog close. "C'mon, sweet thing, it's time for us girls to get some beauty sleep. Night, Dev."

He watched Francyne shuffle to her door and wondered if he should tell her he never learned how to ride a bike.

Jamie peeked through her living room curtains into the deserted courtyard. By the faint glow of the fire pit, she saw one man sitting in one of the patio chairs. Was it Devon?

She should go apologize for running out on him earlier. Instant recall of their time together had her moist and restless, yearning for something she did not usually yearn for: sexual gratification. If not with Devon, who? Maybe he'd take pity on her and at least let her borrow a vibrator.

Shoring up her confidence, she quietly closed her door behind her and edged toward the glowing embers.

"Hi," she said when she was close enough to be heard, "mind if I join you?"

The man turned and jumped up, towering above her. It was not Devon, and panic seized her until she realized it also was not Fred.

He smiled, revealing blinding white teeth that seemed to glow in the darkness. With the firelight gilding his sandy hair, he was easily one of the most stunningly handsome men she'd ever seen. Almost beautiful.

The embers from the fire pit bathed his tanned skin in a warm glow.

"Absodamnlutely, pretty lady," he said in a deep, smooth voice. Sticking out his hand, he said, "I'm Todd. I live in the apartment above yours."

If she planned to ever get over her fear, she had to stay . . . at least a little while.

"Hi, Todd, I'm Jamie." Gauging the distance to her door, should the need arise to escape, she sat down in the chair he offered. After he was seated, she said, "Have you lived here long?"

"About a year." He reached down into the cooler at his feet and brought up two longnecks. "Want a beer?"

She swallowed her usual negative reply. She'd sworn she was through with running, being scared of every shadow. Now was as good a time as any to begin her new life. "Yes, I think I would." He popped the top and handed her the frosty bottle.

The cool beer soothed her parched throat, relaxing her in a way she had not allowed in a very long time.

"How do you like the Surfside Villas, so far?" Todd leaned back in his deck chair, crossing a strong-looking ankle over his smooth knee, exposed by a pair of brief running shorts.

She tried not to stare at the expanse of perfect skin before her. But . . . wow! She'd seen bodies like that only on the beefcake calendars her grandmother loved so much. Boy, if Gram could see what she was sitting next to now. A wave of sadness washed over her. Gram was gone. There was no one to run to anymore.

"Jamie?" Todd's voice broke through her derailed train of thoughts. "Are you okay?"

"Hmmm? Sure. Why?"

"I asked what made you decide to come to this area? A job? Family?"

"Um, neither, actually. I just felt I needed a change of scenery and always thought the beach was relaxing." When he continued staring at her, she shrugged. "After this past year, I could use some relaxation." She glanced down at the empty bottle she held in a death grip. "Is there any more beer?"

Without a word, he reached into the cooler and handed her one.

"No offense, Jamie, but you strike me as a person who is running away from someone or something. I know a runner when I see one." Todd tipped his beer, his Adam's apple gliding in his smooth throat with each swallow. He wiped his mouth with the back of a long-fingered hand. "It's in the eyes, the set of the shoulders. I guess it takes one to know one."

"Oh?" It was definitely not the conversation she'd envisioned when she'd come out of her apartment, but her natural curiosity piqued.

He glanced around the courtyard and said in a lowered tone, "My sister's husband abused her. Nothing stopped him. She was afraid. Afraid of staying and afraid of leaving. Finally I knew we had to get her away and offered to go with her. For over a year, we moved around the country, always looking over our shoulder." A long drag from the beer paused his conversation. Just when she thought he wasn't going to continue, he said, "I saw the same look on your face she used to get on hers when I turned to face you tonight." He leaned forward, forearms on his knees. "Don't be afraid. I'm right above you. If you ever need me, bang on the ceiling. Or, better yet, yell. Hell, as lousy as the insulation is in this place, you could probably just say my name and I'd hear you."

She thought about that, wondering what else he might hear, should she and Devon proceed the way they seemed to be heading tonight. "Don't you work?"

He nodded and popped the top on another beer. "Yeah. I work late, until about two, three nights a week. But I'm home most days, if I'm not catching rays by the pool."

"I didn't see a pool when I moved in. Devon said it's out back, but I get confused when I'm in the courtyard. Where is it?"

He waved his bottle in the general direction of the arch leading to the laundry room. "Out there. And damn inconvenient, if you ask me. I'd have put it in the courtyard. According to the old lady—"

"You mean Francyne?"

"Yeah, her. Anyway, she says she remembers when the complex was new. Seems the architect made an error in the measurements and there wasn't room for the pool. Since they built in the wrong spot, too, there was plenty of space out back and to the side, so they put the pool out there."

"Wow. That's a really major mistake for the architect to make, I'd think." She finished the beer and accepted the new one he opened for her.

He nodded. "Yep. Guess it cost him his reputation. Possibly even his job." He frowned, his blond brows drawn together. "I'm gonna have to ask Francyne what became of that architect."

Jamie fanned her hair off her sweaty forehead. "Does it seem unusually hot to you?"

"Nope." He popped the top on another longneck. "Have another beer. It'll cool you off."

"No. Thanks anyway." She blinked in an effort to focus on Todd. "I'm already feeling a little woozy. I don't usually drink this much, but it tasted so good after the heat of the day."

"You need me to help you to your apartment?" He towered over her, a concerned look on his face.

"No. Please, sit down. I'm fine. I want to stay out a while longer and enjoy the night air."

He stared at her as though he wasn't sure she was telling the truth; then he sat back down and reached for his beer.

"What do you do, Todd?"

His white teeth flashed. "You mean when I'm not drinking beer out here?"

She smiled and nodded. Funny, there was a time when his polished good looks would have had her tongue-tied and she'd have been willing to do just about anything to get his attention. Now that she had it, she found she wasn't all that interested.

"I'm an exotic dancer, to use the PC term."

Her eyes grew wide. "You mean . . . ?"

"Yep." He tipped the beer bottle in her direction. "A stripper." He drained the bottle and set it under his chair with the others. "Are you shocked?"

She thought about that for a moment. "No, not really. Did you want me to be?"

Laughing, he stood and reached for the cooler. "No, it's just that a lot of people are, once I tell them."

"So, you're a trained dancer?"

"No, it was sort of on-the-job training. I could do something else, I have a degree, but for the time being I enjoy it. Hey, don't look so surprised. Most of the guys I work with have degrees."

"Then why—"

"Work as strippers? Better money, it's fun and a great way to meet women. I mean, look at me." He spread his arms and turned. "I'm not stupid. I know my time to do this is limited, so why not? I have the rest of my life to work the old nine-to-five."

"What is your degree in?" She frowned at the slurred sound of her speech.

He stared for so long, she thought he wasn't going to answer. Finally he said, in almost a growl, "Criminal justice."

He turned and began walking toward the stairs.

"Todd!" She knew it was none of her business, but she was curious.

He stopped and looked back at her.

"Did your sister succeed? Did she get away and make a new life?"

After a moment, he shook his head. "No," he said in a voice so quiet she had to lean toward him to hear. "He found her."

13

"And?" She held her breath.

Todd shrugged. "And nothing. The creep is still walking around."

"And your sister?" Her heart pounded while she waited for his reply. Putting herself in Todd's sister's place, she couldn't help but worry. What if Fred found her? Could she get away again? If Todd's sister succeeded, maybe there was hope for her, too.

"Nothing. It's like she disappeared from the face of the earth. This was her last known address. That's why I moved here. It's not much, but I keep telling myself as long as they haven't found her body, there's still hope she'll turn up."

"Oh, Todd," she said on a strangled breath, "I'm so sorry. I can't imagine how you must feel."

"You're right, you can't. I still look for her wherever I go. I know she's alive. I can feel it." He tapped his chest. "In here. I know if she's anywhere, eventually I *will* find her. And once I know she's safe, I'm going after the son of a bitch."

She stared across the courtyard long after Todd disappeared.

What she wouldn't give for a brother as obviously devoted as Todd. Heck, anyone who gave a rat's patootie about her, for that matter, would be good.

There was a time when she thought Fred was that person. In hindsight . . . She shook her head. What had she been thinking?

Remembered fear gripped her at the memory of creeping around her apartment, fearful of saying or doing the wrong thing and incurring Fred's wrath. How she'd stood it as long as she did was nothing short of a miracle.

Still, though, there were times she felt so lonely even Fred would be company. But all it took was remembering why she left and how difficult it had been to get away.

Once she left she'd never looked back. Unless you counted the looks over her shoulder to make sure she wasn't being followed. Again. It was almost uncanny, the way Fred seemed to always find her.

But not this time, she vowed, rising on unsteady legs to stagger toward her door. This time would be different.

Clicking on the tiled courtyard caught her attention a microsecond before something warm and solid hit her behind the knees.

The next instant she was flat on her back on the sun-warmed tiles, her head aching from hitting the hard surface.

"Damnit, Petunia!" Francyne's strident voice echoed from the stucco walls. Or maybe it was just within Jamie's head.

The old woman rounded the corner, her tan legs and sneaker-clad feet coming to a halt by Jamie's head. "Bad dog! Look what you did to our new friend." She leaned down until her nose was almost touching Jamie's. "You all right, sweetie?" The strong smell of alcohol on the woman's breath brought tears to Jamie's eyes.

She nodded and slowly sat up, rubbing the back of her head. "What happened?"

"Oh, that idiot dog of mine got spooked by her own shadow

and took off before I could get the leash clipped. Next thing I knew, she rounded the corner with me in hot pursuit. Then there you were, flat on your back." She glared at the dog, who now sat docilely against the building by Jamie's door. "Didn't take a rocket scientist to figure out how you got that way."

Petunia got up and snuffled Jamie's hand until she'd insinuated her head directly beneath Jamie's palm.

Hesitant, she scratched the big dog's ear and then ran her palm gently over the warm smoothness of her skull. In response, the dog leaned against her leg, almost knocking her sideways.

"Oh, now you've gone and done it," Francyne said with a sour look on her made-up face. "You just made a friend for life. C'mon, Petunia, you affection slut." She tugged on the now secure leash. "It's past time we got our beauty sleep, not that it will help you any." She peered back at Jamie through her trifocals. "You sure you're okay?"

Jamie nodded and smiled despite her headache. "I'm sure. Good night, Francyne." She leaned down and ruffled the dog's sleek head. "And good night to you, too, Petunia."

Before she realized what Petunia was going to do, the dog bestowed a big, slurpy doggy kiss. Yuck, dog germs.

She waved as Francyne and Petunia made slow progress across the courtyard and then let herself into her apartment.

The glare of the new lightbulbs she'd installed caused temporary blindness. Forcing her suddenly heavy eyelids open, she locked the door and the deadbolt and then checked to make sure all the windows and the patio door were securely locked.

Weary steps took her to the bathroom then on into the bedroom where she barely had time to remove the hot silicone pouches from her push-up bra before collapsing on the bed.

He watched through the side window as she reached into her dress and pulled out two globs and then tossed them aside before lying on the bed.

Jamie had altered her appearance since he'd last seen her. He'd hardly recognized her at first. Not that it would help her. She couldn't hide. Not from him. She was his; he was her destiny. The sooner she realized they were meant to be together, the better. She needed to give up all the running and come back where she belonged.

Memories of their last night together flashed through his mind like a movie on fast-forward. He hadn't meant to hurt her. But sometimes she made him so damn mad, it was like she wanted to see how far she could push. It wasn't something he was proud of, but it was her own fault. If she would just realize that and be a good girl, things like that wouldn't happen anymore. But when she was bad, she had to be punished.

Thoughts of punishing Jamie gave him the usual hard-on he had when he thought about her.

He glanced around the deserted courtyard. It was an old complex. Probably the locks weren't all that great. He gave an experimental tug on the window sash. Locked.

"Hey!" Devon rounded the corner of the courtyard and immediately saw the tall man peering into Jamie's bedroom window. "What the hell do you think you're doing? Who are you?"

As he approached, the man turned and ran toward the parking lot.

Devon thought about chasing him, but by the time he checked to make sure Jamie's window had not been tampered with, the guy was gone.

Okay, maybe he did have confrontation issues. Being beaten by bullies on a regular basis as a kid did that kind of stuff to a guy.

After all, he reasoned, it wasn't like the guy actually did anything. Sure window peeping was creepy, but it wasn't really a crime. Was it?

He couldn't resist taking a peek himself, just to make sure she was okay, of course.

Her yellow dress glowed with the weak light from the window. Jamie chose that time to roll over, the short skirt of her sundress bunching up around her hips, exposing her tanned legs and the sweet curve of her ass.

He swallowed a frustrated groan and readjusted his package before walking home.

No doubt about it, it was going to be another long night.

14

Jamie rolled over, shielding her sensitive eyes from the sunshine; its brightness made the screaming yellow walls scream louder.

Disoriented, she sat up, tugging her dress from around her waist. Her teeth were wearing little sweaters. How many beers did she drink?

Crawling to the edge of the bed, she made her way to the bathroom at the speed of turtles stampeding through peanut butter.

A long hot shower made her feel only marginally better. The low growl of her stomach reminded her she'd neglected groceries.

After pulling on baggy khaki cargo shorts and a peach tank top, she pulled her wet hair into a ponytail and headed for the door. A quick stop for root inspection at the mirror by the door confirmed she could go another week before her next touch-up.

Her stomach growled again. Maybe she'd stop at the little corner tearoom by the boardwalk and have breakfast first.

Everyone knew it was a bad idea to buy food when you're hungry.

An hour later, she carried her lone bag of groceries along the beach, thoroughly enjoying the feel of the cooler damp sand between her bare toes when she dug them in with each step.

Her sandals, in the deep pockets of her shorts, bumped against her thighs with each step. She sidestepped a jellyfish corpse and shifted her sack to the other side, looking up to see how far away she was from the distinctive faded-red tiled roof of the Surfside Villas.

A breeze kicked up, blowing grains of sand against her shins. She closed her eyes and tilted her head back to inhale the sea air. She could so get used to living on the beach.

As much as she enjoyed the scenery, it was time to get back to the apartment. She turned back toward the boardwalk and caught sight of a tall man standing to the left, beside a big palm tree.

Fred.

Clutching her groceries to her chest, she ran for the boardwalk. Her heart pounded its frantic beat in her ears; air wheezed in and out of her lungs in strangled gasps. Her first thought was to go back to her little apartment as fast as she could and lock the door. But then she thought again. If she ran directly to the apartment, Fred would follow and know where she lived.

The ice-cream parlor she and Devon went to was directly in front of her. She swerved to dodge a skateboarder and then shoved open the heavy glass door.

Frigid air bathed her heated cheeks. Sweat trickled between her breasts. Her heart still threatening to burst from her chest, she turned and peeked back at the boardwalk. Empty.

A scan of the immediate beach area also produced nothing. Had she imagined seeing Fred? Was the fear so ingrained that she saw bogeymen around every corner?

"Ma'am? You all right?" A teenage boy behind the counter

regarded her with a critical eye. He swallowed, his prominent Adam's apple bobbing with the movement.

"Fine. Thank you. I'm fine." She shoved some hair that had escaped from her ponytail out of her face and forced a smile. "It's just so hot out there. Whew! I thought I was going to pass out for a minute." She took a great gulp of water from the fountain by the door and waved as she opened the door and stepped into the sunshine. "I'm fine now. Have a great day!"

Afraid to look left or right, she put her head down and barreled her way home.

The cooler air of the hallway leading to the courtyard greeted her. She released a breath and picked up the pace.

Bracing for the final sprint across the courtyard, she took a deep breath and stepped out. And ran right into Devon's arms.

"Oh!" She made a quick grab for her bag of groceries.

He steadied her for a moment and then stepped back, his hands still grasping her elbows. "Sorry, I didn't see you." He bent to look her in the eye. "Jamie? Are you okay?"

She started to tell him she was fine, but the lie would not pass her lips. Instead, her lips began trembling uncontrollably. Tears blurred her vision.

He steered her into his open apartment door, closing her in his arms as soon as he shut the door.

She wasn't sure how long they stood like that, but finally the tears ebbed and she sniffed, stepping back from his embrace. "I'm sorry. I got your shirt all wet." She brushed at the dark spots decorating the shoulder and front of his light yellow T-shirt. Sniff. "I'm okay now. Really."

"But you weren't okay. What happened?"

"Fred." She drew a shuddering breath.

"Your ex-boyfriend?" He took her sack of groceries and set it by the door then led her to the sofa and sat down next to her, holding her trembling hands. "What happened? Did he do something?"

"No." She hopped up. "You know, it probably was just my overactive imagination. I'm fine now. I'll just take my groceries and get out of your way—"

She picked up her bag and almost dropped it. The trembling set in again, and she held the plastic sack in a death grip.

He eased the sack from her fingers. "Tell you what, let's put this in my fridge and go take a walk. If we see Fred, we'll call the cops." He returned from the kitchen to find her standing in the same spot, still shaking. "Jamie, sweetheart," he crooned, pulling her into his arms. "It'll be okay. I won't let anything happen to you. I'll be right there beside you."

Nestled in his warmth, it was easy to believe him. But if they walked outside and Fred saw them, she could be putting Devon in danger, too. The hard ridge of his fly pressed against her abdomen. Being so close to her had an obvious effect on him. Maybe they should just stay in and finish what they started last night. . . .

"C'mon, let's go." Devon stepped back, grabbing her hand and tugging her toward the door. "When we get back, I'll let you share my lunch. I made meatballs this morning, and there wasn't enough room in my freezer, so you'd actually be doing me a favor."

While he talked, she noticed the delicious aroma in his apartment. Her stomach growled its approval of the plan.

Out on the beach, the sea air ruffling their hair, fear seemed so overrated. Maybe she hadn't seen Fred after all.

A mile in either direction failed to turn up anything unusual.

Devon observed Jamie as they walked, admiring the way the sun kissed her tanned cheeks and shoulders, adding a peachy glow to her skin. And each time his gaze dropped to the softly rippling flesh swelling above the scoop neckline, his shorts grew another size too small.

He'd love nothing more than to go back to his place and finish what they started. But the stark fear on her face had stopped that train of thought before it left the station. When they had sex, and he prayed it would be soon, he didn't want fear to be in the bedroom with them.

To ensure that, he'd willingly walk the entire beach a hundred times over.

He had to take his mind off of making love with Jamie.

"Kiss me," he said and wanted to kick his spontaneous self. Kissing her was just about the worst way of trying to forget about having sex with her. But the hopeful look in her eyes had him deciding it may have been one of his more brilliant ideas. Possibly even more brilliant than inventing Trent for the hero of his books.

He pulled her into his arms, enjoying the tactile pleasure of her bare arms against the more tender skin of his inner arm. Bodies aligned, her more than ample breasts gently bumped against his excited pecs. Beneath his shorts, his cock did a little happy dance.

A quick glance around confirmed they were alone. He lowered his head, barely brushing her lips with his. When she tried to get closer, to get more of a kiss, he nipped her lower lip with the tips of his teeth, immediately soothing it with his tongue.

She did a little shimmy against his eager body that should have been illegal in most states, her hands gripping his shoulders.

"You call that a kiss?" she asked against his lips.

He deepened the kiss primarily to shut her up, but soon it spiraled out of control. Tongues dueling, bodies rubbing, he staggered back with her until he felt the sun-warmed stucco wall outlining the boardwalk. Against the wall, beneath the shade of several palms and ornamental trees, they were hidden from most views.

Jamie ground against his erection with a single-minded determination to make them both come in their pants if they weren't careful.

He'd pull back. He'd stop. Any minute. Damn, it felt so good to hold her and touch her. It was nigh unto impossible to think straight with her sweet little tongue sweeping the interior of his mouth while her hands squeezed his butt and her hot little pussy rubbed against his denim-sheathed cock in a carnal dance.

But he had to do it. Having sex on the beach was probably against at least three different Texas laws.

She did another sexy shimmy against him, her hard nipples all but burning holes in his shirt.

He looked down at her glistening cleavage, smelled their mutual arousal.

It just might be worth getting arrested.

15

He broke their kiss and stepped back, shoving his hands in the pockets of his shorts. "It's probably safe to go back to the apartment now." He glanced at his watch. "Let's have some lunch."

After a silent walk, he ushered her into his apartment.

"I just need to take Killer out. Then I'll get lunch going."

"Mind if I tag along?"

"No, I don't mind, but I should probably remind you that watching a dog take a leak, or worse, isn't too high on the thrill scale." He bent to clip on the leash as Killer pranced in excited anticipation. Or urgency. With dogs it was hard to tell.

After Devon grabbed some paper towels and a plastic bag, they headed back toward the beach.

"He's really pretty good at this. He doesn't take long to pick his spot and almost never goes on the beach."

She smiled at his obvious pride in his pet's bodily functions.

"You don't have any pets, do you? I can tell by the tolerant look you get, and your eyes glaze over when I talk about Killer."

"I had a cat once. But she's gone now." Thanks to Fred.

"Ever think about getting another one or something else? I

know you probably think I'm weird, but I realized after adopting Killer how much company an animal can be when you live alone."

What a guy. Not only was he sweet and kind, he was an animal lover.

"Not yet," she finally said, "I'm not completely over losing Muffin." She shrugged. "Besides, I move around a lot, thanks to Fred. It wouldn't be fair to subject an animal to that."

They watched the dog lift its leg and then began the walk back. The trip in was as silent as the trip out.

"So what's the deal with Fred?" Devon asked once they were back in his apartment. "He must've done something pretty bad for you to keep running from him."

Memories flashed through her mind. "I left before it got too bad, but I suspect Fred considers me his property, and he doesn't like losing anything. Or sharing. After we broke up, he disappeared, and I thought that was that. Then he showed up again, begging me to take him back. When I didn't, he got . . . well, unpleasant. And he did weird stuff like come in while I was gone and take things. I got a restraining order, but it didn't stop him. I finally realized the only way to get away was to move."

"But you still didn't get away, not really, did you?"

Discomforted by the intensity of his stare, she walked to the window and peeked through the blinds. For a few seconds she watched the people on the beach enjoying the scenery.

"Jamie? You okay?" He was behind her now, his warm hands resting lightly on her shoulder.

It would be so easy to lean back, take the comfort Devon offered, allow him to protect her.

She stiffened her shoulders, along with her resolve. "I'm fine. I just need some space—and time—to adjust and get on with my life." Assuming Fred would ever leave her alone long enough to do that.

"You're safe here, you know." He walked back into the kitchen, still talking. "The guys here are a strange bunch, but you can call on any one of them and they'd help you. They're loyal to their fellow residents."

"Good to know." She followed her nose into the tiny galley kitchen. "I met Todd already." She inhaled the warm yeasty scent of garlic bread and swallowed a moan. "He seemed like a nice guy."

"Yeah, he is. Doesn't seem like a stripper, does he?"

She eyed him. Was he kidding? "Um, Devon, have you ever taken a good look at Todd? I've never actually met a stripper, but I'd have to say he has all the qualification. He's hot!"

He set a basket of bread on the table and walked back to retrieve the bowls of sauce and spaghetti. "Well, yeah, if you go for all the smooth skin and muscle, I guess I could see where some women might find him attractive."

She watched him gather napkins and march out to the table again.

Definitely time to change the subject.

Once seated at the table, they dished up their lunch in silence.

"You're hotter, you know." Embarrassed at having blurted out her thoughts, she concentrated on spearing a meatball and popped it in her mouth.

Fork paused in midair, he looked at her for a moment and then said, "Are you nuts? I may be a straight guy, but even I know Todd is to-hell-and-gone better looking than I am." He put the bite of spaghetti in his mouth, chewed and swallowed. "Hell, if I wasn't such a committed heterosexual, I'd probably be interested in him myself."

"How did we get onto this subject?" She swiped her napkin at the bread crumbs she was sure circled her mouth and took a sip of water. "All I said was, in my opinion, you are much more attractive than Todd. Sure, he's buff and handsome, in the traditional ways." She kicked off one of her sandals and ran her toes up his calf. "But I find you so much more interesting. Really," she said at his incredulous look, "you have so much more . . . substance. I'm comfortable with you in a way I could never be with a person like Todd."

"Great." He frowned. "So I'm comfortable. Thanks. I think I preferred hot." He fed a cut-up meatball to Killer.

"Does Killer have a cage or something?" Realization dawned while watching him gently feed the dog: she wanted his full attention. She wanted to have sex with him, and having a doggy voyeur was not on the agenda.

"Yeah, in the storage closet. Why?"

Shoring up her confidence, she stood and reached beneath the skirt of her sundress. Never breaking eye contact, she grasped the edge of her panties and dragged them down her legs.

Praying she wouldn't trip or wasn't reading Devon wrong, she stepped out of the scrap of silk and walked toward him.

Stopping next to his chair, she leaned down to brush a kiss over his slack mouth. Taking his hand, she ran his palm up and down her inner thigh. "Lose the dog," she whispered against his lips, "and this will be waiting for you when you come back."

Practically tripping in his eagerness, Devon led Killer out of the room.

Jamie wasted no time in closing all the blinds and drawing the drapes, plunging the little living room into semidarkness.

Fingers shaking, she undid her dress, folding her prosthetic breasts safely within the skirt and setting it aside. Naked, she lay on the couch, strategically arranging the throw to conceal the difference in her assets.

She knew the moment Devon reentered the room. The air was suddenly charged. Her heart rate increased; her breathing became shallow. Against the softness of the throw, her nipples beaded to scrape the yarn.

"Are you into fantasies?" his soft voice echoed in the silent room.

Already moist places instantly became moister. Peering over

the back of the sofa, it was a struggle to keep her voice from cracking. "What did you have in mind?"

In answer, he picked up a meatball and slowly walked to stand at her feet. "I had a scene in my book where the hero makes love with food. I made it up, but I've always wanted to try it."

She swallowed and finally managed to nod her agreement. "But you have to get naked, too," she said around the knot of excitement in her throat.

In a flash, he stood before her, magnificent in his nudity.

Her eyes greedily took inventory of everything she'd wondered about for the last few days. His baggy T-shirts hid broad shoulders, a glorious chest, lightly furred with hair tapering down across washboard abs in a delightfully decadent path to widen again around his jutting sex. Mercy! Could she take all that into her body? Doing a quick comparison with the red phallus, she realized she could.

Dropping to his knees next to the couch, he yelped and recoiled.

"What?" Her effort to sit up was met with his palm pushing her back down on the couch.

"Nothing. Just a bunch of junk for my catalog job."

A smile curved her mouth, warming her inside with the remembered activities with the Red Hot and Ready model they'd played with on her last visit. "Maybe we can check them out?"

He returned her smile. "Later." He leaned forward, dragging the meatball against the skin on her chest. "Much." The meatball rolled along the upper swell of her breast while he used the other hand to tug the throw from her grasp. "Much." He dragged it down, exposing her nipples to the cooler air. Using the meatball, he circled each nipple, grazing the sensitive tips with the rough edge of the cooked meat. "Later." His hot breath now fanning her nipple, he swiped at the little trail of sauce with his tongue before taking her nipple deep into his mouth and sucking it in a smooth rhythm that had her hips flexing in synchronization.

After laving her nipples until they were clean and standing in stiff peaks, he continued rolling the meatball down over her stomach and around her navel. His tongue followed the trail, licking every drop from her hot skin.

Squirming and aching for more, she arched off the couch, her legs moving restlessly on the upholstery.

Seated on the sofa between her spread legs, he dragged the meatball back up her stomach, between her breasts to outline her mouth.

More than ready for the play to be over, she opened her mouth and sucked in the meatball, promptly chewing and swallowing it.

Through the dimness, she saw Devon's eyes widen and then crinkle with his smile.

"You ate my toy," he said in a teasing voice. "I guess I'll just have to find another one."

"Please." Her foot on his thigh stopped him from getting up. "No more food. I'm not hungry for any more appetizers. Let's get to the main course." She couldn't believe she was being so assertive, but since Devon hadn't run from the room, she must be doing something right.

He rimmed her opening with the tip of his finger and smiled down at her. "Not quite yet."

His smile was contagious. "Okay . . . what do you have in mind?"

He rummaged around for a few seconds and then sat back up. "Have you ever tried vulva stimulators?"

"Um, no. I—"

"Relax," he said, placing her left leg up along the back of the sofa. "You're going to love it."

She regarded the device in his hand. It looked like an attachment for a mixer. Maybe she wasn't as ready for a sexual adventure as she thought. Before she could sit up or even say anything, cool gel was stroked up and down and all around her labia.

A soft hum filled the air, immediately followed by the delicious sensation of her genitals being gently vibrated. The gel heated, combining with her own excited moisture.

"See? I told you it would feel good." His voice sounded smug, but she couldn't force her eyes open. She didn't want to miss a delightful second of sensation.

"Now I'm going to use the accessory to the stimulators." His voice floated somewhere above her, almost lost in the buzz of her blood rushing through her ears. "This won't hurt, but it may feel a little tight to begin with. Don't worry. You'll love it."

Tight was a bit of an understatement, but as long as the gentle buzz kept going it wasn't all that uncomfortable. "W-what are you doing?" she finally managed to say in a breathless voice. "What kind of accessory?"

"Vulva clamps. They're padded. If they're too tight, there's an adjustment. Relax. If you don't like it, I'll take them off. I just wanted to see what they looked like on a woman and see exactly how they worked."

If she could have formed a coherent sentence, she'd have told him they worked fine.

Cool air bathed her. Poised on the brink of what promised to be a record-breaking orgasm, it felt as though her vagina was a vortex, wanting to suck in any and everything around it.

Coolness filled her, deep within. She forced her heavy eyelids open.

"Flavored gel," Devon said in an equally husky voice before bending to the task.

His hot tongue bathed her exposed labia, flicking her engorged clitoris and then probing her vagina with smooth, sure strokes. After each tongue lashing, he blew softly on her wetness, ratcheting up her heart rate and respiration.

All the while the little stimulator did its thing, keeping her poised on the brink of orgasmic oblivion.

His hot erection bumped her inner thigh.

Suddenly her climax roared through her, taking her breath, altering her thought processes. Fireworks detonated behind her eyelids.

Abruptly Devon sat up, releasing her still vibrating tissue from the loving jaws of the stimulator and clamps. Pushing her legs together and up, he bent and licked her still vibrating pussy.

Small mewling sounds filled the air. She thought they were probably coming from her but didn't care. She wanted him. She wanted him now. She'd never wanted, needed as much as she did at that precise moment.

Unfortunately it was all her overworked lungs could do to continue breathing. Speech was not a possibility.

More cool gel soothed her swollen labia, only to be licked off by Devon's hot tongue.

Out of her mind with longing, she made animal-sounding grunts and tried to pull him up, to position his erection for greater access.

After much stretching, she was able to grasp his penis. But she couldn't guide him to the place that ached for it without contorting. She sighed and stroked him, content for a while to just hold his heat while he licked and sucked her toward another orgasm.

Contentment was short-lived. Soon, achy and restless, she made a decision. If he wouldn't make love to her yet, she could at least return the favor of oral sex. Funny, she'd always abhorred it, but now, for some reason, it was different.

She craved it.

It took some persuasion, but she eventually got him where she wanted him and took his hot length deeply into her mouth.

He groaned.

Against her arm, the big muscles in his thigh vibrated.

His hips paused their rhythmic thrusting for a few seconds while he reached for something on the floor.

The red glow of the Red Hot and Ready vibrator bathed them in its beam. He pushed a button, filling the air with a soft hum.

As they were lying on their sides, he hoped they wouldn't topple from the couch before they finished. While Jamie sucked his cock until he thought he might explode, he positioned the vibrator. He licked the strawberry-flavored gel from her swollen labia and then dragged the tip of the glowing vibrator along the plump folds.

Jamie moaned, her hips bucking against his shoulder, her teeth nipping at his erection.

He found her clit, now swollen from its shield, and fastened his teeth around it, drawing it into his mouth and sucking. As expected, she gasped and arched her hips. He plunged the vibrator deep within her, flicking the nub with the tip of his tongue while he moved the heated phallus in and out in a languorous rhythm.

Jamie screamed, her cum rushing out to wash the vibrator and his hand.

Deftly he switched positions, his mouth firmly fastened on her, his tongue buried deeply within her, licking her slick walls, while the vibrator worked its magic on her clit, bringing her to another screaming release.

She gently bit down on his cock, sucking him deeper. It fueled his excitement, took his breath.

But he didn't want to come in her mouth. It had been too long to settle for second best. He wanted to be buried deep within her tight pussy.

He stood on shaky legs and scooped her up from the couch. As soon as her legs came around his waist, he flexed his hips, burying himself to the hilt in her wet warmth.

Staggering, he walked toward his bedroom. Jamie came twice more before he lowered her to the mattress. Then it was his turn.

It was his new personal best.

16

"I should go home." Jamie stretched and smiled against the pillow at the feel of Devon's renewed erection nudging her hip.

"Mmm," he said, heating the skin on her shoulder. "Not yet."

Rolling over, she held him close and kissed his temple then sighed. "It's getting late. I really should go." She sat up, pulling the top sheet with her.

"Wait." He scooted across the mattress and stood. "I'll walk you home."

Transfixed, she stared at his still inspiring package. What was the hurry? It wasn't like she really had anything to rush back to or do.

She blinked, drawing back to her original plan. No. She had to go home. When she'd walked away from her life with Fred, she'd vowed not to get involved with another man until the whole Fred debacle was over and done. Besides, it was past time she learned to stand on her own two feet and not depend on anyone else. A sigh threatened to escape when she looked at the broad capable shoulders before her. It would be so easy to let Devon help . . .

"You know," he said, pulling up his boxers and reaching for a shirt from the pile next to the bed, "I usually enjoy being stared at. Especially by a hot babe like you. But somehow I get the impression lust isn't what's on your mind."

Their gazes met.

Dang. He was good. Too good to get involved in the mess that was currently her life.

Clutching the sheet to her, she backed toward the bedroom door. "I, ah, was just thinking about everything I had to do. You don't have to walk me back. It's not that far, just across the courtyard."

He paused and then continued pulling the T-shirt over his head. "Not a problem. Just thinking about stuff to do, huh?"

She nodded and stepped into the little hall connecting his room to the kitchen and bath.

He was right behind her.

"'Cause, I thought maybe you were thinking about what's his face. Fred."

His name hung like acid rain in the silence of the apartment.

Dang. She was just such a coward. She was running again. Running from Devon. Running from the way he made her feel. But what choice did she really have? If Fred found her, she could be putting Devon in danger, and that wasn't fair.

Scooping up her clothes along the way, she turned toward the bathroom. At the door, she turned to face him. "I'm not lying to you, Devon. I do have things I need to do. And I have my own apartment, and that's where I need to go. I'll be fine."

He stopped her from closing the door by placing his palm on the edge. "Can you look me in the eye and tell me this has nothing to do with Fred?"

Clutching her side of the door, she took a deep breath. "I could, but I won't. You're going to believe what you want to believe."

He released the door, allowing her to close it just in time to hide the tears she blinked away.

Maybe Fred had ruined her life. Living with him had been torture, and the fear was alive and well, thanks to his relentless pursuit. The question was, what was she going to do about it?

After pulling her clothes on and shoving her feet into her sandals, she took a cursory look in the mirror over the sink.

A blond stranger with terrified eyes looked back at her. Blond, terrified and . . . She leaned closer. And with one boob noticeably smaller than the other. Crap. Where was the errant gel blob?

Devon kicked the adult toys under his sofa with considerably more force than was necessary.

Damn. What was his problem? It wasn't like he didn't have stuff to do. The new catalogs were due to come out soon, and he still had a good hundred items to describe.

Thoughts of his time with Jamie filled his mind. The sex was so damned good, so right. And, the fact was, he wasn't ready for it to end. But he wouldn't beg.

Jamie walked into the room, the sheet clutched in front of her like a shield. Shit, what did she think he was going to do, strip her and have his wicked way with her against her will?

She bent, looking for something. He'd offer to help, but the sight of her firm, tan legs short-circuited his brain for a few seconds.

In his mind, he saw himself walking over and flipping up the sheet, dragging her panties down and off. He'd spread her legs wide, gripping the smooth ass cheeks, and plunge into her hot, honeyed pussy.

She'd scream in ecstasy, pulling his hands around to play with her tits.

He blinked and frowned. Her tits . . . her tits. What was it about them that tugged at his memory, buzzing around his sex-fogged brain like an irritating gnat?

She chose that moment to wrap the damn sheet around her

like a mummy, drawing his attention back from whatever it was he'd been thinking.

What the hell was she doing under there? He watched her gyrations for a few seconds. "Is there something I can help you with?"

She jumped at his question, looking damn guilty, in his opinion.

"No! No," she repeated in a softer voice. "I'm fine. I just realized my top was twisted." She folded the sheet and laid it on the arm of the sofa and then arched her eyebrow. "Or would you like me to put it back on the bed? I can help you make it before I go, if you want. The bed, I mean. I can help you make the bed."

He bit back a grin, watching the color rise up her neck to her cheeks. "No, that's okay. I can do it later."

Her shoulders slumped in obvious relief, and he told himself not to take it personally. Unfortunately he'd never been very good at listening to advice.

He strode to the door and grabbed Killer's leash from the hat rack. "Let me get Killer, and we'll walk you home."

"I told you, that's really not necessary." She hovered by the couch, her body language telling him she wouldn't argue if he just did it.

With a stay gesture that always worked with Killer and Petunia, he hurried to the spare room and took his dog out of the kennel. When they returned to the living room, Jamie was gone.

"C'mon," he said, clicking the leash to the dog's collar. "At least you can get rid of your piss. Nouns are like that. It's the verbs that get to you."

17

Heart thundering in her ears, Jamie power-walked across the deserted courtyard. Eyes wide, she scanned the area constantly, jumping at every shadow.

It had been Fred she saw on the beach. She knew it. Didn't she?

After jiggling her key in the old lock, she threw her shoulder against the door and half fell into her darkened apartment.

A little whimper of fear escaped her. She banged the door shut and threw the bolt home while her other shaking hand frantically felt for the light switch.

The light came on, illuminating the bright decor to a blinding level. As soon as her eyes adjusted, she glanced around. Everything was the same as she'd left it. There was the basket of laundry and her beach sandals.

She forced a laugh at her panicked state and put her groceries in the fridge. But, just to be on the cautious side, she checked all the window and door locks, looked in all the closets and under her bed before going into the bathroom. Maybe a nice hot shower would help her sleep.

* * *

He stepped from the shadows and watched as Jamie's apartment blazed with light. Little fool. He counted to ten, but it didn't help his frustration. Why didn't she realize she belonged to him and stop her stupid little games.

His cock stirred when her bathroom light filtered through the darkened bedroom to the window where he stood, hidden in the shadows. Instant recall of her body, wet and slick in all the right places, raced through his mind.

He stepped back, deeper into the shadow between the units. A group was congregating around the fire again tonight. It wouldn't do for any of the testosterone-laden tenants to see him. Ditto for the old lady and her bloodthirsty dog.

He rubbed his calf, still tender from the rottweiler's nip the day before. He'd take care of the damn dog.

Then he'd find Jamie and convince her he knew what they needed.

They belonged together.

Jamie clutched her towel tighter and edged along the wall toward the side window.

"Stupid," she whispered. "You're being stupid, jumping at shadows." With slow, deliberate movements, she reached out and tugged down the cord, releasing the blind.

The metal sound echoed in the room as the blind unfurled to land with a clang on the sill.

She edged around the corner until she came to the window facing the courtyard.

The amber glow from the fire pit cast her neighbors in a glow, bronzing their buff bodies.

She spotted Todd by the edge of the group and wondered again about his sister and what he would do if he ever caught up with the man who had ruined both of their lives.

The man she recognized as Drew sauntered across the space

and paused to speak to Todd before bending to extract a beer from the cooler by his feet.

Before they spotted her, she let the second blind down and leaned against the cool wall. Whew! She grinned. Her friends back home would be drooling at the sight of her neighbors.

Sobering, the thought hit her. She would probably never see any of her friends again, thanks to Fred. She tucked the towel more securely. At least she knew her friends were safe now. She'd led Fred away from them when she allowed him to chase her far away.

So far away that her old life seemed more like a dream than her past.

Devon logged off and sat back with a satisfied sigh. He'd just sent the latest batch of catalog copy to the Ballbreaker editor. His check should arrive within the next week or so.

He picked up the Float Like a Butterfly, Sting Like a Bee and flipped its tiny stinger with the tip of his index finger, careful to avoid the activation button.

All sorts of hot, raunchy ideas of how he could utilize the innocuous-looking gel insect on Jamie had him shifting in his chair.

He put the bee next to his computer and adjusted his shorts to accommodate his erection; then he flopped back in his chair.

Sex with Jamie was unlike anything he'd ever experienced. That was the only reason he wanted to howl at the moon and crawl to her, begging for more.

He stood and turned off the desk lamp then walked to start picking up the clutter they'd left behind in his living room.

A knock echoed through the quiet apartment, Killer's bark immediately following as he pranced toward the door.

"Damnit, if that's someone wanting an apartment at this time of night, I'm going to kick their ass."

Killer growled his agreement as Devon swung open the door.

A brown cardboard box rested on the doormat. A glance confirmed it was from the Talk Dirty To Me company and probably included the latest models of dildos for the new line the editor told him about last week.

He sighed and picked up the box, absently tapping his finger on its side. The idea of working anymore tonight held no appeal. Still, the sooner he wrote the copy and turned it in, the sooner he'd get another check.

He walked back in, not stopping until he reached the kitchen, where he rummaged around for a knife.

He pulled the first dildo from the box, matching the packing slip with the numbers on the clear wrapper, and began laughing.

Inspiration struck.

Jamie had just finished applying coconut-scented lotion and pulled her nightshirt over her head when a knock sounded, rattling her door.

"Jamie? You up?"

A peek through the peephole confirmed the identity of her late-night visitor.

After struggling a few seconds with the door, she swung it open.

Devon stood smiling at her, a clear plastic container of strawberries in one hand and what looked like a cake box in the other.

"Hi! I'm up." She sniffed at the box, which definitely held some kind of cake, and tried not to look at what else was obviously up.

"Thought maybe we'd have a bedtime snack." He walked past her to set the boxes on the table and then came back to plant a smacking kiss on her forehead before shutting the door. "I brought angel-food-and-strawberry surprise."

"What's the surprise about angel food and strawberries?" She watched him slice the cake and place it on mismatched plates from the kitchen and then spoon the strawberries on top.

What could only be described as a devilish grin flashed her way, his eyes sparkling.

He reached for the hem of her nightshirt. "Ah-ah-ah. We wouldn't want to get your nice, clean shirt sticky and dirty."

"Wait!" She clutched her shirt to her chest and dove for the lights. "Let's light candles." At his look of confusion, she hurried on. "It's much more romantic and also saves money on the power bill." Lame, so lame.

But by the look on his face when she returned from lighting a few candles, he didn't seem to notice.

With a flourish, he grasped the hem of her shirt and drew it up and over her head and then tossed it onto the couch. He waggled his eyebrows. "I've got whipped cream, but you have to get naked if you want any."

Ever since catching sight of his erection as he walked in her door, she'd been wanting to be naked, so it was no hardship.

Hooking her fingers in the string sides of her thong, she shimmied out of her panties and tossed them aside.

"Your turn," she said in a voice turned husky with desire.

His grin could only be described as weird. He made a big production of unzipping his pants.

The tip of his erection was the darkest purple she'd ever seen.

She frowned, but before she could comment, he pulled it out—and off!

"Check it out," he said with an eagerness that was contagious. "First you push up on the balls, like this, while you squeeze, and voilà!"

Streams of what she hoped was whipped cream spurted

from the end of the phallus, forming a frothy pile to cover the strawberries.

Her shrieks of laughter bounced from the old walls, along with his deeper, rumbling chuckles.

Gradually their laughter subsided, replaced by an awareness that heated the room, altering their breathing.

"This," he said, indicating the purple penis, "is from the new kitchen gadget line. It's, um, not for internal use."

"Good to know." She stood looking into his eyes and wondered if she was going to have to make the first move. Assuming any move was made.

"You're so beautiful," he whispered.

"And you," she said, stepping close to tug his shirt from his waistband, "are way overdressed." She pulled his shirt over his head and let it drop.

His hand on hers stopped the descent of his pants. "If I take these off, it will be over too soon." He brought her hand to his lips and kissed her knuckles, pulling her toward the table. "Climb up." He removed the plates of cake and helped her stretch out on the cool tabletop. "Let's play."

He shook the dildo, little droplets of whipped cream flying to spatter her face, eliciting a fresh burst of giggles.

He silenced her with a kiss, dragging his teeth on her lower lip before straightening. "Don't laugh, woman. I'm creating a masterpiece."

Amid lots of squirming and giggling, he managed to finally write his name, in whipped cream, across her flat, tanned tummy.

Taking a plump strawberry, he bit off the tip, allowing the juice to trickle across her breast and down her rib cage. With the piece of fruit, he followed the lines of his name, applying pressure to ensure the juice escaped, coating her torso in its sticky sweetness.

He drew happy faces around each breast, topping the puckered nipples with a dollop of cream, and then licked them clean.

"Devon," she breathed his name with a hitch in her voice, causing his breath to lodge in his chest for a moment.

No one had ever called his name during sex or any act of passion.

"Shhh," he said, shucking his pants and climbing up beside her, hoping the old table would hold their combined weight. "Let's play nice and get you all cleaned up."

His tongue followed the flowing script of whipped cream and strawberry juice, lapping at the combined sweetness of the concoction and her skin.

Beneath his steadying hand, Jamie squirmed, the heat of his palm filling her with a different kind of warmth.

Their breathing sounded unnaturally loud in the quiet apartment.

She reached for him.

The spell was broken as the sound of shattering glass echoed from the walls.

18

Jamie's shriek immediately followed. What looked suspiciously like one of the bricks from the landscaping border lay amid the shards of glass in the living room floor.

Jackknifing to a sitting position, she scrambled for her night-shirt.

Devon rolled from the table. "What the hell?" He headed for the door.

"Devon!" Jamie, now on her feet, grabbed his boxers, waving them in his direction. "You're naked!"

Relief washed through him. He wasn't really a coward. As a sensible, educated adult, giving chase wasn't the thing to do. Yet he'd felt compelled to do so. Thankfully, Jamie's voice called a halt to his faulty line of thinking.

Watching his step in the candlelight, he walked back and took his boxers, stepping into them while he observed Jamie's expression.

Clearly upset, she looked at him expectantly.

He heaved an inward sigh. Of course she was looking expectant. He was the guy. Guys did stuff like rescue damsels in distress, slay dragons, charge fortresses and all that jazz.

The problem with that thought was . . . it wasn't technically his style. Yeah, that was the problem. He was more of a lover than a fighter.

Zipping his shorts, he shoved his feet into his flip-flops and headed toward the door. He could do macho, protective male. After all, in the minutes it had taken for him to get dressed, the guilty party had no doubt beat tracks and made a clean getaway. At Jamie's furrowed brow and her gaze on his feet, he explained, "Don't want to step on any glass."

She nodded, evidently understanding, so he ran for the door. Okay, maybe *ran* is too strong of a verb. Walked briskly would be more definitive.

He flipped the locks and looked back. Maybe he puffed his chest a little, but he was risking life and limb. He needed to look buff.

"Stay here. Lock the door after me." Good grief, did he really just talk an octave lower? How asinine was that?

Outside her door, hearing the lock turn, he released his breath, slumping his shoulders. What now?

Heavy footsteps sounded on the stairs.

Shit! Maybe he should have waited to come out until he put on a shirt. It would have given the thrower more time to get away.

Todd rounded the corner, coming to an abrupt halt in front of Devon.

"Did I hear glass breaking?" Todd looked around and zeroed in on the jagged remains of Jamie's window. "Is Jamie okay? I thought I heard her scream."

Devon stepped in front of Todd, blocking his path to Jamie's door. "She's fine." He glanced at Todd's smooth, well-developed chest and wished again he'd pulled on his shirt before coming out of the apartment. "Someone tossed a brick through her front window and then took off."

"Did she see who did it?" Todd took a step back, looking down the corridor between buildings. "Did anyone see which way he went? Maybe we can still catch up."

"Good idea!" He nudged Todd in the direction of the side parking lot. "You go that way and let me know if you see anyone. I'll check the other side of the complex."

It almost worked. Todd even took a step. Then Jamie opened her door, looking hot and adorable, her robe tied tightly over her nightshirt.

"Did you see him?" she asked in a small voice.

"No. He was gone by the time I got out here." Devon ran his hand through his hair and tried to be concerned more for Jamie than for the hot sex that would not happen.

"I just asked Dev if you saw anything." Todd stepped closer to Jamie, causing Devon's molars to ache. "Do you have any idea who would do this?"

Jamie's gaze found Devon's and held a second or two before she answered. "No, not really. I was, um, busy."

Evidently satisfied with her answer, Todd turned and said, "I'll go this way and check the laundry room and pool area while I'm over there. You go back toward your place and check the front visitor parking lot. You may also want to take a look down the boardwalk, in case he's lurking around there."

Devon nodded and started across the courtyard. Damn, he hoped whoever did it was long gone. He really, really didn't like physical confrontation. Mainly because he had a low pain threshold, which was also embarrassing.

"Be careful!" Jamie's voice echoed in the courtyard.

He grinned, feeling his chest expand. With Jamie, he felt brave, invincible.

"Not to worry," came Todd's deep reply before Devon could open his mouth.

Add stupid to the list of how he felt.

A cursory look around the complex and parking lots failed to yield anything. Thankfully.

He and Todd arrived at Jamie's door about the same time.

She opened the door, fully dressed now, before either of them could knock.

"You okay?" Todd asked, once again beating Devon to it.

She nodded. "I thought I'd go see about buying something to board up the window." She shivered, and Devon felt it in his groin.

"Hey, it's not your responsibility. It's the complex's problem. Right, Dev?"

Damn. Todd was right. He hated when that happened.

"Tell you what," Todd continued, clapping Devon on the back. "I've still got a while before I have to be at work. I'll run upstairs and get my toolbox while you go pick up some plywood at the hardware store. We'll meet back here and board up her window before I leave." Devon tried not to wince when Todd clutched his trapezoid in a viselike grip. "Sound like a plan?"

"Y-yes," he squeaked and then cleared his throat. "I mean, right. Yeah. Good plan." An escape route dawned. "But I can't haul much with my Mustang. And even if I could, I don't have any way to cut the plywood. It was a good plan, though. Other than that." He bent his neck and shook his head in what he hoped was an appropriate amount of disappointment. "Damn." Okay, maybe he carried it a bit far, but it was in direct proportion to his relief. Woodworking, hammering and such weren't exactly his thing either.

"No problem, we can take my truck," Todd boomed right next to his ear. "I have some power tools in the back. I'm sure I have a saw and a nail gun."

"Oh, I don't want to put you out, make you late for work or anything. I'm sure I can manage." Inspiration struck. "If not,

Jamie can always bunk at my place tonight until I get the window fixed."

"It's no trouble." Todd's teeth flashed white in the darkness. "Matter of fact, here." He dug in the pockets of jeans Devon would have sworn were painted on. "Take my key and stay at my place." He tossed Jamie the key he removed from a key ring.

Where the hell did the key ring come from? There wasn't even enough room for pockets.

"Oh, I really couldn't . . ." Jamie began, shaking her head.

"Of course you can! The maid just came today, so it's clean. Fresh sheets on the bed and everything. I won't be home until early tomorrow morning, maybe later."

Todd had a maid? Devon frowned at the dancer's retreating back. Maybe he should take up exotic dancing. He looked at Todd's tight butt and broad back and winced. Maybe not. Just getting in shape for it would probably kill him.

19

"That should do it," Todd's voice boomed in Devon's good ear, the other ear being temporarily—he hoped—deafened by the high-pitched whine of the power saw Todd had used to deftly cut the plywood he and Devon had bought at the hardware store.

"I'll come back and patch the nail holes tomorrow morning." Todd cast a reproachful look at Devon.

"Hey," Devon protested, "I've never used a nail gun before. How was I to know how fast it shot the nails?"

Todd grinned and said in a low, conspiratorial voice, "That's okay. It was worth it to hear you scream like a girl when they went flying into the walls."

"I. Did. Not. Scream." He unclenched his jaw and shrugged. "I was just surprised, that's all." He glanced toward the bedroom where Jamie was packing a bag. "I'm just glad no one got hurt."

Todd grinned and winked. "There you go." He raised his voice. "Jamie? I'm taking off. There's beer and soda in the fridge and plenty of food. Make yourself at home." He gave a two-fingered salute and clicked his tongue. "See you, sport."

With that, he left.

Devon stood in the quiet living room listening to the silence. The boarded-up window muffled all sound from the court-yard.

"Did Todd leave already?" Jamie stood in the doorway, a small duffel bag in her right hand, the other gripping the back of the kitchen chair.

"Yeah," he said, walking to pry her hand from the aged vinyl. "He said he'd see you tomorrow."

Her gaze zeroed in on the plywood. "Thanks for boarding up my window. I'm probably perfectly safe to just stay here tonight."

"But you have three other windows." He shook his head. "I filed a police report before I called the insurance company, but I don't think staying here would be a smart thing to do, considering what happened tonight." Her skin felt warm and smooth beneath his fingertip when he tilted her chin to look into her eyes. "Unless you want to reconsider staying at Todd's and come home with me? Talk Dirty To Me just sent a whole new box of toys. You could be my research assistant," he said with a smile and a wink.

Lowering her mouth to his fingertip, she swirled her tongue around it and then placed a gentle kiss on the end. "I think it's probably a better idea to just stay at Todd's tonight." A step brought her breasts against him. A tug on his shirt lowered his mouth for a light kiss. "It's safer this way." Kiss. "Not as much temptation," she whispered against his lips before his mouth took hers.

He deepened the kiss, doing a full-body grind against her she returned with equal enthusiasm. But she was right. Sleeping together would not be the smart or safe thing to do at the moment. Besides, he'd never had a woman spend the night in his bed, and he wasn't entirely comfortable with the idea now. Not yet, anyway. But the idea had a certain appeal, he conceded when she did a little shimmy against him. Mr. Happy was definitely up for it.

Reluctantly he broke the kiss and took a step back. "I guess you're right. It's better this way. C'mon. I'll walk you up to Todd's. Make sure you're tucked in safe and sound for the night."

She slipped her hand in his and followed him out of the apartment.

Todd's place, being a second-floor unit, had a study in addition to a bedroom. Relief washed over Devon when he saw the twin-size sofa bed made up in the little room in anticipation of Jamie's visit. Not that he didn't trust Todd . . . well, you get the picture.

"Wow." Jamie's eyes were wide as she took in the apartment that resembled the others only in the fact that it was in the same complex and had the same basic floor plan. "It looks professionally decorated." She ran her hand over the gleaming entry table next to the door, walking her fingers over three marble-looking balls in a big silvery shallow bowl resting on top.

Devon's crotch tightened, watching her fingers trace the veins in the shining balls. Why couldn't she just leave the damned balls alone?

"Look at the sofa!" She walked over to the deep red, over-stuffed cushions and stroked the soft-looking fabric, tested the cushions with her fingertips.

"I think Todd plans for you to sleep in here," he said, almost jerking her away from the opulent furnishings. "It probably sleeps like a torture rack, but beggars can't be choosers, right?"

Dropping her duffel, she kicked off her sandals and crawled onto the suspiciously plush-looking mattress.

In his mind, she was naked, her pert little ass taunting him, making him twitch, ready to pounce on her. She rolled to her back. His mind saw her naked breasts jutting toward the ceiling. His mouth salivated.

"Devon? Are you okay?"

He blinked, and she was once again fully clothed. Damn.

"Hmmm? Oh, yeah. Fine. Just tired, I guess." He glanced around the luxurious apartment, refusing to make comparisons. "If you don't need anything else, I guess I'll go on home and start writing the descriptions for the new line before I fall asleep."

Propped up on one elbow, she rested her head in her hand. "How's the book coming along?"

"It's not. I'm sort of stuck right now. Plus, I have quite a bit of work to do for all the companies. Then there's managing this place." He shrugged.

"I'd be happy to read for you, maybe do a little brainstorming, if you'd like."

"Thanks. I may take you up on that. But not right now." He walked to the door. "Make sure you lock up." The door was almost closed before he poked his head back in. "Would you like to have breakfast with me in the morning?" At her nod, he said, "About eight? Great. See you then."

"What the hell's going on?" Francyne stepped from the shadows.

Devon jumped and barely swallowed his surprised yelp. "Do you have to skulk in the shadows like that?"

"Who's skulking? Petunia was helping fertilize the bushes. So. What happened here?" She gestured toward the boarded window and then fell into step with him.

"Some creep threw a patio brick through Jamie's window tonight. Before you ask, no, we didn't see him, and, yes, he got away."

"What were you and Jamie doing during this time?" Francyne's eyes twinkled behind her lenses.

"Nothing. We were just about to have some cake."

Francyne shook her head, clearly disappointed. "Boy, talk about missed opportunity." She clutched his arm. "What does Jamie have to do to get your attention, pumpkin? Parade around naked with a sign around her neck that says TAKE ME?"

"I don't know what you're talking about." He stopped at his door and dug in his pocket for his key.

"Exactly my damn point! The girl is so hot for you, she's practically drooling whenever she's around you. How could you not notice?"

"Francyne, you're exaggerating. Again. Jamie and I are just friends." He stepped inside and flipped on the light. "If you want to wait a sec, I'll get Killer and come with you."

"Good idea, pumpkin." She looked around and shivered. "After what went on tonight, I'd feel safer. Hurry on, now. Petunia is beginning to look desperate."

Jamie woke with the sun streaming across her bed and stretched. The smell of coffee brought her completely awake.

She looked across the immaculate and empty living room. "Todd?" Quiet answered her.

Easing out of bed, she checked the securely locked door. "Todd?"

The plush carpet of the living room caressed her toes with its silky texture before it gave way to the hard, cold slate tile of the kitchen beneath her bare feet. Closer to the shiny black coffee-maker, she saw a bright yellow Post-it note.

Jamie—Hope you slept well. I got home late and had to leave again. Fresh fruit in the fridge. Later. T.

A glance at the pewter clock on the counter confirmed she had time to have a cup of coffee before showering and heading to Devon's apartment.

* * *

"Don't look at me like that," Devon admonished Killer. "I'm not making a big deal. I just thought Jamie looked a little thin last night." That would be when she was stretched out, naked, on the table in her apartment. "So I thought I'd make a bigger than usual breakfast for her. Don't pout. I'll put some in your dish, too."

The feminine knock on his door could be only one person. "Okay, here she is." He pointed a finger at his furry roommate. "I want you on your best behavior this morning, understand?"

Killer dropped to the floor and covered his eyes with his paws.

"Drama queen," he muttered, reaching for the doorknob. "Wow. What a great way to start the day!" He perused Jamie's petite frame, clad in another bright-patterned sundress with a short skirt. "Come in, please. I hope you're hungry. I told Killer he was going overboard with the breakfast menu, but he insisted."

They grinned at each other while he seated her.

"There's a bowl of fresh fruit on the table," he called from the kitchen. "Help yourself. I have to take the biscuits out of the oven and dish up the other stuff. Would you like some juice? I have V8 or orange."

"Is the orange fresh squeezed?"

"What?" He walked back into the dining area and deposited two bowls and a bread basket on the table. "Ah, no. Sorry. Bottled."

She smiled up at him. "Just kidding. You're so organized, I thought I'd tease you a little. Bottled orange juice is fine."

He lifted the lid on a warming plate. "We have three different kinds of eggs, along with sausage and bacon, biscuits and milk gravy."

Before she could reach for anything, he began loading her plate. "Eat. You're too skinny."

"Gee, thanks."

He waggled his eyebrows. "You need to keep up your strength." He reached beneath the table and ran his hand up her thigh before giving her a little squeeze. "I like my women with curves."

Her smile evaporated.

Panic seized him. "What? What did I say? Was it the crack about my women? Because there really haven't been all that many, if that's what's bothering you."

She shook her head and took a tiny swallow of juice and then licked her lips. "No. It's just that, well, Fred always told me I had thunder thighs."

"Yeah?" He made a big production of looking under the table, running his hands up and down her silky thighs. He straightened up and looked her in the eye. "Fred's an idiot. Not to mention a scum-sucking dirtbag loser."

"So true."

He clicked the rim of his juice glass to hers. "To new beginnings." Leaning closer, he swiped his tongue along the orange sweetness of her lip. "And possibilities."

Jamie knew she had a sappy smile on her face as she sauntered along the boardwalk, but she couldn't help it.

Breakfast with Devon had been so special. So right. Not to mention fun and sexy. A fresh wave of arousal swept over her as she thought of the product testing they'd done after breakfast. Whew. She didn't know if it was Devon's expertise or if she was experiencing hormone surges, but she just couldn't get enough of him.

And although she most likely would be naked during most of their future dates, she realized that morning she needed more clothes.

Shirl looked up when Jamie walked through the door of *Play It Again, Ma'am.*

"Hey, girlfriend!" Shirl's big smile revealed a smudge of tangerine lipstick on his/her front tooth. "Well, look at you. Don't you just look like the cat that ate the canary." Outrageous penciled eyebrows moved up and down. "Or was it something more interesting?"

Heat seared Jamie's cheeks. Averting her eyes from Shirl's knowing ones, she flipped through a rack of marked-down tank tops and shorts. "I need more clothes."

Shirl's chuckle vibrated the air. "Not if you play your cards right, sweetie." She/he heaved a sigh. "Oh, fine. We just got a big shipment from an estate sale." A long finger tipped with a bright orange, talonlike nail directed her to the back wall, where several boxes were stacked. Shirl glanced around the deserted store, and then said in a lowered voice, "I haven't even inventoried any of it yet, if you know what I mean."

"Not really."

Shirl sighed again. "Since I haven't inventoried it, I have no idea what is there . . . and what isn't." At her continued blank stare, he/she growled. "For cripes' sake! Take whatever you want. Since there's no inventory, no one will know if any are missing."

"I couldn't do that! It wouldn't be right."

"Doll, I'm going to tell you a little secret." He leaned closer. "It doesn't matter. I can let you have anything I want." He glanced at the door and then back at her. "I own the store. Don't spread it around."

"But why—"

"My ex-wife. She bled me dry. All I had left was the store, and I was determined she wasn't going to get that. So, after my 'suicide,' my sister Shirl inherited the store."

"But I thought you were—"

"Shhh. This is our little secret, okay? I really do have a sister named Shirl, by the way. She hated the bitch I was married to almost as much as I did, so she didn't mind me using her identity for a while. Now. Take the clothes. Wear them for your boyfriend in good health."

"I don't know what to say." Jamie wiped a tear from her eye. Why was Shirl being so nice to her, a virtual stranger?

"How about 'Thank you, Shirl'?"

"There are some killer shoes in the back that would look superb with that dress, doll," Shirl said several minutes later when Jamie exited the dressing room. Shirl twirled his finger, indicating she should turn around. "You know, not many girls could wear that and not have their asses look big. On you, though, it looks perfect."

Jamie glanced uneasily in the full-length mirror and resisted the urge to tug up on the plunging neckline and down on the short tight skirt of the lime-green raw-silk cocktail dress. "I'm not sure it's me."

"Do you think your guy will like seeing you in it?"

"Probably, but—"

"Does it make you feel sexy?"

Sexy didn't begin to describe the way the dress made her feel. Lined with the softest silk imaginable, it gave her a full-body caress whenever she moved. She nodded.

"Then I guarantee your boyfriend is gonna love it. It'll give him an instant boner."

20

Devon shut the oven door with his heel. The warm sweetness of chocolate filled the air in the small kitchen, hugging him in a cocoon of well-being.

The sound of chocolate-chip cookies sliding onto the wire baking rack on the counter next to the stove echoed in the quiet apartment.

Killer, lying by the apartment door, rolled over and resumed his doggy snoring.

A glance at the clock confirmed Jamie had been gone for almost three hours. Should he be worried? Should he go check on her? Right. And say what?

He grabbed a warm cookie and took a big bite, only to open his mouth to let air cool the melted chocolate chip burning a hole in his tongue.

The cool milk carton slipped from his hand just as he lifted it to take a swig. Helpless, he watched as, in slow motion, it bounced on the tile floor, sending a plume of white liquid to rooster tail over him, drenching his shirt, rapidly soaking into the running shorts he'd pulled on after Jamie left. The milk swam around his bare feet, darting between each toe, cold against the sensitive skin.

A swipe of his hand confirmed that not only was his face drenched, so was his hair. As soon as he cleaned up the mess and put another batch of cookies into the oven, he'd grab a quick shower. If Jamie had not returned by the time he was out of the shower, he'd go look for her.

The bell above the door of *Play It Again, Ma'am* rattled against its brass hook.

Jamie clutched the pile of clothing to her chest at the sight of Francyne walking into the boutique and cast a frantic glance at Shirl.

He waived a negligent hand and tottered on his size-twelve high-heeled pumps to meet the older woman.

"You're gonna have to leave, old woman. Management doesn't allow dogs in here."

"Maybe she's a seeing-eye dog," Francyne retorted, shoving past Shirl's bulk to the sale rack.

"Yeah, and maybe she's not. You see just fine. Take your dog and get out."

Hands on hips, Francyne whirled to face him. "You old cross-dressing goat! I have as much right to be in this shop as anyone. Petunia isn't hurting a thing, and you know it. Now get out of my way." Peeking around his arm, she waved and smiled. "Hi, Jamie! I was just telling this old goat Petunia wouldn't hurt a fly and she's not doing anything wrong. Is she bothering you?"

Jamie blinked. "Ah, no. I was just about to leave anyway."

Francyne pulled a string bikini, in a shocking shade of orange, from the rack and held it up for inspection. "What do you think? Is it me? I bet the boys at the pool would really sit up and take notice if I wore this when I sunbathed."

"No offense," Shirl said, "but I think the days of men sitting up to take notice when you wear a bathing suit ended with Prohibition. Besides, you already look like a piece of shoe leather. Haven't you ever heard tanning is bad for your skin?"

"Hey, *Cinderfella*, haven't you ever heard a tan hides cellulite?" Francyne countered.

"I believe, in order to have cellulite, you have to have something other than skin and bones." Shirl straightened to his full height and placed his fists on his ample, silk-clad hips.

Francyne regarded him for a few seconds and then broke into a grin as she patted his hip. "You'd know more about that than I would, for sure, bless your heart." On tiptoe, she gave him an affectionate hug. "How've you been, *girlfriend*?"

"Fine until you and your mutt walked in."

While the obvious friends shared a laugh, Jamie wilted in relief. She hated arguments and any kind of confrontation. For a few moments, she'd feared having to rescue the older woman.

"Jamie, I'm going to try this on while you finish your shopping; then I'm going to treat you to an ice cream on our way home."

After she'd slipped behind the curtained area, Jamie walked to the counter.

"What are you doing?" Shirl gave a mock look of disgust and shook his head. "Here. Put that stuff in one of these shopping bags and take off."

"But I thought I'd pay for at least some of it—"

Shirl leaned across the counter, his beak nose close to Jamie's. "Did I ask for any money? No, I did not. I don't need your money." He gestured around the store at the bulging racks and shelves. "And I sure as hell don't need any more inventory. You'd be doing me a favor by taking that junk off my hands."

"Shirl, I don't know how to thank you. I—"

"No thanks necessary, doll. Just enjoy the clothes and stop by occasionally for a visit, okay? Deal?"

"Deal."

"Okay, you old reprobate," Francyne said as she toddled up to the counter. "I'll take it and this pair of walking shoes. They're a perfect fit! Total up the damages."

"Are you losing your mind, old woman? You donated those shoes two weeks ago."

"Horsefeathers! Why would I give away a perfectly good pair of walking shoes?"

"Beats me," Shirl grumbled as Jamie stepped out into the sunshine with Petunia at her heels.

The bench on the other side of the boardwalk was vacant, so she sat on it, the dog as close as she could get to her left leg.

"We'll wait here for your mommy, Petunia. How would that be?" She scratched the silky warm fur beneath the dog's ear. Within seconds, Jamie's eyes began watering and her nose burned. She sniffed. Yes, it definitely was Petunia's fur getting to her. But the big dog was such a gentle giant, she didn't want to not touch her. "Do you like ice cream?" she asked, smoothing the warm, silky coat.

"'Course she likes ice cream, she's female." Francyne walked up, shifting her shopping bag to grasp the dog's trailing leash. "Just let me get situated. Don't want another ticket for not having Petunia on a leash."

The dog's hackles rose, a low growl echoing deep in her throat.

Both women followed the dog's gaze.

A tall man stood by the corner of the surf shop. With the sun in her eyes, Jamie couldn't make out his features, but Fred immediately sprang to mind.

She blinked, and he was gone; she could breathe again.

Petunia immediately quieted and settled into a slow, lumbering gait beside them as they made their way to the ice-cream parlor.

"Did you know that fella back there?" Francyne held the door open and motioned Jamie into the cool interior.

"I don't think so. I didn't really get a good look at him." At least, she hoped she didn't know him.

"Well, whoever he was, Petunia didn't care for him." She motioned for the dog to sit by the door and shuffled over to the counter. "Hey, Tommy, how're you doing? How're your mama and daddy these days?"

"They're fine, Miz Anderson, Just fine. And yourself? What can I get for you ladies today?"

"I'll take a triple scoop of mocha cheesecake in a cup, with marshmallow sauce. And give it a blast of hot fudge while you're at it."

"Make mine the same but with boysenberry cheesecake ice cream, please."

"You got it. I'll get it as soon as I give my favorite customer her cone." Tommy scooped a huge mound of peach ice cream into a sugar cone and then walked out from behind the glass counter to offer it to Petunia.

The dog practically vibrated her joy, her bobtailed rump wagging so hard it lifted her hind legs off the floor in a happy dance.

A sudden lump rose in Jamie's throat. How had she lucked out to land in a place with so many nice people? Not only did they all know each other, they even knew and were kind to the animals. Blinking back sappy tears, she accepted the cup of ice cream from Tommy and followed Francyne to a table by the door.

"Tommy's a good kid," Francyne said between bites, as if she'd read her mind. "His mama's first husband, Tommy's father, was a policeman. Got killed in a drug bust. Tommy was just a baby. Rita, his mother, lived in the Surfside for a while. Until she met Wes. He owns the market down the way. All the merchants gathered round to help Rita and little Tommy, donating their goods and time. Pretty soon, we noticed ole Wes spending a lot more time around her than any of the rest of us."

Francyne grinned and tossed her empty cup into the trash and then wiped her hands. "Nature took its course, and they've been married now, oh, 'bout fifteen years, I'd say. Gave Tommy two little sisters." She dabbed at her eyes and then settled her glasses back onto the bridge of her nose. "I just love it when things work out."

"It sounds like Rita was very lucky to have such a supportive group around her." Jamie stood, tossing her cup in the trash and holding the door for Francyne and Petunia.

"Nah, not lucky. That's just the way it is around here. Those that have help the ones that have not. What goes around comes around."

Jamie thought about that on the way back to the complex.

"Want to take a walk with me and Petunia?"

Jamie shook her head. "I can't right now. But thank you anyway."

"Fixin' to do some more product testing with our young stud Devon?" Francyne wiggled her eyebrows and grinned.

Heat streaked up Jamie's neck to puddle in her cheeks. "No, I, ah, I mean, I just told him I'd let him know when I got back. We're just friends, Francyne." Wow. That didn't even sound convincing to her.

"Sure, sure. I get it." Francyne shrugged. "I just had high hopes for you two. You look so cute together and all. You don't have a boyfriend or anything, do you?"

"No! But I just came off a long-term relationship, and I'm not ready to get involved with anyone. Yet."

The old woman patted Jamie's cheek. "You just keep telling yourself that, sweetie. C'mon, Petunia. Let's get this show on the road or we'll miss our soaps."

Devon placed the cookie sheet in the dishwasher and glanced at the clock on the stove when a knock sounded. Running a hand through his shower-damp hair, he made his way to the door, sidestepping a yapping Killer.

Jamie resisted the urge to throw her arms around Devon when he answered the door. Barely.

Stepping inside, she took a deep breath. Warm and cozy, his apartment smelled inviting and mouthwatering.

"Are you baking?" She set her packages by the door and followed him into the kitchen.

"Yeah, I do that a lot these days."

"Oh?" Taking the cookie he offered, she took a bite, forcing her eyes to remain open when the flavors burst on her tongue. "Oh, wow. This is fantastic! It's the best chocolate-chip cookie I've ever tasted. What did you do to the recipe?"

"Added a couple extra things, used real butter, stuff like that." He opened and shut the refrigerator. "I was going to offer you a glass of milk to go with that, but I forgot I don't have any."

"I wish I'd known," she said, reaching for another cookie. "I could have picked some up. Wait. I have a gallon at my apartment. I'll go get it."

"No! I don't want you going back there until I get the window fixed. The glass place couldn't get to it until tomorrow."

"Devon, I'll be perfectly safe there. I'm sure it was just some kid making mischief." She gave a little shudder. "The worst part is I keep wondering if he saw, you know, us. On the table."

He brightened. "That reminds me. Check it out." He pulled another phallus from the fridge, this one green. "I was trying out some of the new shipment and found this. It's really cool."

He removed the lid from a stainless-steel cake plate and grabbed an unfrosted cupcake. Setting the cupcake on the counter, he gripped the base of the green thing, balancing the length on the fingers of his right hand. Green frosting came out of the tip in delicate ruffles.

He reached for a shaker and sprinkled multicolor sugar

sparkles on top. "It's actually not a bad frosting tube. There are interchangeable tips to make other designs, but I haven't tried them yet."

Their gazes met and held. The kitchen got hotter.

"Want to play with the various designs? I could use the research."

"You mean play with each other and the frosting or play by decorating more cupcakes?"

He edged closer to her, close enough for her to smell his soapy, clean skin. "Whatever you want. . . ."

Suddenly she knew what she wanted and it had nothing to do with frosting and everything to do with the sexy man before her.

21

Jamie lay panting, sprawled naked on Devon's bed, and glanced over at her discarded halter top, wondering if her gel blobs were still in the built-in bra and if Devon had noticed the disparity.

She found that this took too many brain cells. Brain cells that were recently fried by her last full-bodied orgasm.

Beside her, Devon frowned as he examined the frosting rosette he'd recently created on each of her nipples. "Definitely not my best work." He sucked one off and reapplied the frosting, his brows drawn in concentration.

She would have laughed, but it required too much oxygen.

"I can't tell if it's the tip or my technique. Hold still." He licked the frosting from her right breast and then the left.

Somewhere along the way, he became sidetracked and began licking and sucking the clean nipple, blowing on the distended tip in a very distracting way.

"I love your breasts," he said, his hot breath sending shafts of desire to spear through to her core. "Especially your nipples. They're so perfect." He circled each with the tip of his tongue as though to demonstrate. "I love to play with them." He licked them and then blew lightly. "See how responsive they are? Look how they pucker and get hard."

Rallying her strength, she closed her hand around his erection. "Looks like they're not the only things hard around here." Had she more oxygen in her deprived brain, she was sure she'd have been scandalized by her aggressive behavior. When had she ever been so brazen?

His pulse stroked her palm, short-circuiting her train of thought.

"Are you finished playing with the frosting?"

"Why? What did you have in mind?" She loved it when his voice was low and sexy like that.

With her other hand, she grasped the frosting dildo and tossed it across the room, where it bounced against the closed door.

"What I have in mind does not require gimmicks, aids or batteries." She smoothly flipped their positions, straddling his lean hips. "I want to screw your brains out. The old-fashioned way."

Guiding him to the spot once again eager for his heat, she lowered her hips until she'd taken him fully into her body.

Their eyes met.

She brought his hands up to hold her breasts.

He caressed her rigid nipples with the pads of his thumbs, causing her hips to buck.

Her moisture made his abdomen slippery. She had to clench her knees to his hips to stay on.

His hands kneaded her breasts, his hips encouraging her wild ride.

Higher and higher she went, nothing anchoring her but his hands and his body buried so deeply within hers. Close, so close. Her breath came in short, agonizing gasps. The only sounds in the room were their panting, the soft slap of skin against skin, the subtle answering moan of the springs.

After moment after agonizing moment of being poised on the brink, she tumbled, free-falling into the abyss of supreme sexual satisfaction.

Devon's hips thrust once, twice and held, his grip on her breasts a pleasure/pain. Back arched, he made a guttural sound, his warmth spreading deep within her belly.

Collapsing on his sweat-slicked chest, she gasped for air, his heartbeat thundering in her ear.

His hands moved, smoothing, petting every spot he could reach, his fingers outlining the edges of her breasts where they pillowed outward. Never still, they kept moving until, miraculously, the stirrings began again.

At first it was a small, dull ache between her legs that caused her to squirm a bit. That squirm brought an answering movement from the penis buried deeply within her.

His caresses became more obvious, firmer, touching certain areas more than others.

Moisture gathered. Again.

His mouth took hers in a carnal kiss, telling her without words what he wanted to take, what she wanted to give.

Devon lay in the dark, watching Jamie put on her clothes. "You don't have to go, you know. In fact, it's probably a waste of time. I'll just follow you and we'll start all over again. Why not skip the preliminaries and just come back to bed?"

She walked to the side of the bed and bent to brush his lips in a fleeting kiss. "You're probably right, but I just think I need to go."

"Are you going to spend the night at Todd's again?"

"Does it matter?"

"Hell, yes, it matters!" He propped his head on a wadded-up pillow and did his best to glare at her and not notice the slight flush of stubble burn tingeing the delicate skin of her chest or how his hands all but itched to tear her clothes off and haul her naked body back to his bed where it belonged.

Wait. Since when did he think she belonged in any way, shape or form to him? That was not the deal.

With a sigh, he threw back the covers and stood. "Let me grab some clothes and I'll walk you back to Todd's."

"You don't have to do that. I—"

"Yes, damnit, I do! I—"

A little whimper and a definite scratch on the door stopped him from making a fool of himself.

"I have to go walk Killer anyway, so it's no big deal to walk you back."

"Oh. Okay." Cheeks heating, she averted her eyes and made her way to the door. "I need to use the bathroom. Then I'll wait out there."

She leaned against the closed door and sighed, listening to him move around in his room. Of course he would walk her home. He was a gentleman, and besides, he had to take his dog out. It didn't mean anything.

Sure, he was a nice guy. A great guy. But he wasn't interested in her as anything other than a temporary sexual indulgence. She thought she was okay with that, going in. Really, how long would she stick around anyway? Casual sex had never appealed to her, but the idea had had infinite possibilities once she'd met Devon. They would use each other for sex and then go their separate ways. She was cool with that.

So why did it feel so . . . disappointing?

Glum, Jamie shuffled from the bathroom in Todd's apartment the following morning, feeling only slightly more refreshed after her shower.

Todd was still mysteriously absent. Jamie snickered as she

poured a cup of coffee and picked at a bowl of fruit he'd left on the counter for her. Maybe Todd had gotten lucky.

Of course, one would say she had, too. But she'd insisted on coming back to sleep alone. On hindsight, not one of her best ideas.

Thoughts of Devon caused a needy ache between her legs. An ache only he seemed able to appease.

"Enough," she said to no one as she loaded her cup and fruit bowl into the dishwasher. If she didn't see Devon after she went back to her apartment and hung up her clothes, she'd take a walk on the beach. Or go find the pool and refresh her tan. Anything but mope around and miss him.

The air off the Gulf, as usual for mornings, was brisk. Jamie took an appreciative breath and skipped down the stairs, her key firmly in one hand, the bag of new clothes in the other.

It was a gorgeous day. Way too nice to hang out indoors. Humming to herself, she rounded the corner of the building to stop dead in her tracks. Her heart stumbled. Her blood ran cold.

A perfect yellow rose lay on the welcome mat of her apartment.

22

"Uh-oh," Francyne's voice singsonged from the other side of the complex, where she stood in her doorway with Petunia, her voice echoing in the deserted courtyard. "Looks like someone's got a secret admirer!"

Jamie grabbed the flower and hurried inside, firmly shutting the door, throwing the bolts home.

In the still air of the darkened apartment, the rose smelled cloyingly sweet.

After looking at it in horror for a few minutes, she strode to the kitchen and dropped it in the garbage disposal, flipping the switch and running the water until the sound told her it was devoured.

Fred had always given her a yellow rose after they fought. Obviously he still thought it would work on her. And, just as obviously, he was wrong.

Clutching together her shaking hands, she sat on the couch, in the dark, gathering her courage to go out in the sunshine and enjoy the day as planned.

She yelped at the sharp rap on her door.

Halting steps took her to the peephole.

Shoulders slumped with relief. She could breathe again. It was only Devon.

Mustering her courage, she threw back the locks and opened the door.

Upon seeing him, however, all her bravado deserted her and she fell into his arms, a mass of shook-up nerve endings.

"Hey, hey," he said softly, holding her at arm's length. "Are you okay? Did something else happen?" He grinned down at her. "Or did you just miss me?"

She gazed up at him through her tears. It would sound so stupid and pathetic to tell him she was afraid because someone left a rose at her door. Besides, maybe spending time with Devon would take her mind off Fred.

"I guess I missed you." She pulled him down for a kiss that instantly heated.

Gathering her close, he stepped through the door and kicked it shut, never breaking the kiss.

Reluctantly she stepped back. If they stayed there, they would no doubt spend the day in bed. Not what she had planned.

"It's such a gorgeous day, I thought I'd go out. In fact, I was just on my way out." She stepped toward the door to give him a hint.

"Hey, great minds think alike. I'm playing hooky today. Wanna go to the beach?"

"What about the leasing office?"

"Francyne said she'd watch it while I'm gone." He lowered his voice, "I think she has the hots for my big screen. She says her soaps come in better on it."

"In that case, yes, I'd love to go to the beach! Just let me grab a few things."

He playfully pulled her into his arms and said, "I'd like to grab a few things, too, if you get my drift. You know," he said, rubbing his pelvis against her, "I know a spot where bathing suits are optional."

"I'll keep that in mind." She brushed her lips over his mouth and stepped out of his arms. "But I'm taking my suit just in case."

A few minutes later, she skipped into the room with her tote bag. "I'm ready."

"Great. Let's stop off at my place on the way out so I can grab the picnic basket."

"A picnic basket?" She turned and shimmied the door unlocked.

"Sure. Being out in all that fresh air and sand makes me hungry. Actually," he said as they made their way across the courtyard, "you're saving me from myself. If you hadn't agreed to come, I'd have had to eat all the food alone."

"Ugh, I'm stuffed." Jamie flopped down on the blanket and rubbed her stomach. "Why did you let me eat all that?"

"I told you, you're too skinny. Besides, I like watching you eat."

She raised her sunglasses and looked at him. "That's weird."

"No, not really. I like the fact you enjoy your food. It's even—"

"What? You think I eat like a pig or something?"

"No! Of course not. I just meant I think it's sexy to be with a woman who likes to eat for a change. Hell, I've dated weirdos who would get full on a few grapes. So. Are you ready for dessert?"

In response, she clutched her stomach and moaned. "Didn't you hear me? I'm stuffed." She warily watched him unwrap two pieces of molten chocolate cake. "What's that?"

"Leftover cake from the other night. I brought us each a piece, but you don't want any so I guess I'll have to eat both of them. Too bad. I even brought whipped cream."

"All right. Fine." She sat up and pulled a plate from his hand and then made a rolling motion with her fork. "Don't forget, I like lots of whipped cream."

"I thought you didn't want anything else."

"I'm only doing it for you. I know you don't want to get fat, so I'm helping you out. Don't be so stingy with the whipped cream."

He reached out and rimmed her mouth with the frothy concoction then quickly licked it off. "We could save it for later. Maybe use it when we try out a few of the new sex toys. It might inspire me."

"Shut up and eat your cake."

Jamie wiped a trickle of sweat away from her eye and tried not to squint at the relentless sun.

"Want me to put more sunscreen on you?" Devon's voice ruffled the hair by her ear, sending a shiver over her heated skin.

The idea of his hands, cool with lotion, gliding over her hot skin was heavenly.

She moaned. "I'd love it, but I don't think that's a good idea."

"Oh?"

"If you start rubbing lotion on me, I won't want you to stop . . . and we're in public."

"Look around, sweet thing." He lifted her sunglasses, his hot gaze melting her resolve. "I told you I knew all the secluded spots." A flick of his wrist had her bikini strings untied; then he brushed aside her cups.

She grabbed unsuccessfully for the top. "Devon! Someone could walk up and see us." Despite her words, the thought excited her, and she relaxed against the soft warmth of the blanket.

"Possible but not probable." He nudged her legs apart and

settled against her. Even through her bikini bottom, his hardness pressed into her weeping flesh. He reached between them and tugged on the side ties of the bottom. As soon as they fell by her side, he pulled on the fabric. "Lift your hips. C'mon. No one will see you. And even if someone walked up, I'm on top, shielding you."

All the reasons why it was a bad idea left her in the thrill of feeling his hands on her flesh. Canting her hips, she allowed him to drag her suit away from her lower body, leaving her naked beneath his hot, hard body.

She hooked her thumbs in the elastic at his waist. "If I'm going to risk getting caught buck naked out here, you need to lose these, too."

She didn't have to say it twice. In seconds, he was back, his hot erection probing her willing flesh. Their combined heat amplified the coconut scent of the suntan lotion to waft up between them, creating an aromatic sensual cocoon.

His kiss was soft yet demanding and tasted of chocolate and sin.

Sex on the beach used to be one of her secret fantasies. The floodgates opened, bringing to life all her old longings and dreams. Within her arms was the epitome of every fantasy or daydream she'd ever had. She'd have to be a special kind of stupid to pass up what he so strongly wanted to give.

His fingers walked up her ribs, between their chests, to roll her hardened nipples while his tongue continued to sweep her mouth in languid strokes.

The urge to feel him inside her grew until it reached fever pitch.

Clutching him close, she spread her legs and thrust her hips on the off chance he didn't understand what she wanted.

A sexy moan vibrated her mouth. She had no idea if it came from her or Devon. The tip of his penis teased her.

She nipped his lower lip in frustration and spread her legs

wider. The hard muscle beneath the smooth skin of his buttocks burned the palms of her hands. Grasping a cheek in each hand, she flexed her hips, burying him to the hilt.

They sighed and stilled for a moment and then began a slow in-and-out glide. With each smooth thrust, Devon slid his lotion-slicked chest against hers. Her nipples hardened to tight, sensitive peaks. Each slide of hot, slick skin over skin caused an answering surge of moisture.

She hooked her feet behind his knees for more leverage, her soles pushing on his calf muscles.

He pushed up on his hands, looking down at her, while he reached down to massage her mons.

Her back arched as wave after wave of release washed over her.

Devon seized the opportunity to tickle her nipples with the tips of his teeth. Rhythmically he sucked and laved each nipple. Before she realized it, she was ready to climax again, her hips pumping vigorously along with his.

He reached beneath her shoulders, gathering her close while he increased the speed of his thrusts.

"Yes, that's it," he whispered in her ear, his breath harsh against her heated skin, "come for me again, baby. That's right, just like that. I love—"

"What the hell is going on here?" a deep voice boomed.

Devon strained to look back over his shoulder, careful to shield Jamie from view. "Hello, officer."

23

"That had to be the most embarrassing thing in my life," Jamie muttered as she and Devon made their way toward the exit of the Surfside police station. Her steps faltered. "Hey, is that Todd?"

Devon, who had been schlepping along beside her, looked up. Sure enough, there was their neighbor. He increased his pace. "Todd?"

Todd looked up from a clipboard he'd been reading. For an instant, Jamie got the impression he was just as surprised to see them.

"Hey, you two." Todd set the clipboard aside and walked toward them.

"What are you doing here?" Jamie stepped forward and grasped his hand. "Are you the one who bailed us out?"

He grinned down at her, blue eyes twinkling. "Well, someone had to do it."

"Thank you," she said in a strangled whisper, blinking back tears. "I've never been so humiliated! The policeman wouldn't even allow me to get dressed."

Todd's smile disappeared. "What? Which one brought you in? That's against the rules to—"

"Well, he did let me pull on Devon's shirt," she amended, "and he was allowed to pull on his swim trunks."

Todd's eyes narrowed. "Just what was it, exactly, you two were brought in for?"

Devon mumbled and shuffled his feet.

"Say what? I didn't hear you." Todd stepped closer.

"I said, lewd and lascivious conduct on a public beach."

Todd's lips tightened, and he looked suspiciously like he was trying not to laugh. "I see," he finally said in a curt voice.

"I'm just thankful to be out of here and going home!" Jamie walked to the window marked PROPERTIES and rang the bell.

A woman who looked like she'd rather be anywhere else trudged up to the window. "Name? Last name first, first name last," she said in a tinny drone through the little stainless-steel speaker in the thick window.

"Jamie. Jamie Cartright."

"I *said*, last name first, first name last."

"Oh, sorry." She repeated, this time in the correct order.

"And McCloud, Devon," he said, leaning over Jamie's shoulder.

"Sir, step back behind the line. I can help only one person at a time." She blinked drowsy looking, mud-brown eyes at him until he complied. Her gaze shifted to Todd, standing a bit behind Devon. She blinked again. "What are you doing here?"

"I'm with them," Todd replied. "I don't need anything, but thanks. I'm just giving them a ride home."

"Uh-huh." She stared for a while and then turned and made slow progress. Then she disappeared into the labyrinth of shelving behind her.

Forty-five excruciatingly long minutes later, they'd signed for their belongings, dressed and exited the station, Todd in tow.

"Wow. It's dark already. I guess I kind of lost track of time.

Where are you parked?" Devon looked up and down the deserted street.

"I had to park a ways out. Wait here and I'll come around and pick you up." Before they could respond, he took off at a fast jog.

"I'm sorry," Devon whispered, close to her ear, while they waited.

After a moment, she sighed and looked up at him. "It's not your fault. Well, not entirely. I'm an adult. I should have known better than to get carried away like that in public. We're both to blame."

Standing in silence, she thought about her actions and subsequent arrest. Talk about reality slapping you in the face. But in the grand scheme of things, although it was an embarrassment, getting arrested was nothing compared to what might have happened if Fred had been the one to walk up on them. For that, she was profoundly grateful.

"Yeah," Devon was saying next to her, "but I'm the one who kept assuring you it was okay, that no one would see us." He shifted and looked down the street. "I still don't know how he saw us. I've lived in this area all my life and know for a fact that area of the beach is secluded, hidden from view from just about every angle."

"Well, if you knew it, don't you think other people—like policemen—might also know it?" She tightened the grip on the bag on her shoulder. "Is that Todd?"

He looked in the direction she pointed. "Yeah, that's his red truck."

Todd squealed to a stop at the curb, causing them to hop back. The door locks clicked.

Devon opened the door and helped Jamie up into the cab. "Thanks again, Todd, for coming to our rescue. But how did you know we were here? I just called Francyne a few minutes ago."

"I was out, so when she called my cell, I just hightailed it on over."

"Well, it's lucky for us you were in the neighborhood and available." Devon settled Jamie against his hip and held her in place with his arm slung over her shoulder.

"Yeah." Todd put on his signal and merged onto the highway.

The air-conditioned cab was cool, making Jamie grateful for the warmth of Devon's body next to hers on the saddle leather seat.

She watched Todd's face, bathed in the light from the dash. For some reason, she couldn't shake the feeling he wasn't telling them something. Maybe he'd been there looking for his sister and Devon didn't know about her. That must have been it. Since Todd was alone and looking none too happy, it was a safe bet his sister was still missing. Poor guy.

The passing lights mesmerized her, and the next thing she knew, Devon was shaking her shoulder.

"Jamie? Jamie, we're here. Wake up."

"I'm awake." She stretched and reached for the door handle.

The door opened, and Todd reached in to lift her from the cab, not releasing her when her feet touched the pavement of the apartment parking lot. "Are you staying with me again tonight?"

"I—"

"Not necessary," Devon said, tugging Jamie in the direction of the building. "Francyne said the glass people came and replaced Jamie's window this afternoon. I'll just walk her home and make sure everything is okay before I leave. Thanks again for picking us up. Oh, wait. How much do I owe you?"

"Owe me?" Todd stood like a deer in the headlights.

"Yeah, you know, for bailing us out."

"Oh! Right." Todd avoided eye contact. "Here's the thing. I have some friends on the force, and I, well, I got the charges dropped. So you don't owe me anything."

"Oh, man, that's awesome. Thanks! We both really appreciate it. Don't we, Jamie?"

"Hmmm? Oh, yes, thanks." Funny, Todd had the same look her students used to get when they were lying. But why would he lie about something like bailing them out? It didn't make sense.

24

___

Jamie stepped into her apartment and looked around. All the glass had been cleaned from her carpeting, and the new window was sparkling clean. So clean, in fact, it would be like living in a fish bowl, with anyone who desired being able to look right in at her.

She strode to the curtains and jerked them closed. Next she did the same with the other window, not stopping until every curtain in the apartment was snuggly closed.

"You know," Devon told her, "you don't have to stay here tonight if you're uncomfortable."

A denial was on the tip of her tongue. Her shoulders slumped. Who was she trying to kid? The idea of spending the night in her apartment again was definitely unappealing.

"I don't have anywhere else to stay." She held up her hand to stop whatever he was about to say. "And before you say it, no, I don't think it's a good idea for me to stay with you." A quick smile flashed across her face. "Too much temptation. That's already gotten us into enough trouble lately."

He gave a slow nod and wry grin. "Much as it pains me to

suggest this, maybe you should stay another night at Todd's."
He glanced back at the door. "Meanwhile, I'll get someone out
here to install a new lock and dead bolt."

Jamie hummed and carried her second cup of coffee into the
bathroom the next morning. Devon was right. Spending another night at Todd's was exactly what she needed. The morning sunshine had woken her with new hope for the day, and she
was anxious to get back to her little apartment and begin making it her home.

After her shower, she wiped the steam from the mirror and
inserted her contacts and then brushed her teeth.

Towels around her torso and head, the empty cup in her hand,
she opened the bathroom door only to come to an abrupt halt.

An impressive backside, encased in worn denim, faced her as
its owner bent to look in the refrigerator.

"About damn time you got out of the shower, *princess*," the
deep voice said from within the interior of the fridge. "Man,
Todd, don't you ever eat anything that's not healthy? I feel like
I should be grazing or something." The man shoved stuff
around on the shelves. "I just got back to town about an hour
ago and came straight here after checking in. Sorry, bro, it was
another dead end. Hey, how old is this pizza in the back?"

He straightened and turned. Dark hair framed a face made
for magazine covers. His front was even more impressive than
his back. He was holding a withered-looking piece of partially
tin-foil-wrapped pizza. His eyes widened. "Whoops. Didn't
know Todd had company. Who are you?"

"Jamie." She edged toward the door of her temporary room.
"I live downstairs. Todd let me stay here while my apartment
was being repaired." She reached the edge of the study and
gauged the distance to her cell phone. "Who are you, and how
did you get in? The door was locked. I checked it twice before
I went to take my shower."

"Oh, man, I'm sorry—Jamie, was it?" She nodded. "Todd and I have keys to each other's places. Since I've been out of town, I came over here to grab something to eat before I crashed. Didn't feel like stopping for supplies on my way home. I didn't realize anyone was here. When I heard the shower, I assumed it was Todd. I didn't mean to scare you. Oh, yeah." He wiped his hand on the leg of his jeans and took a few steps toward her, hand extended. "My name's Rick. I live downstairs on the other side of the laundry room. Todd and I work together."

She stared at his hand until he dropped it to his side.

"You're a dancer, too?" she asked.

A strange look passed over his face, almost a wince, but it was gone so quickly she didn't have a chance to decide.

"Ah, no." He turned to lay the pizza on the counter. "Did I say we worked together?" He gave a short bark of a laugh. "I meant we *used* to work together." He shrugged. "I guess I'm still not used to the idea of him being a stripper."

"Well, it was nice meeting you, Rick." Clutching her towel to her chest, she backed toward the door to the study. "I'll tell Todd you stopped by. Now, if you'll excuse me, I need to get dressed and go home." The apartment was suddenly crowded.

Safely behind the closed door, she paused, willing her heart rate to slow down. With his shiny black hair and deep turquoise eyes, Rick was even better looking, if that was possible, than Todd.

After throwing on a pair of white denim shorts and a tank top, she shoved the remaining clothes in her beach bag and headed for the bathroom for her shampoo and toothpaste. To her relief, Rick was nowhere to be seen.

She hurried and stripped the bed. A cursory look turned up no clean sheets, so she scribbled a note telling Todd she'd wash and return the bedding.

With a last look around, she stepped into the sunshine and locked the door.

* * *

Devon stared at the blinking cursor. "C'mon, Mac, you can do this. You know you can." Trent had just had his big love scene, and the girl was putting her clothes on. Unbidden, his mind pictured Jamie, sexily rumpled as she pulled on her clothing. What kind of underwear would she have on?

With a sigh, he rocked back in his desk chair and swiveled to look out across the courtyard. If he leaned just so, he could see her door.

Funny, she never mentioned the rose he'd left on her mat. Maybe she didn't like roses. Maybe someone else had walked by and taken it before she found it. It could happen.

Leaving a rose was kind of a sappy thing to do, but his budding relationship with Jamie had put him in a sappy kind of mood.

A trip to the kitchen failed to yield anything of interest, so he returned to his chair. Jamie should be home by now. Maybe he should go see if she needed anything.

Decision made, he saved what few words he'd written and shut down his computer.

Jamie bumped the oven door shut with her hip and set the cake on the stovetop to cool. Inhaling the warm, lush scent of homemade pineapple upside-down cake filled her with a sense of well-being she hadn't felt in quite a while.

A knock sounded. With a glance back at the cooling cake, she made her way to check the peephole and then opened the door to Devon.

"Hey, wow! Is that pineapple upside-down cake I smell?" He bussed her cheek on his way to the kitchen. "When can we have a piece?"

She laughed. "Not until it cools a little. Is does smell good, doesn't it?"

He nodded and drew her into his arms, nuzzling her neck.

"So do you," he said against her skin, sending goosebumps down her arms. "I can think of a great way to pass our time while we wait for the cake to cool."

He bumped her with his pelvis, taking playful nips of her neck.

Instead of reciprocating, she stepped out of his loose embrace. "I don't know if that's such a good idea."

"Really? 'Cause I think it's one of my more brilliant ones." He ran the tip of his finger along the caramelized edge of the baking dish and then licked it clean. "Mmm. This is seriously good cake. And I can tell it's from scratch. You bake a lot?"

"Whenever I can." She shrugged. "I guess it's my version of stress relief."

Finger in his mouth, he stopped and looked at her and then slowly dropped his hand. "Really? So do I."

"No way."

"Yes, way. I started baking when I was in college. Before long, I noticed I baked when I was stressed. I also noticed it helped, so I ignored my friends razzing me. And they didn't have a problem with eating the bounty, so eventually they got used to it."

"My grandmother loved to bake. She always said troubles lessened when her hands were busy. I guess that's why I started baking more and more as my relationship with Fred deteriorated."

"That bad, huh?"

"Oh . . . yeah. But I don't want to talk about it. The sun is shining, and I'm finally settling into my new place. For an old oven, this one cooks great. I think if Fred will just drop off the face of the Earth, I could like living here."

The haunted look in her eyes was not masked by her bright smile, so he had no choice. He gathered her in his arms and kissed her. The mercy kiss deepened until they were both breathing hard.

Jamie did a little shimmy that made his blood boil.

"How long does the cake need to cool?" Nipping kisses took him up her neck to lick her earlobe. A graze of his teeth had her grinding against his erection. "I could probably come up with something for us to do to pass the time." He snaked his hand under her top to tweak her hard nipples.

Within two minutes, he had her naked.

"Oh . . . yes," she whispered, widening her stance, while his fingers did wicked things to her.

Hooking her thumbs in the waistband of his shorts, she tugged until they and his boxers fell to his ankles. His polo shirt joined them, to be kicked aside with his sandals.

"You're all I've been able to think about," he said in a husky whisper, running his hands all over her body. "I missed you. Missed this."

Holding her high against his chest, his fingers still working their magic deep within her, he staggered in the direction of the bedroom.

"Can't. Wait," he said, panting, while he let her slide to her feet. "I can't make it to the bedroom. Would it be okay if we did it here?"

While he talked, his hands remained busy, sliding over her skin, squeezing her breasts, lightly pinching her nipples.

It wasn't enough.

Hand in hand, she led him to the dining room table.

But instead of climbing up with her, as she'd envisioned, he pushed against her until she lay sprawled before him, her legs dangling on either side of his hips.

The look of intensity on his stubbled face took her breath. With a gentle touch, he parted her, running the pad of his thumbs in slow motion over her wet, swollen folds.

"So pretty," he whispered, petting and probing. "Lush is the only word I can think of to describe it. Maybe delicious." He bent, his breath hot against her weeping flesh, and then swiped his tongue in a long, languid movement up and down. Down and up. Only occasionally varying by pausing to suck her swollen nub or insert the tip of his tongue in the spot begging for him.

The cool, hard surface of the table bit into her spine while she writhed, vacillating between clutching his hair to pull him closer for more and wanting to drag him up for a kiss that would align the parts for the perfect penetration she knew was imminent.

Close, so close. But she didn't want to come without him inside her.

Frustrated, she bit her lip, spreading her legs wider, tugging on his hair.

Her blood roared in her ears, her heart thundering to every nerve ending in her body.

Just as she thought she could stand no more, he flipped her over. The table cooled her heated breasts.

Behind her, Devon spread her legs, canted her hips and plunged into her.

Her climax roared through her, wetting the table, making the surface slippery.

Gasping for breath, she tried to remain an active participant while Devon continued to pound into her receptive body. The edge of the table dragged along the front of her thighs with each thrust. Her sensitized labia and clit slipped back and forth on the wet surface. It wasn't unpleasant.

Then Devon reached around her, insinuating his hand between her and the tabletop, to flick and pinch her nubbin to screaming awareness.

She'd have sworn her previous orgasm had milked her of all her strength. But climax number two had her total attention now as it set flames of sensation streaking through her.

Outside her window, he took a deep breath and counted to ten, fists clenched. He needed to see this, to see her fucking someone else, to heal. If he was ever going to get over her and get on with his life, he had to stop reacting to the hurtful things she did.

The edges of his nails cut into his palms. The little cunt actually seemed to be enjoying it. She'd never been that active when his cock was inside her.

Despite all he'd learned, he felt the anger bubbling up inside until it was a white-hot rage threatening to engulf him.

He should be the one fucking her brains out.

"Oh!" Beneath him, Jamie stiffened. She struggled in an obvious attempt to get out from under him. He should move, let her up. And he would. In a minute. As soon as his muscles once again obeyed his command.

"Shhh," he said, stroking the side of her breast. "Let me catch my breath. Then we'll go for our new personal best in the bedroom." He kissed her between her shoulder blades, where his head rested.

"Devon!" She wiggled again, severing their connection and squirming to the side until she broke free. "There's someone outside the window!"

Instantly alert, he jerked to a standing position. "Where? Did you see who it was?"

Hopping around while attempting to put on his pants, he watched Jamie. She was genuinely upset. In all probability, no one was outside, unless it was Petunia again, but he would look like a hero if he went to investigate, so he made a big production of finding his shoes.

Jamie clutched his shirt to her chest, eyes wide.

Being a basic coward had its disadvantages. Like now. He'd really prefer to stay right where he was, but one look at Jamie's stricken face had his feet moving toward the door.

"Where are you going?"

He paused and looked back. "I thought I'd take a look outside . . . unless you would prefer me to stay in here with you?" She hesitated, and he heaved an inward sigh.

One hero coming up.

"Stay inside while I go take a look around." He turned the knob and looked back. "It's going to be all right. I'll just take a quick look and be right back. I promise."

It came as no surprise, but it was still a giant relief when he found no one loitering outside Jamie's apartment.

By the time he'd checked the almost empty parking lots and worked his way around the complex back to her door, Jamie was once again fully dressed.

It helped only marginally that she rewarded his bravery with a huge piece of the best pineapple upside-down cake he'd ever eaten.

After they'd cleaned up the kitchen, she gave him another reward. Gratitude sex may be pathetic, but it was very . . . gratifying.

25

Devon stretched and rolled to his back on Jamie's bed, smiling at her. "Thanks, I needed that."

In response, she grinned and snuggled close to his heart, her arm slung over his chest. "No problem."

After some quiet snuggling, she said, "Do you think it was Fred again?"

He thought about pretending he didn't know what she meant for about two seconds and then decided they needed to be truthful with each other.

"I don't know, Jamie. You were the one who saw him. Do you think it was him?" He held up a chunk of her hair and watched it curl around his finger.

"I thought so at first, but now I'm not so sure. I don't want to be a fraidy cat, seeing bogeymen around every corner. For instance, Fred always gave me a yellow rose after we fought. I hated seeing those dang roses almost as much as I hated being so afraid." She shuddered. "I don't know, maybe it was because I knew what was coming. He'd always give me the rose and then expect make-up sex. Then when I found a yellow rose at my door yesterday, I freaked. It may or may not have been from him, but it brought back all my old fears." She kissed his shoulder. "But Fred is real, and what he did to me was real. I have a darn good reason to be afraid of him."

He held her closer, enjoying the fresh citrus scent of her hair, tamping down guilt for not telling her he'd left the rose. "Of course you do. And I promise I'll do my best to try to protect you." Since he was part of her fear, it was only fair to vow his protection. He'd tell her about the rose in a few minutes.

She stretched to kiss his jaw. "Thanks, I know you will."

Now he knew how the Grinch felt when his heart expanded. With a start, he realized he'd spoken the truth. He'd do whatever it took to keep her safe.

Wow. He sure hoped it didn't involve danger to life or limb.

Beside him, Jamie was wiggling in a most interesting manner. Her hand stroked him to instant hardness.

"Devon?"

"Hmmm?" He reciprocated by outlining her breast with the tip of his index finger. Funny, now that they had been intimate a few times, her breasts didn't seem nearly as full as when he'd first met her. Must be because he was used to seeing and touching them.

"Remember that song, 'Save a Horse, Ride a Cowboy'?" She was up on her knees now, beside him.

Damn. He had thought he was going to get lucky again. Why was she wanting to talk about songs?

"Yeah, but why—"

His question was short-circuited along with his thought processes when she climbed on top and straddled him. His erection slipped home, and they both sighed.

Their gazes met.

"Giddyup, cowboy," she said with a grin.

And their third wild ride of the night began.

* * *

Several hours later, Devon stepped into the courtyard and shut Jamie's door.

The men were congregated around the fire pit, but he was not in the mood for bullshit tonight. Skirting around in the shadows, he took a circuitous route to his apartment, not taking a deep breath until he'd gained the sanctuary of his home.

"'Bout time you got back." Francyne sat in his recliner, the TV on mute. She stood, stretched and then yawned. "I took both dogs for a walk and then dropped Petunia off so she could get some sleep. Killer finally gave up on you and fell asleep a few minutes ago." She came to a stop in front of him. "You look like you had a nice time tonight."

He grinned. "I had a great time. Thanks for asking. And thanks for taking care of things."

"My pleasure, pumpkin. Say, why don't you take the day off tomorrow, too, and go do something with Jamie? I don't mind watching the place again. I've been worried about her. She's skittish as a cat, worried about running into that Neanderthal she used to date. And nothing takes your mind off a man like getting it on with another one."

"Francyne! Too much information there."

"Oh, horsefeathers! You young people didn't invent sex, you know. Don't be such a prude."

"I'll check with Jamie tomorrow and let you know. Thanks again. Oh, and Francyne?"

"Hmmm?" She paused in the open door.

"Thanks, too, for calling Todd to bail us out. I really appreciate it. Did you call him because he has connections in the police department?"

"Um, yeah. Something like that. You're welcome. See you tomorrow."

After he shut the door, it hit him. He'd forgotten to tell Jamie about the rose. He'd meant to tell her, but the sex thing had wiped out pretty much every other thought from his brain.

* * *

"Todd?" Francyne called from her doorway. "Could you come here for a minute, please?"

Todd set his bottle of beer on the cement next to his chair and got up. He said something to his friend with the dark hair and then ambled over.

"Yes, ma'am?"

"I need some help reaching something. Come on in for a sec, would you?"

As soon as she closed the door, she wheeled on him. "What did you tell Devon? Why does he think I called you to bail him out?"

"Francyne, I thought we went through all this before." He shifted his stance and stared at the ceiling a second before meeting her gaze. "I was at the station when he and Jamie came out to collect their stuff. They thought you called me. I just let them think it. Then I gave them a ride home."

"Your car wasn't parked in the police lot? How'd you manage that?"

"Yeah, but I had them wait and drove around the block to pick them up."

"And they bought that you were just there for them?"

"Seemed to. Am I right in my guess that you paid their bail?"

"Who the hell else would do it? I swear, I think all that hair dye has leached into your brain."

"Aw, c'mon, Francyne, you know you love me." He grinned and patted her on top of the head.

"Cut that out, you'll ruin my do!" She swatted at him and stepped out of reach. "I saw Rick is back. I take it he didn't turn up anything new?"

"Nope." He shook his head. "It's like she's fallen off the face of the Earth."

Francyne touched his arm. "Sweetie, maybe it's time to face

the fact your baby sister may not still be alive. I know, I know, you don't want to believe it. But she always talked highly of you. She loved you. I can't help but think if Alexis was still alive out there somewhere, she would've contacted you by now. That's all I'm saying. And I think she would want you to get on with your life."

He forked his fingers through his hair and stalked to the end of her living room and back. "No! She's out there, I know it. That's why I'm staying here. This was her last address. If she's alive, I know sooner or later she will come back here."

A knock sounded.

They looked at each other.

"Are you expecting anyone?" Todd stepped back behind the door.

Francyne shook her head and shuffled to the door. "It's Jamie," she whispered after looking through the peephole.

"Get rid of her. I don't want her to see me here. She ran into Rick at my apartment today. She's not stupid. It wouldn't take much more before she put two and two together."

"And that would be bad because?"

"Duh. If everyone knows I'm undercover, don't you think it might mess things up a tad?"

"Oh. Good point. I'll get rid of her."

Francyne cracked open the door. "Oh, hi, Jamie. I was just fixin' to go to bed. Is there something you need?"

"Oh, sorry, I didn't realize how late it was. I was going to do some laundry, and there's a sign on Devon's door saying to come here for the tickets. But I can come back tomorrow if—"

"No, that's okay. I was watching the office today and forgot to take down the sign. Just give me a sec to find them." She reached into a bowl by the door and handed a pile to Jamie. "Here you go."

Jamie stepped closer, and Francyne held the door to prevent her from entering.

"Francyne, is that a fireplace?"

"Um . . ." She looked back at Todd, who made the sign to speed things up. "Yes, I guess it is."

"I didn't know any of the apartments had fireplaces."

"Mine is the only unit with one. The builder decided it wasn't a good idea."

"Do you mind if I take a look?"

"No! I mean, I was just about to go to bed. Come back tomorrow." She closed the door and glared at Todd. "I hope you're happy. I probably scarred that poor child for life. She probably thinks I don't like her now."

"Can't be helped. I just need you to keep your mouth shut a little while longer. Can you do that? You're the only one here who really knew Alexis. You were probably the last one to see her."

"Actually I think Devon was the last one to see her. According to him, she came in, all upset, and broke her lease. He had enough petty cash to give her the deposit back, but the rent refund is still lying in a bowl on his desk. I saw it the other night."

"Has he ever said anything else about her?"

"We've been over and over this. No, he did not. Now get on out of here so I can get my beauty sleep."

Petunia came shuffling out after the door shut. She yawned and stretched and then looked at her bowl expectantly.

"Forget it. You're on a diet, remember?" Francyne turned the dead bolt and paused. "I wonder if I should have mentioned Devon saw Alexis get in the car with a man the day she disappeared?"

26

Bright and early the following morning, Devon knocked on Jamie's door.

"Hey," he said when she opened the door for him. "It's going to be a great day. Want to try the beach again?"

She pursed her lips and shook her head.

"No? How about the pool? When I checked the chemicals earlier, there was no one there. We could have it to ourselves."

"The pool sounds nice. But no funny stuff, okay? I've had enough embarrassment for a while."

"No funny stuff. Just two people enjoying the day and the pool."

"Okay. Let me put on my suit."

"Don't do it on my account," he said with a grin and then held up his hands. "Just kidding. No funny stuff. Got it. Stop begging, woman, and go get your suit on. We're wasting sunshine."

Jamie pulled up the straps of one of the bikinis she'd bought at Play It Again, Ma'am and then adjusted her gel packs.

"I sure hope these puppies don't melt," she muttered, turning to check the fit of the suit. Satisfied, she slipped an oversize T-shirt over her head and grabbed a towel on her way out of the bathroom.

The pool was located by going through the hall between the buildings on the other side of the laundry room. Next to the back parking lot, it was secluded by a lattice fence. The corners of the pool area had large palm trees. Planter boxes along the side fences overflowed with an abundance of blooming tropical plants.

Jamie stopped inside the gate and pulled her shirt over her head and then stuffed it in the canvas bag she carried. She paused to sniff a potted honeysuckle.

Devon almost tripped over his own feet, struck by how hot she looked in her barely there, orange hibiscus print suit.

He watched the golden globes of her breasts rise and fall above the tiny triangles covering her nipples and felt his cock swell.

Down, boy. We promised no funny stuff. He discreetly rearranged his package. Trailing behind her, he watched her select a chaise, spread a threadbare beach towel and lie down.

Shielding her eyes, she squinted up at him. "Aren't you going to find a chair?"

"Sure." He grabbed the one next to hers and plopped down on the ancient webbing . . . which immediately gave with his weight, causing a ripping sound to echo within the pool area.

"Shit!"

"Devon, are you okay?" Jamie hopped up and grasped his arm while he struggled to extract his behind from the shredded webbing with as little loss of skin as possible.

"Wait!" He licked his lips and eyed the cleavage so close to his face he could probably touch it with his tongue. He would have tried, except he'd promised no funny stuff. Unable to totally resist, he leaned forward and brushed a kiss on the top of each breast. "You need to remove these—"

"What!" She looked so freaked out it would have been funny had he not been so turned on.

"I meant you need to not get them so close to my mouth unless you mean business." He smiled at her shocked expression. "I know I promised to be good, but you're making it very difficult." He waggled his eyebrows and said, "Notice I didn't say 'hard'? See, I'm abiding by your wishes."

She thumped his forehead and then straddled the broken chair and gripped his upper arms. "We need to get you out of here. When I pull, you push yourself up as far as possible. Ready?"

"Did I ever tell you my fantasy about having sex on a chaise longue?"

"Devon, keep your mind on the problem at hand." She giggled. "And technically, you're *in* a chaise, not *on* one."

"Okay, did I ever tell you my fantasy about having sex *in* a chaise longue?"

She sighed and put her fists on her hips. "Okay, if it will make you move, tell me your fantasy so we can get you out of this thing."

"Well . . ." he began, running the tip of his index fingers up the insides of her thighs and along the elastic leg of her bikini bottom. "Actually, my fantasy involves you on the chaise, on your hands and knees, sans bottom, and me behind the chair. The only way to get to you is by pushing my cock through the squares in the webbing." He dipped his fingers beneath the elastic to slip up and down her slick folds.

She shuddered and moved a little closer, eyes shut.

Mr. Happy did a little dance of joy within the liner of his trunks.

"O-oh?" She licked her lips, her breathing shallow.

"Uh-huh. But now that I can feel how scratchy the webbing is, I'm a little worried about penal lacerations." He dipped into her and was rewarded with a little moan. He thought she was the one who'd moaned but wasn't totally sure about it.

Her hand squeezed him through the fabric of his bathing suit and then pulled the elastic down to let Mr. Happy get a tan.

This time, he definitely knew he was the one doing the moaning.

She drew a little circle around his engorged head, spreading the telltale drop of excitement around. "Too bad. Maybe we can think of a way to improvise?"

His heart rate jumped to warp speed. Mr. Happy was developing a headache.

"You said no funny stuff. Sweetheart, right now, I can't think of anything more fun to do."

Glancing around, she leaned closer and whispered, "I just don't want to get caught again."

Inspiration licked.

27

"Turn around."

"Excuse me?"

"Trust me. Turn around, facing away. No, keep your legs on either side of the chair. That's right. Okay, now sit back. A little more. That's it. Ahhh!"

Jamie's eyes widened when Devon shoved aside the leg of her bottoms and shoved his hot penis into her. A second later, she was squirming to get closer, to increase the sensation rushing through her.

"Scoot back a little more," he said against her ear. "That's right, baby, just like that." His voice was almost a purr. "Oh, yeah, that feels so good." He took nibbling kisses along the side of her neck, his hands pushing on the underside of her top.

Collecting her wits enough to move his hands to the neckline, she leaned against his chest and let the sun and Devon worship her.

His hands gently kneaded her breasts; then his index fingers and thumbs dipped in to squeeze and roll her nipples. All the while, his hips performed languid thrusts. In the distance, the waves could be heard rolling to the shore in perfect accompaniment to the sensual push and pull of his penis deep within her.

Her head lolled against his shoulder. Devon heated her inside while the sun heated her skin.

She whimpered and wiggled her hips for a closer, deeper union. Her completion was elusive, dancing just out of reach, in and out with each thrust.

Beneath his fingers, her nipples hardened to twin peaks of pleasure/pain. She was so wet, so primed, it was amazing his penis didn't slip out.

Just as she was about to cry her frustration, a wave of pleasure crashed over her, drenching her, drowning her, in the intensity of her release.

Devon pulled on her aching nipples, rolling them, prolonging her ecstasy.

Wrung out, she stilled, impaled on him, limp and panting. The sensation of her vagina opening and clenching around his erection stimulated her, but she was too sated to do anything about it.

Devon's thrusts became harder, deeper, faster. His grasp on her nipples tightened to the point of more pain. His harsh gasps of air huffed into her ear, ruffled her hair against her neck.

A tickle of arousal blossomed deep within her. Within seconds, it was in full bloom, driving her to her second orgasm in as many minutes.

Devon plunged into her, his hands clutching her breasts, plastering her back to his chest. He growled and then groaned his completion, every muscle in his body hard against hers.

The blood roaring through her ears subsided enough to allow her to hear the surf again. Sweat-slicked and panting, she tilted her head back to look at Devon, who still held her tightly against his heaving chest.

His eyes were closed, nostrils flared, as he gulped in air.

One by one, his muscles relaxed against her, his grip on her breasts slackened. His fingers moved in little caresses up and around the cups of her suit, occasionally outlining the top edge, his touch burning her as though they hadn't just had mind-blowing sex.

Deep within her, his penis moved, causing an answering wiggle of her hips.

"I could stay like this forever," she said with a sigh.

"I know what you mean," he said against her ear, "except I think I may need a couple of Band-Aids."

Despite his argument, Jamie managed to get him into her bathtub, where she then tenderly washed the abrasions scoring each side of his waist and hips.

"Why didn't you say anything?" she asked when he hissed at the feel of soap and hot water as she washed off the droplets of blood.

"Hey, it was my fantasy. What's a little pain compared to that?"

"Men," she said under her breath as she helped him stand and patted him dry. "You can be such weirdos. Didn't it hurt each time you moved?"

He gave a fake macho laugh. "That wasn't the sensation I was focused on."

"Go lie on the bed while I get the ointment and gauze pads. Good thing for you I bought some when I went out."

"Okay, but I don't want you to think I'm easy." He grinned back over his shoulder as he walked to the bedroom.

"Oh, please." She swatted his bare butt. "That train has left the station."

On his stomach, he breathed in the fresh scent of laundry detergent and fabric softener while he waited for Jamie to come back. He should probably go home and get some writing done after he let her tend to his sex injury. He'd left Trent in a pretty tight situation, plus he promised his editor he'd fax the ad copy for the kitchen line by the end of the week. Unfortunately he lost all creative ambition when Jamie walked back in and climbed onto the bed next to him. Well, creative ambition as pertained to writing. He found he could still be plenty creative sexually.

"Put that hand down!" Swatting his hand away, she continued smoothing the cool ointment onto his fevered, abused skin. For good measure, she swatted his left buttock. "I mean it, Devon! Cut it out. Now lie still while I get the gauze taped down."

"Are you finished yet?"

Her cheeks heated. Good thing he wasn't looking at her. He would have caught her ogling his bare backside. She took another peek. Oh, yeah, it was in fine shape.

"Caught you!" Grabbing her, he rolled until he had her pinned beneath him. "You were looking at my butt!"

"Was not!" Laughing, she made a halfhearted attempt to roll him off.

"Were, too!" His laughter died as their gazes locked. He kissed the tip of her nose. "Your nose is sunburned. You should have worn sunscreen."

"I didn't have the chance to put any on. Some horny guy wanted to do it in the lounge chair."

"It's called a 'chaise,' and watch who you're calling a horny guy."

At that moment, Mr. Happy rose to the occasion.

Jamie arched an eyebrow and grinned.

"Okay, point taken. But it still hurt my feelings."

"Poor baby."

"That's right. I'm not just some horny guy . . . am I?" At her silence, he hurried on. "I mean, I'm more than your sex toy, aren't I? Not that there's anything wrong with that." He ran the tip of his finger down the wrapped front of her robe, leaving a trail of fire, branding her. "I could live with being a sex object."

She raised her head and brushed a light kiss across his lips. "You're the only 'horny guy' I'd consider letting do the things we've done."

He reached between them and untied the sash of her robe. "Prove it." Cupping her breasts in his hands, he licked the tip of her nipples. He blew on the wetness, watching them pucker. He gave a little squeeze she felt all the way to her core. He ran the tip of his tongue around each nipple and then drew one deeply into his mouth.

He placed a string of kisses around each areola and then dragged his tongue between her breasts, up her neck to her mouth. "I love to kiss them," he said against her mouth. "And I love kissing you," he whispered and then proceeded to do just that.

When she felt his erection slip between her spread legs, she wedged her hands between their bodies and pushed on his chest. "Stop. We need protection. We've already taken too many chances."

He stared at her blankly. "I didn't bring anything with me. Please tell me you have something." He glanced between their bodies. "Don't send me out into the cold like this." A slow smile crossed his face. "We don't have to actually do it, you know."

"We don't?" Disappointment washed through her. For someone who never really cared for sex, she'd suddenly become addicted to it with Devon. The thought of abstaining wasn't a happy one.

He shook his head. "Nope. There are other ways to have sex. Ways that don't include penetration. Besides, I thought women liked to cuddle?"

"That's true. . . ." The idea of just cuddling lost a lot of appeal, now that she knew what she'd be missing. She ran her hand across his abdomen and grasped his erection, sliding her hand up and down.

He gently disengaged her hand and moved to the side of the

bed. "If you keep doing that, I can't make any promises." Standing, he reached for her. "Okay, slide to the edge of the bed. No, don't get up. Okay."

He parted her robe, draping it on each side of her breasts. "Lean back a little, resting on your hands. That's it." He touched the tip of each breast, which obediently puckered. "So pretty," he whispered before kissing each one.

His hands were hot when they caressed her thighs apart, spreading them. Dropping to his knees, he stared at a place few men had ever seen.

"I want to touch you," he said in a husky voice, "everywhere." His hands slid up the inside of her thighs, spreading her wider, his fingers dancing along her moisture. "I want to kiss you," he said, softer still, as he trailed tiny kisses up the inside of each thigh, stopping just shy of the place that wept for him. "Everywhere," he whispered and took her aching folds in his mouth, sucking and running his tongue up and down until she was clutching the sheets in her fists to keep from grabbing him and demanding more.

Tucking her legs up onto his shoulders, he tilted her hips for better access and flicked her clitoris with the pointed tip of his tongue.

The muscles in the backs of her thighs vibrated with her arousal.

He ran the tip of his tongue around her opening, eliciting a moan, and then pierced her once, twice, three times with quick, hot thrusts.

Frustrated, she grabbed his hair and held him tight while his mouth continued to ravage and please her. On the edge, she tried to tug him upward, but he persisted.

His teeth closed around her aching nub, sucking it deeply into his mouth. He suckled the tender morsel while he inserted his finger and echoed the rhythm deep within.

On the brink and pretty much out of her mind with lust, she

spread her legs wider, holding his head in place, her hips bucking wildly, toes curling.

Her orgasm shook her to the core, wetting the sheet beneath her, wringing her out.

And still he continued to pleasure her.

Wild now, she clawed at him in an attempt to pull him up and into her body. A body that craved what only he could give her.

Finally, finally, he paused and looked up at her, his face set in grim lines, his thumbs continuing to pleasure her. "I want you to suck me, but I can't risk it. I want you too much."

"What do you want?" Her voice was a raspy whisper. "Tell me."

"I want to fuck you."

Leaning back on her elbows, she tugged him up to her, spreading her legs to accommodate his hips. Placing her hands on each side of his head, she gripped his hair and said in a low, growling voice, "Do it!"

28

Devon pulled the sheet over Jamie and kissed her cheek. She mumbled something and turned over.

After pulling on his trunks, he stepped out of her door and locked it. The new dead bolt turned much smoother than the old one. He glanced down at his key ring. Maybe making his copy of her new key in pink was kind of hokey, but it made it easier to find.

Whistling, he headed across the dark courtyard. A glance at his watch confirmed he'd been out longer than he'd told Francyne. It wouldn't do to take advantage of her neighborly goodwill.

A Post-it note on his door fluttered in the ocean breeze. He grabbed it and unlocked his door. Inside, he read the spidery handwriting:

Took your mutt. Return tomorrow.

The note was simply signed with an *F*. He chuckled. That was Francyne for you, a woman of few words. Unless, of course, she was giving advice.

Alone in his apartment, he wandered around, wondering what he'd done before adopting Killer. Funny how empty the place was without the little guy.

Suddenly hungry, he turned on the oven to preheat and then began pulling ingredients from the pantry and refrigerator. A homemade pizza would taste good, and if there was any left he could either have it for breakfast or give it to Killer tomorrow.

He prepared a whole-wheat crust, brushed extra-virgin olive oil on the pizza pan and spread the dough to cover it. After he'd mixed tomato sauce and chunky picante sauce and poured it over the crust, he opened and drained a can of chicken breast meat and spread it on top of the sauce. Fresh chopped mushrooms came next, along with green pepper and a thick layer of colby jack and mozzarella cheese.

After popping it into the oven, he poured a glass of Lambrusco and walked to his desk to bring up his work-in-progress on the laptop.

Settled in his chair, he watched the cursor, typed a word or two and then deleted them and sat and watched the cursor blinking for a while longer.

The pizza began to fill the apartment with a mouthwatering scent. As if on cue, his stomach growled.

A timid knock barely registered until it came again.

Just in case he'd written anything substantial, he hit SAVE and got up.

Jamie stood, shivering, when he opened the door, her pink robe wrapped snugly around her, arms crossed. She shifted from one bare foot to another. "Aren't you going to ask me to come in?"

He bowed and stepped back, waving her into the apartment. "What's up?"

"I woke up, and you were gone." She looked toward the kitchen and sniffed the air. "And I smell pizza."

"You smelled that all the way across the courtyard?" He

grinned down at her and tried not to think about what she might or might not have on under the robe.

"No," she said with a smile and batted her eyelashes at him. "But I am hungry."

"Still haven't gone grocery shopping, huh?"

"Yes, I went, but there isn't anything good at my place." She sniffed again and moved farther into the apartment. "Not as good as that pizza smells, anyway."

He bit his cheek to keep from laughing. "Would you like a piece of pizza?"

In response, she walked to the dining room table and sat down. "I thought you'd never ask. Is it almost done? I'm starving!"

After eating, she helped clean up and then wandered back into the living room, apparently in no great hurry to go home.

"Am I keeping you from working?" she asked when he glanced at the computer screen for the second time since they'd sat down.

"Unfortunately, no." He settled back on the couch and pulled her against him. When she rested her head on his shoulder, he realized he was doing exactly what he wanted to do. "I opened the file with my book but couldn't really get into the story. Then I thought about writing the descriptions for the kitchen-line gadgets, but then I realized I was hungry, so I made the pizza. Then you came over."

"I don't want to be the cause of you not writing." She tried to sit up, but he held her firmly against him. "Really, Devon. I can go home. It's getting late." She glanced down at her robe. "I can't believe I walked over here in my robe. What was I thinking?"

He grinned and gave her a one-armed hug. "Don't worry about it. Francyne does it all the time. Hell, she even has been known to walk Petunia like that."

"Wow. Is that how she maintains her tan?"

"Nah. I don't know if you noticed or not, but there is no apartment above hers or mine. She made a tanning deck on her roof." He gave an exaggerated shudder. "That's a sight to see first thing in the morning, I'll tell you! She usually walks Petunia after breakfast and then tans for the rest of the morning." Their eyes met. "Afternoons, of course, are reserved for her soaps."

Jamie giggled. "Don't tell me, she wears a bikini."

"I wish! The first time I saw her, I was afraid I'd have to jab out my eyes. Miz Francyne likes an even, all-over tan, if you know what I mean."

Their laughter echoed within the quiet apartment.

Jamie wiped the mirth from her eyes and stood, tightening her belt. "I should go. Thanks for the pizza."

He caught her belt as she walked toward the door and pulled her back and into his arms. "You could stay and help me research the toys."

"I thought you said you were going to write up the descriptions for the kitchen gadgets."

"If you stay, I could do the sex-toy work instead. Which I vote for, since it would be much more fun." He tugged her belt, and her robe fell open.

She was naked.

"Ms. Jamie! You're plumb nekkid under there!" The grin made his alleged shock a lie.

She shrugged. "I thought, maybe . . . Well, I guess I should go."

"Wait!" He hauled her into his arms. "I think something just came up. Let's not be too hasty about leaving. After all, you came ready and willing to help me test the products. I think that's what we should do. So, what would you like to help me test first?" He gestured at the array of products spread over the coffee table.

She picked up the candy dish of condoms. "How about we test to see which one of these really glows in the dark?"

Jamie woke with a slight headache and the taste of strawberry and latex in her mouth. Looking around, she realized she was in her own bed. Alone.

Slowly the night before came back to her. She and Devon had tried out every condom in the candy dish. They glowed in green, orange and yellow. The pink one didn't glow as brightly but felt more substantial than its brighter counterparts. She and Devon agreed the flavored condoms interfered less with tactile pleasure than the glow-in-the-dark ones. Which explained the aftertaste.

Realizing her legs were wobbly, she giggled and walked gingerly into the bathroom. They'd probably had more sex last night than she'd had in her entire life.

She leaned closer to the mirror and examined the slight discoloration at the base of her neck, unable to stop smiling.

She couldn't wait to "help" Devon again.

After a quick shower, Jamie braided her hair into a single braid and headed toward the boardwalk. Maybe Shirl would have a new shipment of dresses in. Devon was taking her out to dinner, and she wanted to look her best.

"Hey, doll," Shirl called in his distinctive deep raspy voice when the bell jingled to announce her arrival. "I just got some stuff in that's your size!" He toddled on orange-sequined heels to the door of the stockroom and pulled out a rolling rack. "Check it out while I make a couple of calls to customers."

Today Shirl was dressed in a pair of lime-green stretch capri pants that were stretched to the max. His obviously waxed chest didn't improve the neckline of the plunging neon-pink tank top. The edge of his fake boobs, clearly visible through the bra he wore, pushed against soft knit, giving his chest a boxy look. His outlandish red hair was piled on top of his head, secured with what looked suspiciously like a big swizzle stick topped with a little pile of fake fruit. Tiny clusters of bananas hung from each pierced ear, giving him the appearance of a Caribbean queen on testosterone overload.

Obviously noticing her stare, he did a slow turn and then flicked one earring with the tip of a bright coral fingernail. "What do you think? Too much?"

"Well, it's certainly, um, eye-catching."

Shirl nodded and looked thoughtful, so Jamie took it as a sign to try on a few dresses she snagged from the new items.

With Shirl's voice rumbling in the background, Jamie tried on three dresses and a pantsuit that reminded her of a costume from *The Brady Bunch.*

Disheartened, she walked out to rehang the clothes, shaking her head at Shirl's questioning look.

"Hold on, sugar." Shirl covered the receiver and whispered. "Did you see the black number on the other end?" He made a shooing motion with his hand and then went back to his conversation.

Jamie held up "the black number." Tiny sparkles woven into the fabric caught and reflected the light coming in through the plateglass windows. The dress looked tiny, but the tag confirmed it was her size.

She tested the fabric by giving it a little tug. It stretched and then popped right back.

In the fitting room, she stared at her reflection. She looked like she was wearing black-glittered shrink-wrap.

After confirming that no one else was in the store, she hurried out to the three-way mirror. By light of day, it really wasn't bad.

She turned, observing the dress from every conceivable direction, light reflecting her every move. The long sleeves were sheer with the same tiny sparkles woven in. The neckline was low. Very low. It dipped almost to her belly button, while the back stopped just shy of being too revealing. A jaunty bow of the same fabric saved the back from being risqué by hiding the telltale slope of her derrière.

The hem was shorter than she usually wore, and she had to resist the urge to tug it down.

"Okay, doll, if you don't take that dress, you are banned from this shop for eternity." Shirl walked over and motioned for her to turn. Then he let loose a loud wolf whistle. "Damn, I wish I had it in my size."

"I can't imagine how anyone taller could wear it without being exposed." Jamie frowned at the expanse of leg showing and wondered if she had the nerve to wear it that night.

"Truth be told, I think it may be a tunic top, doll, but it's the perfect dress for you." He pointed at her. "Stay right there. I think I saw some heels in the box that would go perfectly with it."

For a big man, he moved pretty fast in high heels.

"What size do you wear, doll?" he called from the back room.

"Five or five and a half, but you may as well forget it," she called back, "because it's almost impossible to find that size anymore." Which was fine, because she preferred flip-flops anyway.

Shirl emerged, waving a pair of the highest black heels Jamie had ever seen. "They're a six, but they're so high you'll probably need the extra room to keep from pinching your toes. Gravity, you know." He shoved the shoes toward her. "Look, they even have the same little sparkles as the dress."

Jamie kicked off a flip-flop and slipped on one of the shoes. She would have immediately fallen over had Shirl not reached out to grab her. "I'll never be able to walk in these things!"

"Sure you will, doll. If I can do it, so can you." He held up the remaining shoe, light-leather sole out. "They don't look like they've ever been worn, so maybe you should walk out on the sidewalk and do a few practice laps in front of the store to roughen up the soles while you get the hang of walking in them."

Devon paced around his living room and checked the clock for about the fifth time in as many minutes. Killer was having another sleep-over with Petunia and Francyne, and it was surprising how much he missed him.

He glanced at the dark screen of the laptop and tamped down the guilt for not working on his book. After he had walked Jamie home last night—okay, so it had been closer to this morning—he had come home and written up enough descriptions to keep the editor of the Midnight Fantasies company happy for a while; then he'd faxed them.

But his mind wasn't on his work anymore. Hadn't really been, since he and Jamie got together.

Just the thought of his impending date had Mr. Happy ready to ride.

Images of the previous night flashed through his mind, tightening his pants.

Damn. With the way his life had been going lately, maybe he should try his hand at writing porn.

29

Jamie wiped her sweating palms on the sides of her new dress and eyed her reflection in the full-length mirror on the back of the bathroom door.

The dress was so formfitting, she had not been able to wear any underwear. The back was too low for a bra, and the fit would reveal panty lines, regardless of the scantiness of the undergarment. She knew because she'd tried on every thong she owned.

The good news was, due to the elasticity of the dress, she was still able to wear her gel augmentation. Just to make sure they were secure, she jumped up and down a few times. Both breasts remained at the same size and location.

A part of her told her it was stupid to continue wearing the hot, uncomfortable things. After all, she was going to be with Devon. He'd seen and felt the real her plenty of times by now. He hadn't even seemed to notice the disparity in size.

But they were going out in public. Fred could be lurking. That's why she had splurged on a new hair coloring kit and renewed her blondness that afternoon. Devon had been busy, so she'd also slathered on self-tanning lotion and then gone and sat by the pool to speed along the process. She'd discovered that the sun helped the self-tanner look more like a real tan. It also helped dissipate the smell somewhat.

Her shoulders slumped. What was she doing? She and Devon had been having a perfectly lovely, intensely sexual relationship. Why had she let him talk her into going out on an actual date? She liked him too much. It would be too easy to fall for him. And she didn't want to do that.

She couldn't afford to get emotionally involved with anyone until she was certain she was safely away from Fred forever.

The air clicked on, giving her a definite draft. She guessed going pantyless would do that for a person. She critically eyed the hemline again and then dragged a kitchen chair into the bathroom and sat down in front of the mirror. Nothing showed.

Just to be sure, she got her compact and pretended she was stepping in and out of a car. Again, nothing showed except an expanse of tanned leg.

Thank goodness.

She glanced at the clock on the oven. Devon would be there soon. Had she brushed her teeth?

She ran into the bathroom again and swished mouthwash and then rebrushed her teeth, just to make sure.

Of course, then she had to reapply her lipstick. She leaned close to make sure there was no red stain on her teeth. The bright red lip color had been Shirl's idea. Jamie personally preferred softer shades and the lightness of a gloss.

She frowned at her reflection and then grabbed a tissue and scrubbed the bright junk off. Digging in her little makeup bag, she finally found her Clinique Ripe Apple lip gloss and swiped it across her lips and then smiled. That was more like it.

*　*　*

Rick and Todd were sitting, talking quietly, in the courtyard when Devon headed for Jamie's apartment. He noticed they stopped talking as he approached.

"Hey, guys, how's it going?" He stopped just shy of the fire pit and observed them. What was going on?

Todd shrugged and took a swig of his beer. "Not much." He eyed Devon. "Got a date or something?"

Devon nodded and cast a nervous glance at Jamie's apartment. Should he tell who he was taking out?

"Rick, when did you get back to town?" Diversion was always a good tactic. "I thought I saw your truck in the back lot yesterday, but then it wasn't there, so I thought maybe not." His watch confirmed he had a few minutes, so he pulled up a chair but shook his head when Rick held up a beer.

"Yeah, I got in yesterday. Had a bunch of errands to run, so I went back out right away." Rick stretched and looked at Todd and then slumped back in his chair. "Anything interesting been going on while I was gone?"

"New tenant." Todd nodded in the direction of Jamie's apartment. "I met her. Seems nice." He grinned. "Hot stuff, right, Dev?"

Beneath his crossed arms, Devon clenched his fists. He made a noncommittal shrug. He knew by the smile on Todd's too perfect face that he was razzing him, but his relationship with Jamie was too new to discuss with anyone.

That thought brought his brain to attention. Did he and Jamie have a relationship? Sure, they enjoyed great and varied sex, but did that mean they were involved in a relationship? The thought was sobering, to say the least.

He wasn't sure he was ready to get involved with anyone. After all, he had his writing career to consider. He'd always planned to settle down someday, maybe even get married and have a family. But he'd also planned to write and sell his books.

While he didn't intend to wait until he hit the best-seller list, he'd always thought he wouldn't begin to seriously look for anyone until he'd at least published his first book. Hell, he could barely support himself and Killer; forget a wife and potential future children.

Yet now that he'd gotten to know Jamie—and he didn't mean only in the biblical sense—he couldn't really imagine life with anyone else.

Pretty scary thought.

"Dev?" Todd's voice broke into his thoughts. "I said we're going to P.O.'s, maybe grab some barbeque and play some pool. Wanna come?"

Devon made a show of looking at his watch. "No. Thanks, anyway. I've got something else to do in a bit."

Todd's grin flashed white in the firelight. He gave Devon a playful punch on the shoulder. "Go get her, tiger."

He and Rick laughed as they walked away like they thought the idea of him scoring with someone like Jamie or anyone for that matter was a big joke.

Was it? He'd spent most of his life with his nose stuck in a book or daydreaming. Or cooking. Not exactly potential stud material.

Jamie jumped when the knock echoed in her apartment and gave herself one more once-over. Deciding it was probably too late to change her dress, she tightened her butt muscles to avoid wobbling as she walked to the door in her new shoes.

A glance in the old mirror on the living room wall made her stop for a second. If she'd thought she didn't recognize the new her in the mirror before, what she saw tonight was even more of a stretch.

She took a deep breath and continued toward the door.

"Take no prisoners," she whispered and opened the door.

Devon paused in the process of spraying his mouth and started coughing.

"Devon!" She rushed to him and pulled him into her apartment. She closed the door and watched as he continued to cough. "Are you choking? Can I get you a glass of water?" He shook his head. "Call nine-one-one?" That earned her a glare. Relief washed over her. He was going to be okay.

"Just give me a sec," he wheezed.

He took a deep breath and straightened up, wiping the tears from his eyes. "Sorry about that. You surprised me. I didn't think you'd answer the door so soon so I decided to take a shot of breath spray." He shrugged. "Guess I inhaled." He brushed a kiss across her lips. "But at least I know my breath is fresh," he said with a smile.

"Yes, it is." She stood smiling up at him, her smile telling him it was okay to behave like an idiot with her. She understood.

Then again, maybe her smile just said he was an idiot. He wasn't all that adept at reading female body language.

"Are you ready to go? Our reservation is for nine."

"Sure. Just let me grab my purse." She turned and picked up a miniscule black object not much bigger than a number-ten envelope.

He squinted. Was she wearing any underwear? He sure couldn't see any panty lines. Or any other lines, come to think of it.

Pausing at the door, she looked back at him. "What? Is there a problem?" She looked down at her shoes and dress. "Don't I look all right? Is what I'm wearing too much? Too little?" She gave a nervous-sounding laugh.

"How can you walk in those shoes?" he finally blurted out and then could have bitten his tongue when her face fell. "I mean," he racked his brain for a way to soothe her obviously hurt feelings, "they're nice. Pretty. They match your dress, don't they?" He nodded like a Bobble-Head doll. And felt about as intelligent. "I just asked because I wouldn't want you to fall and hurt yourself." He closed his eyes and took a deep breath.

When he opened them again, she was smiling shyly up at him.

"Don't worry, I've been practicing walking in them all afternoon. But you can hold on to me, if you want, just in case."

Great. If she knew how he wanted to hold on to her, she wouldn't be smiling. She'd be screaming and running. Then again, with her wearing those shoes, he might be able to catch her.

He watched her lock the door and then walked her to his car, one hand on her elbow and the other at the small of her back.

She smiled up at him and thanked him for helping her into the bucket seat of his Mustang.

He closed her door and wiped the sweat from his forehead as he walked around the car.

Was Jamie really that clueless?

Heaven help him. He was dating a woman in a fuck-me dress if he'd ever seen one.

30

Jamie had a difficult time enjoying the delicious meal. At least, she thought it was probably delicious. She was too busy concentrating on keeping her legs together. As if that hadn't been bad enough, the hostess had seated them on the upper level of the rotating dining room. She felt like people were looking right up her dress.

From the leering glances of some of the men at the bar, they probably were.

"You're not having a very good time, are you?" Devon looked down at his plate, shoving food around with his fork. "I should have taken you somewhere else. The food is good, but—"

"No!" She reached across the starched white tablecloth and touched his arm. "It's great. Really. I just, um, have a little problem with heights. And it's made worse by the rotating." She shrugged. "I can't look out the window or I'll get dizzy."

He dropped his fork to his place and heaved a sigh. "Like I said, I should have picked another place." He looked over at her. "I had no idea you had a problem or I'd have picked a stationary restaurant. On ground level."

She squeezed his hand. "Of course you would have. But you didn't know. And this is really a very nice place." She picked up a lump of something and popped it in her mouth, chewing appreciatively. "And the food is delicious," she added after swallowing.

"You look pretty," he said and flashed a small smile.

"Thanks. So do you." She put her hand to her mouth. "I shouldn't have said that, should I? I meant you look handsome."

He grinned, and she was once again struck by his features. Handsome was too mundane for the way he looked. By day he was sexily scruffy, but when he cleaned up and wore something other than shorts and flip-flops, he took her breath away.

He took a sip of his drink. "I'll settle for pretty. Handsome might be a stretch."

"Not really." Had he no idea of how attracted she was to him?

"Thanks." He stood up and extended his hand. "Would you like to dance?"

The idea of dancing in the high heels filled her with terror. Besides, she knew what was beneath his starched shirt and tie and conservative sports coat. Before the evening was through she planned to touch and kiss and lick every inch of the skin hidden from view.

The thought made her achy in places that hadn't ever ached before. Last night had been wonderful.

She fully intended for tonight to be even better.

He paused at the top of the spiral staircase. "Maybe we should ask if there's an elevator."

"I don't want to wait. Let's go home." When still he hesitated, she said, "Tell you what, why don't you go ahead of me? That way, if I slip, you can catch me."

He thought about that for a second and then nodded. "Good plan."

After he'd descended a couple of steps, she placed her hands on his shoulders and began her decent, trying not to look down.

Evidently, she didn't lift her foot quite high enough on the second step.

The tip of her heel caught on the edge of the carpeted step. Thinking it was just picking on the fiber of the carpet, she pushed out with that foot a little harder. Her foot connected with air, and before she could do more than squeak her surprise, she was beginning a bumpy descent down the stairs.

Devon reacted, turning on the steps and reaching out, closing his arms around her.

Unfortunately all he caught was her dress as it slid up around her armpits.

The cool breeze wafting around her privates told her she'd just flashed all the patrons of the Dockside Steak Emporium and Bar.

31

A collective gasp came from all the restaurant patrons. Jamie kept her eyes squeezed shut, too mortified to react, while Devon's shaking hands tugged her dress back down to protect what little modesty she had left.

When he helped her to her feet at the base of the stairs, she kept her gaze firmly on the toes of her shoes, concentrating on placing one foot in front of the other. Just as they reached the door, an employee rushed up.

"Ma'am? I believe you dropped this."

The flesh-colored glob of silicone entered her field of vision.

Her hand shot out, grabbing the telltale augmentation and shoving it into her dress in one—she hoped—lightning-fast motion.

Devon cleared his throat, drawing her attention. He glanced pointedly at her chest, so she looked down.

Darn. She'd shoved the falsie into the wrong side of her bodice, resulting in a horribly lopsided bosom.

Without a word, Devon guided her to his car. After helping

her in, he slid into the driver's seat and started the powerful engine.

As they entered Interstate 45, he finally spoke. "You want to tell me about what you stuffed down your dress?"

Even though she'd immediately shifted the misplaced form, she glanced down at her chest and tugged on her neckline. "Not really."

What sounded suspiciously like a smothered laugh echoed in the silence of the car's interior. "It really wasn't necessary, you know. I've already seen you naked, up close and personal." He chuckled. "And, now, so has everyone in the restaurant."

She punched his bicep.

"Ow!" He made a show of rubbing the offended spot. "You're not only an exhibitionist, you're violent."

Burying her heated face in her hands, she wished he'd just push her out of the car on some deserted stretch of highway. A person could take only so much humiliation in one's life.

The car pulled onto the shoulder of the road, making her wonder if Devon had read her mind.

"It's past time you told me what you're really doing in Surfside." Devon leveled his gaze on her as the car rolled to a stop, the glow from the dash casting him in harsh relief.

"What do you mean?" She chewed on her lower lip and wondered how far they were from the apartment. Her stomach sank—she'd never make it more than a block in the grotesquely high heels. What had she been thinking? The shoes were so not her style.

"Jamie, don't look so worried." He reached and took her hand in his much warmer one. "I had hoped we knew each other well enough not to have secrets."

Without warning, he dipped his free hand into her bodice and removed a traitorous gel pack. "Want to tell me why you feel you need to wear these ridiculous things?"

"Give me that!" Her grab was unsuccessful. "I mean it, Devon. This isn't funny."

"I know." His quiet voice filled the silence. "What I don't know is what you're doing."

Shifting on the seat, she glared at him.

He glared right back.

Defeated, she slumped back in the red bucket seat. "I told you I'm trying to keep a low profile because of Fred." At his nod, she continued. "I thought maybe if I changed the way I looked, Fred wouldn't be able to find me so easily."

"And you thought a bigger bosom would do the trick?" The tone of his voice told her what he thought of that idea. "What is he, some throwback, a true 'breast' man?"

"Of course I didn't think just a bigger chest would throw him off my trail. I also changed my hair and eye color. And I began wearing clothing the old Jamie would never wear, more flamboyant types of things." Not to mention acting a way that was also foreign to her old lifestyle. Ironically, she found she liked the new hedonistic Jamie.

She pulled a strand of hair from his toying fingers and leaned back against the passenger door. His touch was too disturbing.

"Yet you keep thinking you've seen him," he pointed out. "Obviously the disguise thing isn't working too well for you."

Her sigh filled the car. "I don't know what else to do, Devon. Everything I've tried in the past hasn't worked. It's spooky the way he keeps finding me. If you have any other ideas, I'm all ears."

"Could he be finding you through your bank or credit cards?"

"I canceled my credit cards and have been accessing my trust fund through a personal banker in Denver. He transfers the funds to a checking account, and I use my ATM. I don't even have an e-mail account for Fred to hack into anymore."

"Is Jamie Cartwright your real name? Maybe that's how he's

finding you. A lot of things are public record, you know. It's just a matter of finding out a way to access it."

"Actually, my real name is Jamie Lambert. Cartwright is my middle name. It was my mom's maiden name."

"But your driver's license said Cartwright. I saw it when you signed the lease."

"It was pretty easy to get a new license. All I had to do was apply for a new one and use my birth certificate. My mom and dad were fighting when I was born, so Mom put her maiden name on my birth certificate and listed my father as unknown. They made up, of course, but she never got around to having the birth certificate changed."

"Does Fred know this?"

She thought about that for a moment and then shook her head. "No. He's never had any dealing with me that would have required the use of my full name."

"Your name wasn't on the lease when you lived with him?"

"No. Fred has control issues."

"Which is why you left him in the first place."

"Exactly."

He started the car and glanced over at her with a grin. "Have you ever done it in a Mustang?"

The question shot heat through her. She checked out the space and then shook her head. "No, and I don't think it's logistically possible, even if we tried."

"There's an old saying, where there's a will, there's a way."

Tempting as the thought was, she shook her head. "Ah, that's the thing. I'm not willing. And you're still injured from our little lawn-chair sex experiment—"

"—I'm a fast healer—"

"Plus," she continued as though he hadn't spoken, "I've had enough humiliation for one night. Maybe for a lifetime."

His chuckle warmed her more, adding to the flush of desire

blazing through her. "I hear you. I was embarrassed on your behalf. While I, personally, enjoyed the view, I wasn't too happy about the rest of the crowd. And I knew you had to be dying."

"You can say that again! I can't recall ever being so mortified. Thanks, by the way, for your fast reaction in helping me get my dress back down."

"You're grateful and yet not willing to have sex with me in the car?" He tsked and put the car in gear, checking for traffic as he pulled onto the road. "What ever happened to gratitude sex?"

"Oh, come on! I think you're making stuff up. Really. Have you ever actually had *gratitude* sex?"

"Well, no. But that doesn't mean I wouldn't be *grateful* for it," he said with a smile in her direction.

"Just shut up and drive."

"Want to come to my apartment and rub more gunk on my sex injuries?" Devon helped her out of the car and then locked it.

"No offense, but I think I'll pass. We got sidetracked the last time I did that. I ended up rubbing a lot more than your injuries."

He waggled his eyebrows and kissed her temple. "That's what I'm counting on."

"And that's why I'm not going to do it," she shot back with a saccharine smile.

Devon hung his head and trudged toward the courtyard. "You're a hard woman, Jamie."

"I still have some pineapple upside-down cake, if you can behave yourself." Even without sex, she found she liked spending time with him and was surprised to realize she wasn't ready for the evening to end.

His smile caused a returning one from her. He saluted her. "Scout's honor. I'll be on my best behavior."

* * *

Devon rolled from her sweat-slicked body and heaved a sigh. "I know, I promised. But the sight of you serving whipped cream with the cake caused all this. It did me in. You know, in some countries whipping cream is an aphrodisiac. Sixty-three percent of couples prefer their sex with whipped cream."

"You're making that up!" She would have swatted at him, but her arm refused to obey her command.

"Okay, maybe I am, but if it's not a fact, it should be." He rolled close to her and ran his fingertip along the outside of her breast. "If I promise to behave, may I have seconds?"

"Oh, no, you don't! I'm not falling for your word games. Seconds of what? Cake? Or sex?"

"Yes."

He popped an antacid in his mouth and chewed vigorously, his eyes narrowed at the darkened bedroom window. How long did it take to eat cake? He'd seen Jamie and the guy go into the apartment, heard them discussing cake, saw them eating at the table. Then they'd disappeared. It didn't take a rocket scientist to figure out where they went. Jamie had turned into a real sex maniac since they separated.

The thought made him sick, and he chomped down on another chalky mint.

He took a deep breath. He could control his temper. He'd been doing so well. Why did she have to be such a slut?

Footsteps sounded on the courtyard. He turned and walked toward the back parking lot.

"Hey!" a deep voice shouted. "Hey, you! Are you looking for someone?"

He picked up the pace and then sprinted to his car, not looking back as he took the exit on two wheels.

* * *

Bang, bang, bang.

Devon jackknifed to a sitting position, dipping the mattress and jiggling Jamie.

Bang, bang, bang.

"Whoever it is sounds anxious." Devon pulled up his pants and stepped around the pile of clothes on the floor. "Stay here. I'll go see who it is."

As soon as he left the room, she vaulted from the bed and grabbed her robe. No way was she going to allow Fred to pulverize or otherwise bully Devon.

She hurried into the living room as Devon opened the door. Her shoulders slumped with relief when she recognized Todd's friend Rick.

"Everything okay in here?" Rick scanned the room while he talked.

"It was, until you started banging on the door," Devon answered with a wry smile.

Rick's gaze zeroed in on Jamie, raking her from bare feet to the top of her head and back. "I didn't mean to interrupt." He stepped back over the threshold. "I just saw some creep loitering outside by the bedroom window and wanted to make sure everyone was all right."

"Did you see who it was?" Jamie pulled the lapels of her robe tight against her neck.

Rick shook his head. "Nah. Too dark. All I saw was a dark silhouette, tall, male. Buzz cut. That's about it. As soon as I yelled at him, he made tracks for the parking lot. By the time I got out there, he was a speck of taillights."

"Well, thanks for coming by," Devon said, closing the door. "Appreciate it."

Rick stared for a moment and then nodded and walked away.

"Do you think it was Fred?" Jamie was right behind him when he closed the door.

He pulled her into his arms and rested his chin on her head. "Calm down. No reason to think it was him." Of course, there was also no reason to think otherwise, but he wasn't about to tell her that. "I'm going to go home now and try to get some work done. How about breakfast tomorrow; then we can catch some rays on the beach." He held up his hand. "Don't worry, I plan to keep my distance from you so we don't get arrested again. Besides, I need to be back in time for Francyne to watch her soaps. She claims subbing for me at the manager's office cuts into her viewing time."

"Okay. Should I bring anything? Orange juice, suntan lotion? A chastity belt?"

"Ha. Ha. Very funny. Why don't you be there around eight; then we can be on the beach by nine."

A chaste kiss was followed by a steamy gaze, and he walked away.

After pausing to listen for the dead bolt being thrown, he whistled tunelessly and set off across the courtyard.

A metal scraping sound drew his attention. It sounded like it had come from the corridor running next to Jamie's bedroom.

Even with the light of a full moon, it was difficult to see once he progressed a few steps toward the interior.

Out of nowhere, a fist connected with his face.

32

When Devon opened his eyes, he was flat on his back next to Jamie's window. It hurt, but he turned his head. He was alone.

Good thing, too. If he'd seen the coward who'd clocked him, he'd kick his ass.

He stood and grabbed the wall until the wave of dizziness left him.

Okay, maybe the guy's ass was safe.

Right now, he needed a stiff drink, a soft bed and an extra-strength pain reliever. Not necessarily in that order.

A glance confirmed that Jamie's lights were still on.

He sighed. Rest would have to wait. He needed to make sure she was okay.

Jamie dried her face as she walked from the bathroom, pausing until she heard Devon's voice call through the door.

She swung the door open to see him leaning against the frame, his hand covering his face.

"Are you all right?" She tugged until he was inside the door and then shut it again. "What's wrong?"

"Nothing," he said in a muffled voice. "I just wanted to double-check that you were okay before I went home. Night."

"Wait! What's going on?" She grabbed his arm as he passed, turning him toward the light. "Oh, my gosh! What happened? Do you need to put ice on it?"

Devon's nose was swollen beneath both eyes a shade or two darker than usual.

"No," he assured her. "I'm fine. Really. Just had a little accident, that's all. After I picked myself up, I decided I should check on you one more time." He grinned and winced and then touched his nose and winced again. "I wanted to make sure my clumsiness hadn't rubbed off on you."

Tugging him until she could reach the freezer, she took out a small bag of frozen peas and handed it to him. "You're not going anywhere until you put something on that."

While he sat with the bag on his face, she rummaged around in the drawer until she found the small bottle of Tylenol she'd bought at the grocery store. She shook some into her hand and got a glass of water. "Here. Take these. And drink the whole glass of water."

He peeked around the plastic bag and took the pills, throwing them into his mouth and gulping the entire glass of water. "There," he said, handing back the empty glass, "are you happy now?"

"Not really. Not until you tell me what really happened."

"I tripped."

"Why don't I believe you?"

He stood and tossed the peas back into the freezer section. Walking back to her, he gripped her shoulders and pulled her into a kiss that curled her toes.

"Because," he said when he finished kissing her senseless, "you are a suspicious person." He kissed the tip of her nose and stepped back. "I have some work to do, and then I'm getting a good night's sleep. I suggest you do the same. See you bright and early tomorrow, sunshine."

She stood staring at the door after he left. It certainly looked as though someone had punched Devon in the nose.

With a sigh, she walked over and locked the door. If he didn't stop lying to her, she might be the next person to punch his lights out.

"I smell bacon," Francyne said as she walked into Devon's apartment the next morning. "You didn't tell me you were making breakfast for me. I already had a bowl of All-Bran. 'Course, I wouldn't turn down a cup of coffee—holy shit! What happened to you?"

She reached and turned his face to the light. "You're working on a set of black eyes. Somebody punch you?"

"Nah. Just clumsy. Here."

He grinned and handed her a filled mug with the flavored creamer she favored already in it.

"You're a good boy," she said, patting his cheek. After taking a sip, she sighed and looked up at him. "You're going to make someone a good wife someday."

"Very funny."

"So," Francyne said, leaning against the counter, "who's coming for breakfast, as though I didn't know?"

"Jamie," he answered, his head bent over the biscuits in the oven. He straightened, wiping his hands on the towel tucked into the waistband of his shorts. "We're going to go to the beach for a couple hours after we eat. I printed up some lease applications, in case you get a rush while I'm gone."

That earned a snicker.

"Yeah, I don't think I'll hold my breath on that. Did Rick tell you his faucet is leaking again? I'll call the plumber as soon as I'm finished with my coffee."

"I can take a look at it when I get back."

Francyne snorted. "Like I said, I'll call a plumber."

"What's that supposed to mean?" He stirred the gravy and put the lid on the tureen.

"It means you're a great guy, pumpkin, and we love you, but a fix-it man you are not. Remember Drew's shower fiasco last year? It's cheaper to call a plumber."

"It's open," Devon called a few seconds later when a knock sounded.

Jamie entered, looking very tan and sexy in a white fishnet cover-up over a very revealing bright yellow bikini.

"Hi, Francyne!" Jamie looked genuinely pleased to see the old lady. "Where's Petunia?"

Francyne gave a dismissive wave of her hand. "Ah, she and Killer frolicked most of the night. Finally had to separate them. They're sleeping in. Soon as I finish my coffee and make a call, I'll go get them and take them out and then bring them back here."

"Good morning, Dev—oh, my! Have you looked at your face this morning?" Jamie walked close enough for him to smell her coconut suntan lotion. It conjured up ideas of licking her delectable body, which brought a fresh stab of pain in his nose.

"Yes, as a matter of fact, I have. Yes, I am aware both of my eyes are black. And, yes, I think my nose is probably broken. And, no, I do not plan to go to the doctor. I plan to sit down and enjoy our breakfast and then brush my teeth and head for the beach. The sun will help my headache and your tan. Now sit. Eat before it gets cold." He pulled out a chair for her. "Francyne? Would you like something? There's plenty."

"Oh, no, thanks. If I don't watch my figure, no one else will."

"I'm sure they try not to," he whispered in Jamie's ear, eliciting a smothered giggle.

"Well," Francyne said as she walked to put her empty cup in the dishwasher, "I'll get going and leave you two lovebirds to your breakfast. Killer and Petunia will be hopping around with their legs crossed if I don't get them out soon."

They ate their breakfast in silence after Francyne left and then cleaned up and left for the beach.

Jamie took a deep breath of ocean air and grinned. "I could get used to living by the beach."

Panic, totally disproportionate to the length of time they'd known each other, gripped Devon. Was Jamie planning to leave Surfside?

"Don't worry," he said with feigned nonchalance, "you'll get used to it pretty quickly. Pretty soon you'll be like everyone else and forget it's here." He grinned. "It's a great little town, and the beach is one of the best-kept secrets of south Texas. I'd live here even if I didn't work here."

"It is nice," she agreed, stepping down onto the sand. "But I don't know how much longer my money will last. I can't stay unemployed forever." She watched a group of children building a sand castle. "Besides, I miss teaching." She glanced his way. "I was good at it."

"I'm sure you could be good at just about anything you tried." The blanket he brought flapped in the breeze. Smoothing it in place, he sat and patted the spot next to him. "Have a seat. Is this spot all right? We're in public, so we can't get too carried away, and we're also close to the boardwalk in case we get hungry or thirsty."

"It's fine." She sat down and pulled her cover-up over her head. "Did you remember to bring a copy of your book for me to read?"

"No, I forgot. But don't feel like you have to read it just because we're, ah, friends." He narrowed his eyes and leaned closer. "We are friends, aren't we?"

In answer, she ran the tip of her finger along the edge of his lower lip and then met his gaze. "Of course we're friends. More than just friends, I hope."

He picked up his suntan oil. "You mean like BFF?"

She laughed and lightly punched his arm. "You are such a dork."

Stretched out on the blanket, they relaxed and let the sound of the surf and the warmth of the sun lull them.

A shadow fell across Jamie's face. When it didn't move after a few minutes, she realized it was not a random cloud and opened her eyes.

Fred stared down at her.

Fear froze her vocal cords. Her hand refused to obey her command to nudge Devon. Now she knew what it meant to be paralyzed with fear.

She closed her eyes, praying for strength. When she opened them, Fred was gone. A look around found him walking down the boardwalk, away from them.

"Devon," she finally managed to say. "Devon!" She touched the sun-warmed skin on his shoulder and gave a firm shake.

"Hmmm?" He raised his head, the imprint of the nubby blanket on one cheek. "What?"

"Were you asleep?" How could he lie there and calmly doze off when Fred was lurking?

He yawned and stretched. "I guess I was. Why, is there a problem?"

"Um, no." No point in telling him about Fred, who was now out of sight. At least now she knew she had not been imagining things. "I just thought maybe we should pack up and go home."

Devon stretched again and picked his watch out of the pile of clothing. Shielding his eyes, he squinted at the dial. "Yeah, I didn't realize we'd been gone so long. I promised Francyne I'd be back by now." He stood and stepped into his shorts, pulling his shirt over his head before speaking again. "Sorry we had to cut it short today. Maybe we can come back tomorrow or use the pool. Assuming you want to, that is."

Shaking the sand out of the blanket, she took her time folding it, scanning the beach area and boardwalk. "Sure. Why don't we try the pool tomorrow?" She touched his hip, lifting the hem of his shirt and turning him to the side. "Your scratches are just about gone. But that doesn't mean you can get frisky again at the pool," she warned when he grinned over his shoulder.

He pulled a mock defeated look. "Aw, you're no fun."

In reply, she stood on tiptoe and brushed her lips over his. "I'm plenty of fun. I just choose to keep private things, well, private."

He gave her shapely butt a playful swat as they headed up the stairs to the boardwalk. "Okay, party pooper, let's go back to my place and give you a chance to prove it." He slung his arm over her shoulder, resisting the urge to pull her close for a kiss. "My apartment is *very* private, especially at this time of day. Tell you what, I'll even put the CLOSED sign on the door and let you prove how much fun you are. What do you say to that?"

She stepped away and grinned. "First one to the apartment gets to shower first."

He stood and watched her sprint toward the complex, enjoying the view, and then made his way slowly back home. Jamie didn't know it, but it really didn't matter who got there first.

They were still going to shower together.

33

By the time he closed the apartment door, Francyne had already left and the shower echoed from the walls of the bedroom.

Wasting no time, he shucked out of his shorts and trunks on the way into the bathroom.

Killer stood guard by the bathroom door, tongue lolling as he gave his master a doggy smile.

"Hey, buddy. How about a nice little nap? I know you didn't get a good night's sleep. I bet you're tired. C'mon."

Killer looked at him for a few seconds and then gamely followed him into the storage area and into the kennel.

Tamping down his guilt for imprisoning his dog, he made a silent promise to give Killer extra treats after supper.

The bathroom was steam filled, the warm smell of soap and shampoo permeating the air.

Through the frosted shower doors, he could see Jamie lathering her luscious body.

Mine.

He slid open the door and stepped into the tub with her.

She jumped and turned to him, eyes wide.

He took the soap from her hand and began lathering her breasts, taking special care to massage them thoroughly.

"I already did that," she said in a strangled voice.

"But I bet it didn't feel this good, did it?"

She shook her head.

He slid the soap down her abdomen, appreciating her exfoliation.

Her breath hitched when he slid the soap between her legs.

He put the soap on the soap dish and bent his knees, rubbing his chest against her soapy one.

"I'm saving soap," he said against her mouth and then kissed her.

On a scale of one to ten, he'd rank the kiss as about an eight, but it seemed to really rev Jamie up, so he continued kissing her, all the while rubbing against her and slipping his hands up and down her torso.

Water sluiced over them, ran between his legs, further inspiring Mr. Happy.

"Let's get you rinsed," he said around the constriction in his throat. He'd showered with plenty of women in his time. Well, okay, maybe plenty wouldn't be exactly accurate, but he'd shared a shower a few times. And never, never had he felt the things he felt when he showered with Jamie.

It couldn't be love. Could it?

Nah. He'd just been celibate for too long. Now that he'd found a playmate, he was just so grateful, it was easy to get confused. That's all it was. Gratitude.

He turned Jamie until she faced the water, her back against his chest. He rinsed her breasts and then slid his hands slowly up and down her torso, sluicing all the water from her gorgeous body. In response, she did a little shimmy, rubbing her bottom against his erection.

Gratitude sex. He could live with that.

* * *

Jamie leaned heavily against the warm wall of Devon's chest, glad he was supporting her. His hands slicked over her, rubbing, caressing, taunting until she thought she'd scream with sexual frustration.

On tiptoe, she rubbed her buttocks against his hot erection, wishing she was tall enough to take him from behind while standing up.

He splayed his fingers, spreading her legs. Eager, she complied and then shivered when his fingers slipped up and down, teasing her opening.

He held her open, the warm water running against her engorged folds, causing her hips to thrust, wanting more.

His thumb massaged her clitoris, weakening her knees. Pressure built. Impatient, she was all but dancing, riding his hand.

He plucked the hardened nub, bringing her to screaming release.

"Okay, that's it!" Devon's voice echoed in the enclosure.

He reached past her and twisted the shower control off. Grasping her by the waist, he picked her up and stepped from the tub.

"Wait!" She twisted in an attempt to reach a towel. "We're all wet! We're going to get the sheets wet. I—"

"Not a problem. I can't make it to the bedroom."

"You mean—"

"Yep. Right here. Right now."

"Shouldn't we at least dry off a little?"

He sat on the closed toilet seat lid and pulled her to him. "No time."

His mouth closed over her nipple, sucking it deeply into his mouth as he pulled her onto his lap. He flexed his hips, burying himself to the hilt.

The feel of him deep within her body set off a new wave of pleasure that threatened to drown her in its intensity.

He held her tightly, thrusting deep, deeper than he'd ever been.

She loved it.

Clamping her knees against his lean hips, she rode him, meeting him, thrust for thrust.

He released her breast, clutching her to his heart while he pumped into her.

Their labored breathing echoed from the tiled walls. Harder. Faster.

He pushed his hand between them and flicked her nub, grinned when she gushed with renewed moisture.

He rubbed the pad of his thumb over her sensitized flesh. Once. Twice. Three times.

Devon watched the expression of bliss on Jamie's beautiful face. No woman had ever responded to his touch the way she did. It was empowering as well as a gigantic turn-on.

Her back arched, her knees gripping his hips, her nipples erect as she shuddered her release.

Feeling her velvet clamping his cock, milking him, sent him tumbling over the precipice to free-fall along with her.

Once their breathing slowed down, they heard a small "Lark! Lark?" muffled by the door, followed by the distinctive sound of a dog pawing on the door.

Laughter rumbled in Devon's chest, setting off chuckles in Jamie. "Either I didn't latch it or he figured out how to open the door of his kennel."

"Poor Killer," she said, getting off Devon's lap with as much dignity as she could muster. "He probably thinks we're hurting each other in here."

Devon reached for the sweatpants he kept hanging on the back of the door. "While I take him out and feed him, why don't you think about what you would like for lunch."

"Oh, that's not necessary," she said, slipping her cover-up over her head. "I can fix myself something at home." Assuming she could concentrate enough to eat anything, knowing Fred was out there somewhere.

"Okay, how about this? I'll take Killer out and then walk you home and wait while you get ready. Then we can decide where we want to go."

She chewed her lower lip. "To tell the truth, after our last dinner date, I'm not sure it's such a good idea." Humiliation flared whenever she thought about it, in fact.

"Okay, how about this? I have some macaroni and tuna salad in the fridge. We can have that; then you can go home or stay here and watch TV or take a nap while I get some work done. Then, later, we can go out to eat. I know a little Mexican place down on the other end of the boardwalk. Very casual, so you can wear your flip-flops." Slipping his feet into his flip-flops, he smiled up at her. "And it's safe. No stairs." He pulled her into his arms for a brief hug. "C'mon! We have to eat. Why not do it together?" He frowned. "Or is this your way of telling me you're sick of me?"

"How can you even ask that, after what we just did?"

He shrugged. "I'm insecure."

Her snicker echoed from the tile. "Yeah, right."

Killer pawed at the door again, so Devon opened it. The dog trotted in, prancing in a circle around them.

Devon knelt and scratched the dog's ear. "Do you need to go out? Tell Jamie you want her to come with us." He looked up at her. "It won't take long. What do you say? You wouldn't want to disappoint Killer, would you?"

Killer smiled expectantly. Who could resist that little face?

"Okay. But let's hurry. Suddenly I'm ravenous. I love macaroni and tuna salad. I think I'd like to just hang out around here, if you're sure I won't bother you. And I can't remember the last time I had Mexican food. So I guess you have yourself a dinner date, too, assuming you're not ready to be rid of me by then."

Holding hands, they headed toward the beach, Killer trotting along. Devon had to remember their relationship was temporary, at best, and strictly sexual.

But, walking with her, holding her hand, it was getting more and more difficult to remember.

Damn, it sure felt like more.

"Aren't you ready yet?" Devon bellowed from the living room, bringing a smile to Jamie while she wrestled her hair into a braid.

"Just a sec!" She surveyed her reflection. The yellow terry halter dress set off her new tan and had the added benefit of not wrinkling while she lounged on Devon's couch. She could still look presentable when they went out later.

Devon whistled when Jamie walked out of the bathroom. "You look," he said, going to her and pulling her into his arms, "good enough to eat." He pretended to take a loud bite out of her neck, inordinately pleased when she squirmed and giggled in his arms. After brushing a kiss on the tip of her nose, he stepped back. "I just hope Killer can keep his paws off you."

After lunch, Devon booted up his computer while Jamie settled onto the couch with the remote and Killer. Lucky dog.

After watching the blinking cursor longer than he'd care to contemplate, he looked over at Jamie.

Killer had moved. In fact, he'd left the room.

Jamie lay on the sofa, her bare feet crossed at the ankles, eyes closed, the manuscript she'd insisted on reading resting on her stomach.

The temptation was too much to resist.

Saving his work, he closed the laptop and walked to join Jamie.

A small smile curved her lips when he sat down next to her, the cushion dipping with his weight, but she didn't open her eyes.

"Are you asleep?" he whispered.

"No," she whispered back. "Just resting my eyes. Are you quitting already?"

"Taking a break. You can keep your eyes closed. I just want to check out a few things."

She cracked open one eyelid. "Like what?"

His hands reveled in the tactile pleasure of her satin-smooth skin as he slid them up her arms to the back of her neck. "Like," he said, unfastening the button behind her neck, "whether or not I can flip the top of your dress down independently or if both sides would come down together."

"And this is important how?"

"Shhh. Relax. It's research. Just research."

With slow, deliberate movements, he dragged one side of the plunging neckline down until he'd exposed her right breast, its nipple immediately puckering in the air-conditioned air. Bending, he ran the tip of his tongue around and over the hardened tip, finally taking it between his teeth, running his tongue back and forth.

Her breathing became shallow, and she arched her back slightly, but kept her eyes shut.

He drew the other side of the dress down to her waist and admired the size and shape of the newly exposed breast before taking it into his mouth.

She whimpered a little but kept her eyes closed.

He pulled her dress back up, covering temptation, and secured it once again. "Can I ask you a question?"

She blinked lazily at him. "Hmmm?"

"I was wondering . . . why did you wear those things? Your breasts are perfect, just as they are."

Shifting on the sofa, she partially sat up before she answered. "I was trying to disguise myself."

"By having big boobs? No offense, but that's not much, as disguises go."

"I told you I also changed my hair, my eye color and the

way I dress and act. In the process, I was trying to reinvent myself, I guess."

"I've been thinking about that. . . . So you're not a real blonde?" Not that it mattered, but he couldn't imagine her with any other color of hair. And, since she practiced total body-hair removal, there was nothing to compare it to.

"Sorry, no." She struggled to sit up.

He stopped her with his hand on her shoulder. "How could I have missed that? Wait. I need to take a closer look."

Scooting to the end by her feet, he lifted her skirt and peeked under at tanned legs and panties the same shade of yellow as her dress.

"I don't think we should have sex right here in the open, on the couch, during the day," she warned, squirming against the cushions.

"Who said anything about having sex?" he said from beneath her dress. "I'm conducting research, woman. Now hold still. I'm going to have to remove these in order to see more clearly."

"Couldn't you just push the leg opening aside and check out what you need?"

In response, he nipped her mound through the sheer fabric of her panties. "Hush," he said, his breath hot against her. "I have to be thorough."

She shivered as he drew her panties down her legs, an inch at a time, and watched them float across the room where he tossed them.

Her back arched off the cushions when his finger probed her, teasing her with what she knew would come.

His tongue replaced his finger, and she bowed off the couch, her hands clutching his hair, holding him firmly in place.

Delicious sensation danced along her nerve endings, setting wildfires to ignite along the way.

Just as she hovered, poised on the brink of fulfillment, Devon sat up, smoothing her dress down.

Their eyes met. She was sure hers were shooting flames.

"I promised we would not have sex, and I'm a man of my word." He made an adjustment and grinned. "Besides, I know once would never be enough. For either of us. And then we'd end up missing dinner."

Suddenly she wasn't hungry—not for food, anyway. But she didn't tell him. The no-sex thing had been her idea. Now she would just have to live with the consequences.

After she'd retrieved her underwear and Devon resumed his work, she picked up the manuscript and continued reading.

A few minutes later, she glanced at him. How could she diplomatically tell him his writing . . . stunk? Not an easy thing to do, under any circumstances. When you were sleeping together, it was even harder.

"Well, how do you like it so far?" Devon stood beside the couch.

With careful movements, she tidied the stack of paper and set it on the coffee table, wracking her brain for something constructive, if not kind, to say.

She licked her lips and took a deep breath. "Well, truthfully I was having a hard time concentrating. I can't think very well when I'm hungry. Is it almost time to eat?"

For a moment, she thought he wasn't going to let her get away without telling him exactly what she thought of his book. Relief washed through her when he smiled and nodded.

"Just let me take Killer out one more time. Then we can go." He glanced at his sport watch. "If we hurry, happy hour should still be going on. Casa Lopez makes the best frozen margaritas around. You like margaritas?" He clipped Killer's leash onto the dog's collar.

"Love 'em, especially strawberry ones."

Tinny strains of "It's Five O'clock Somewhere" sounded.

Devon extracted a black cell phone from his pants pocket and flipped it open. "Hey, Francyne. I'm just taking him out now, and then we're going to eat at Casa Lopez." He glanced at Jamie. "That would be great, if you're sure you don't mind." He opened the door and motioned for her to go in front of him and then stepped out and locked the door. "Okay, we'll be right over. Thanks." He clicked the phone shut and repocketed it. "Francyne says she and Petunia are having a slumber party and want Killer to join them. I told her we'd bring him over after he did his business."

Jamie walked quietly along the boardwalk with Devon and Killer. Without Killer waiting at home, would Devon plan to spend the night at her apartment? And, more importantly, was that what she wanted?

Devon carried on a running conversation with his dog as they walked. Jamie couldn't help smiling at the nonsensical things he said. There was something so appealing about a guy who clearly loved his dog.

Before she knew it, they were standing outside Francyne's door.

Francyne's apartment made Jamie's apartment look like it should be condemned.

Besides the obvious difference of the beautifully carved mantel and fireplace, it looked professionally decorated.

Francyne was dressed in her usual brightly colored muumuu, tonight paired with pink fuzzy slippers shaped like flamingoes. In her hand was easily the largest margarita glass Jamie had ever seen.

"Come in, come in." Francyne tugged them in and closed the door and then held aloft her glass. "Want a 'rita? I just made a fresh blenderful. Best batch to date, if I do say so myself."

Devon glanced at Jamie. She gave a little shake. Petunia's dander was already getting to her. Besides, if they were going to get to the restaurant before the end of happy hour, they probably wouldn't have time.

"We'll catch the next batch; thanks, anyway. Happy hour is still going on, and we need to get going if we want a booth before the crowd arrives."

"Do you have time to take a look at the statement my stockbroker sent me? I can't make heads nor tails of it."

"Sure." Devon followed her into the kitchen, their voices becoming background noise.

Jamie wandered over to the fireplace, admiring the high ceiling and large windows facing the beach. No doubt about it, this was prime real estate. No wonder the owners were thinking about selling. It had to be worth a fortune.

And speaking of fortunes . . . Francyne must have had some serious bucks to afford the high-end furniture displayed in her living room. Jamie squinted at a painting. Van Gogh? She touched the surface. If it was a print, it was a dang good one.

On a round cherry end table Jamie was sure she recognized from "Antiques Roadshow" was an oval framed sketch. On closer inspection, she saw it was a nude and realized it bore a striking resemblance to a much younger Francyne. The signature was barely visible, but it sure looked like it said Picasso. Surely not.

A knock sounded. The door immediately opened, and the man Jamie recognized as the one who'd had sex by the fire when she first moved in entered.

Tall and well built, like all the male tenants seemed to be, he wore his dark hair short and slicked back, which emphasized his tan and the brilliant blue of his eyes. She wondered if he wore colored contacts, too.

"Francyne," he said as he shut the door, obviously oblivious to the fact that Francyne had company, "we have a problem. Rick and Todd are—"

Devon walked out of the kitchen and stopped short.

"Grant," he said, "what are you doing in Francyne's apartment?"

34

"Ah, um . . . Grant!" Francyne hurried over and threw her arms around him. "It's okay, pookie. They're my friends, they won't tell anyone about . . ." she put her hands on each side of his head, staring straight into his eyes, and said, "us." Then pulled him down for a deep, passionate-looking kiss.

"I think I just lost my appetite," Devon said close to Jamie's ear. "Let's get out of here. I think I need that drink, and I need it right now." In a louder tone, he said, "Bye, Francyne, Grant. Your secret is safe with us. See you tomorrow."

Outside, they looked at each other and began to laugh as they made their way to the restaurant.

Casa Lopez looked like every other hole-in-the-wall mom-and-pop Mexican restaurant Jamie had ever seen. Somewhat dingy, it boasted mismatched chrome tables with scarred Formica tops and a ragtag assortment of dinette chairs surrounded by plastic padded booths.

The hostess looked to be about eighty if she was a day. She toddled over when they stepped into the restaurant.

"Seen-yor Dee-von," she said, giving him a hug. "We have

not seen you for a long time. And you have a new beautiful lady." She winked. "For you, we will give the best table. Come!"

Frankly Jamie thought all the tables were about the same, but she smiled gamely at the old lady when she waved them to a corner booth and handed them the menus.

"Buenos noches, Devon." A young woman, younger than Jamie, strolled to their table. Her black hair, scraped back into a tight bun, shone in the dim light. Full figured, she had pouty red lips and sported so much eye makeup it was a wonder she could hold her eyes open.

"Hello, Anna," Devon said after they hugged. "This is Jamie." The women nodded at each other. Jamie noticed that the waitress refrained from giving her a welcoming hug.

"Margaritas. Grande? Frozen, no salt?"

Devon nodded and then added, "But make the lady's a strawberry."

That earned a dirty look, but Anna walked toward the bar. Jamie watched closely to make sure the waitress didn't do something mean, like spit in her drink.

She wondered if Anna and Devon had ever gone out, but she'd bite her tongue off before she'd ask.

"I tutored Anna and her sister in English when they first came here from Mexico. As a favor to the Lopez family. I've known the Lopez brothers since junior high."

Anna returned to place their drinks on the table, along with a basket of chips and two bowls of picante sauce and guacamole. "Are you ready to order, or do you need a few minutes?"

"I know what I want," Devon said with a smile.

She smiled back.

"Chef's special," Anna and Devon said together.

"What's the chef's special?" Jamie dipped a chip in the green sauce and took a bite. Blinking back tears, she took a gulp of ice water.

Anna wiped the smirk from her face. "Is good. Grilled cheek-on, fajita steak, shrimps, much grilled vegetables, seasoned with bacon. It comes with bean soup and flour tortillas."

"That sounds good. I'll have that, too."

The waitress looked at her for a second and then nodded and left.

"Did I do or say something to offend her?" Jamie reached for another chip but avoided the cups of sauce.

"No, she—"

"Hey! Hombre!" The booming voice belonged to the man striding toward their table, a blinding white smile on his dark-skinned face. His thick hair shone blue-black in the low lights. "I saw the order and knew who was here!"

The man pulled Devon from his seat into a bear hug and thumped him on the back and then looked expectantly at Jamie.

"Jamie, this is my good friend, Moises Lopez. Mo, this is Jamie Cartwright. She just moved here."

Moises executed a formal bow and kissed the back of her hand. "A pleasure, señorita. If this guy acts up, you tell me and I will take you away."

Heat climbed into her cheeks, but she kept smiling and nodding. The men talked for a few minutes, and then Moises left with a wave of his hand.

"I take it he's the chef?" She stuck her tongue against the roof of her mouth to dissipate the recent surge of brain freeze from her drink.

"Are you kidding?" Devon popped a chip, laden with guacamole, into his mouth. "I wouldn't touch anything that klutz cooked. I'd probably get poisoned. Nah, his twin brother, Miguel, is the chef."

Sizzling filled the air, along with a mouthwatering aroma.

Anna walked to the table carrying a huge metal serving tray with steam coming from several of the dishes. One by one, she set the food on their table until almost the entire surface was covered. Without a word, she walked away.

Jamie closed her eyes and inhaled the tantalizing scent and then opened them and speared a plump jumbo shrimp that lay on top of the pile of food.

"Ohhh, this is so good!" She chewed appreciatively and then swallowed.

Another round of jumbo margaritas was consumed before she pushed her plate away.

"Oh, man, that was good!"

"You didn't finish." Devon nodded at Anna when she dropped their bill on the table.

Anna looked at the half-full plate and then at Jamie. "You want a to-go box?"

Jamie shook her head. "No. Thank you, though. It was delicious. But I couldn't eat another bite."

She thought she heard Anna mutter something like "too skinny" but wasn't sure.

"Enjoy the rest of your drink." Devon stood, reaching for his wallet. "I'll go pay the bill and come back."

She sat, half asleep, with her stomach full of the best food she'd had in ages and savored the remnants of her margarita.

Someone stopped at her table.

Assuming it was Devon, she looked up with a smile.

Her heart tripped. The sip of frozen drink lodged somewhere in her throat.

Fred.

35

"Hello, Jamie." He leered down at her, icy hatred in his brown eyes. "I see you've moved on."

Instincts kicked in, and she screamed.

Fred got a panicked look on his face. It looked like he was trying to say something, maybe calm her down. But she was so far gone, all she could do was keep screaming.

She grabbed the steak knife still lying on the table and lunged for him.

His eyes widened, mouth slacked. He turned and ran.

He'd just disappeared when Devon ran back into the dining room, followed by what looked to be most of the waitstaff.

Within seconds, Devon was beside her, gathering her into his arms.

"Jamie, sweetheart, what's wrong? Are you all right? Are you hurt?"

She shook so badly she could barely speak but finally was able to say, "Fred."

"Fred?" She nodded. "He was here? In this restaurant? Are you sure?"

"Of course I'm sure! Why do you think I screamed?"

He looked around. "Did you see which way he went?"

In response, she pointed a shaky finger in the direction of the patio doors.

Moises jogged over to the table. "I called the police. They should be here momentarily."

The police arrived, sirens blaring, and did a thorough search of the restaurant and surrounding area. After taking the report, they gave Jamie a card with a case number and their phone number. Like that was going to do her any good if Fred got hold of her.

She couldn't stop shaking.

Wrapped in Devon's arms, she walked home. And when he asked if she'd like to come in, she didn't hesitate.

It was not the time to be brave. Or alone.

While Devon locked the door, she wasted no time. By the time he walked into the kitchen, she was naked. Sex may not be the answer for everything, but it sure helped.

"Are you sure you're up to this?" Devon managed to say between kisses while she tugged at his shorts.

"Yes," she breathed against his lips, her hand snaking into his boxers. "And so are you."

"But where? What do you want—" His teeth clicked against hers.

"Anywhere. Anything. I'll do whatever you want to do. We can play with the toys. Get down and dirty in the tub. Whatever you want."

Although he'd waited most of his adult life to hear those words from a willing female, suddenly it was no big deal.

The only thing he wanted, really wanted, was Jamie. Naked, preferably. Warm and willing in his bed.

"While I appreciate the offer, and I admit I've had some kinky thoughts of late, what I'd really like is to just make love to you. Without gadgets, without flavor enhancers or tools of any kind. You. Me. Naked. In bed. How does that sound?"

She blinked back tears. "Heavenly."

After lighting several candles, which was really very heroic, considering his innate fear of fire, Devon stretched out next to Jamie and began by kissing the silky, fragrant skin of her shoulder.

From there, he trailed kisses down her arm to the tips of each finger, biting back a smile when he felt her shiver.

He worked his way to her toes, the arches of her feet and then back up again, determined to taste every delicious inch of her.

When he had her writhing on the sheets, he brought her to a climax with his mouth and then his hand.

Damn, he loved it when she screamed.

"My turn," she said, tugging him away from her wetness.

"No," he whispered, poised between her legs. "Tonight it's all for you."

She lay panting after Devon rolled away. The air clicked on, cooling her sweat-slicked skin. The last orgasm had more than rocked her world. It had been almost an out-of-body experience. Shoot, they may have even wiped out a few brain cells.

The mattress dipped. Devon walked into the bathroom and then returned a moment later to pull her close and kiss her forehead.

So content she almost purred, she snuggled against him, listening to his breathing as it changed.

Her lips brushed his shoulder.

"Thank you," she whispered against his skin. "I hope you don't mind, but I think I'm falling in love with you."

Devon lay in the dark long after her breathing told him she slept.

She had said she was falling in love with him when she thought he was asleep.

In the past, he would have run screaming if a woman had said that to him. Oddly that urge was not present.

Did that mean he might be falling in love with her, too?

He turned to his side, cradling her against his chest, and kissed the back of her neck.

No, he wasn't falling in love with Jamie Cartwright.

He'd already fallen.

36

Sunshine woke Devon the next morning. Or maybe it was the persistent pounding on his door.

Beside him, Jamie stretched and hitched one smooth leg over his as she snuggled closer to his side.

Last night had been unique. Special. He wasn't totally sure what it meant or where it would lead, but he did know one thing: Jamie Cartwright had done something last night no other woman had ever done before.

She'd spent the night, the entire night, in his bed.

And even though he'd come to the realization he was in love with her, the fact that she'd spent the night in his bed still had the ability to scare the crap out of him.

The pounding continued. He disengaged from Jamie and eased out of bed.

Tugging up his shorts from last night, he padded down the hall to the door. A glance at the clock on the microwave as he walked through the kitchen revealed it was still two hours until office hours.

He swung open the door and gaped at the tall man looming

on his doormat. The guy had to be an easy six-foot-six or -seven. Curling brown hair frizzed on the ends, no doubt from the Gulf air.

Although he'd never seen the guy up close and personal, he knew immediately who he was.

"I want to talk to Jamie," Fred said in a booming voice. "Now."

Devon's first reaction was to slam the door in Fred's face, but he stopped. Fred was a bully. Devon may not have ever had a serious relationship, but he'd had an ongoing familiarity with bullies his entire life.

It was past time to stop letting the bullies of the world push him around. Beginning with Fred.

"I'll tell you a little secret, Fred. It is Fred, isn't it?" The man nodded, and Devon continued. "Jamie doesn't want to see you. She doesn't want to talk to you or have anything to do with you. If you don't stop harassing her, we're calling the cops. Stalking is a crime."

"I need to see Jamie. I have to talk to her." Fred crossed his arms over his muscular chest in an obvious attempt at intimidation.

"Fred, I really don't give a rat's ass what you want or need. Leave." He closed the door and held his breath in anticipation of Fred beating it down.

After a few minutes of silence, he peeked out. Fred was gone.

Jamie woke to the smell of fresh-brewed coffee. It took a moment to realize she was in Devon's bed. Frowning, she got up and walked into the bathroom.

She'd spent the night with Devon. In hindsight, probably not one of her brighter ideas. It wouldn't do for him to read too much into it. Although she knew she was already more than halfway in love with him, she didn't want to push.

Pasting a smile on her face, she opened the bathroom door and headed for the kitchen.

"Hey, sleepyhead!" Devon got up when she entered the kitchen and took a mug from the cupboard. "You look like you could use a cup of coffee." He handed her the steaming cup and gestured toward the fridge. "Creamer is in there, if you want it. There's half-and-half and a couple of the flavored kind."

"What's in your coffee?" She opened the refrigerator door, amazed at the amount of food. Most single guys she knew had sparse supplies.

"Amaretto. I also highly recommend the white chocolate."

Once she'd stirred the creamer into her coffee and joined him at the little bistro table in the corner of the kitchen, he put down the paper and smiled at her. "Sleep well?"

She nodded and set her cup on the blue and yellow plaid place mat. "Yes, thanks for letting me stay over. I knew I wouldn't get any sleep if I went home." She shuddered. "I still don't know how Fred keeps finding me."

"That's not too difficult to figure out." He took a sip of coffee and said, "He's obviously been following you." He took a deep breath. "In fact, he's already been here this morning, wanting to talk to you."

He watched the panic cross her face, the color leach from her cheeks.

"Well," she finally said, "that settles it, doesn't it? I'm going to have to move again."

"Why?"

"You just said it! Fred has found me again. I have to get out of here." She jumped up, but he caught her arm.

"No, you don't. Not if you don't want to leave. I handled it."

"Excuse me? How, exactly, did you 'handle' it?" She sank back into her chair.

"It was pretty easy, actually. I just told him to leave you alone or we'd call the cops. Stalking is a crime, you know, and the guy's obviously been stalking you. Also, it's a pretty safe bet he's the one who threw the brick through your window, which is another crime. I must have made a believer out of him, because he left."

"Just like that?"

"Yep. Just like that." Feeling pretty smug, he finished his coffee. "Now, how about a quick shower and then we'll go grab some breakfast. I'm not really in the mood to cook, and I know a great little tearoom on the boardwalk that serves an unbelievable brunch. If we hurry, we can beat the crowd."

"Let me run home and take my shower there. That way, I can change."

His eyes narrowed. "Are you sure you don't want to take a shower here? I'll let you decide if you shower alone or not. Then I can go with you while you change."

"No, that's okay. I'll be fine. You said Fred left. Even if he isn't gone for good, it's unlikely he will come back so soon. Besides," she said, standing and kissing his forehead, "it's time I developed a backbone. See you in about half an hour?"

"Sure. I'll give Francyne a call and make arrangements for Killer and then come get you when I'm ready."

"Don't ever kiss me like you did last night," Grant warned as he let himself into Francyne's apartment.

She looked up from her newspaper with a coquettish grin. "Oh? Then how would you like me to kiss you, sugar?"

"No kisses at all would be good." He shuddered. "Damn kiss gave me nightmares."

"Oh, poor baby." She shuffled to the coffeemaker on the snack bar and held up a mug. At his nod, she poured and returned to her Chippendale breakfast set, handing him the mug as she sat down. "I've been thinking about Todd and Rick. Why don't you just tell them you're FBI, and then you could all work together."

"I don't work with civilians, for one thing. And before you say it, yes, I realize they're cops. But that still makes them civilians to me. For another, we don't know for sure Todd and or his friend Rick are entirely innocent in the vic's disappearance."

"The 'vic' has a name. Her name is Alexis. Use it. And for that matter, do we even know for sure she is a victim? There is a possibility, however slight, that she left of her own free will." She reached for a tea cookie on the Dresden plate and offered Grant one. After he shook his head, she took a bite. "I admit, I don't believe it, but it's a possibility."

Grant nodded and placed his cup on the lace tablecloth. "I don't believe it either, Aunt Francyne." He held up his hand as though he anticipated her giving him an argument. "I know she broke her lease. I know she told the manager she couldn't take the sexual harassment and that was why she left. I know all her clothes are gone." His forearms on the table, he leaned toward her. "But I also know how close she was to her brother. She would never have just up and disappeared without telling him. And she sure as hell wouldn't have stayed gone without getting word to him."

"You think she's dead, don't you?"

"Until we find a body, we have to assume she isn't."

"But that's your gut feeling, isn't it?"

When he nodded and silently took another sip of his coffee, Francyne had to force her cookie past the lump restricting her throat. She'd known Alexis. From what little interaction they'd had, she'd liked her. Now she couldn't help but wonder if she'd made more of an effort to get to know the pretty young woman with the troubled eyes, if things might have turned out differently.

The phone rang, jerking them both from their reflections.

Francyne picked up the cordless phone and checked the caller ID. Devon. "Hi, pumpkin," she said after pressing the TALK button. "Sure. No problem. Killer and Petunia are still sleeping. We watched an 'I Love Lucy' marathon last night and then had to take an extra walk. You mean Grant?" She looked across the table and winked, just to mess with him. "Oh, I don't think it'll work out. He's too old for me."

Grant spewed coffee, and she chuckled.

"Take your time, sweetie. Killer will be fine. Bye."

Jamie took a leisurely shower and got dressed, reflecting on her night in Devon's bed. It wasn't like her to spend the night with someone without some kind of emotional commitment. For that matter, it also wasn't like her to have wild sex with a virtual stranger either. But she'd acclimated fast.

A flush heated her cheeks at the memories of all the things she'd enjoyed doing with Devon. Things she would never have dreamed of doing with anyone else. Besides being sexy and hot, Devon was also fun. Fun was something she'd never experienced in relationships.

True, she had trust issues. And they had probably started way before she met Fred, if she was honest. Trust wasn't something she gave easily. Never had been.

Yet she trusted Devon. Completely. What was it about him that made her want to trust him as well as jump his bones at every opportunity?

Could she trust Devon to protect her from Fred? In her heart, she knew he could.

She'd just completed her makeup and done a quick inspection in the full-length mirror on the back of the bathroom door.

Now that Devon knew about the gel packs, there was no use in wearing them. She'd inserted them out of habit. Reaching into the bodice of her pink and purple hibiscus-print sundress, she plucked them out, tossing them into their storage box.

The dress didn't fit that much differently, other than the fact of having noticeably less cleavage.

Three sharp raps on the door told her Devon was ready.

Grabbing her purse, she hurried to the door. On the table, the pages of Devon's manuscript fluttered with the breeze of the door opening.

She hoped he wouldn't ask her opinion of his work. Private-eye novels weren't her usual reading fare, but even she knew a stinker when she read one. In her opinion, his catalog copy for the sex-toy manufacturers was more entertaining.

Serenity Tearoom and Bake Shoppe was a tiny place situated at the end of the boardwalk. Backing onto the main street of Old Towne Surfside, it was packed with antiques and just plain cute and interesting things. Jamie would have liked to spend the day there, just looking at everything.

Before she had a chance to do more than look around at the plethora of goods available for sale, they were seated.

Their waitress handed them what looked to be a newspaper but turned out to be a menu and then returned with their drinks.

After ordering the Sawmill special, which consisted of eggs, bacon, grits and baked cinnamon apples with biscuits, they settled in to wait for their food.

"What a cute place!" Jamie tried to take it all in. The hostess stand sported a ship's wheel. The walls were covered in sea- and beach-related things, including a myriad of shells and vintage sand pails. Heavy rope topped the windows, the valances they held made of what looked like fishing nets. "Do you mind if I look through the gift shop before we leave?"

"Sure, knock yourself out." He smiled back at her. "We're not in a rush."

The waitress set their plates on the table and hurried to her next customer.

Jamie inhaled the delicious aroma wafting from the big platter before her. She found she couldn't stop smiling, especially when she looked at Devon, so she concentrated on her food.

"So," Devon began, several minutes later, "did you get a

chance to finish *Darkness Becomes Her*?" He forked a pile of scrambled eggs into his mouth and swallowed. "What did you think?"

The piece of bacon she'd just swallowed threatened to come back up. She coughed in an effort to get it to go in one direction or the other while she tried to think of something nice to say.

"It was, um, interesting. But I'm no expert." She took a sip of her Diet Coke and licked her lips. "Devon, what do you think about writing a cookbook?"

"A cookbook? You or me?"

At least he hadn't acted hurt or insulted, which gave her the courage to go on.

"You, of course. You're a fabulous cook! I've never tasted anything you made that wasn't fantastic. Especially your baking."

"You bake, too," he countered.

"Yes, but I follow recipes. You make them up as you go along." She pushed her plate aside and leaned forward on the oak table. "Seriously. I think it could be a huge success. You might even turn out to be another Emeril."

He laughed. "Yeah, right."

"You won't know until you try. Think about it. That's all I'm asking."

He sat for a moment, staring into space, and then blinked. "You know, you may have something. I've always liked to cook. Hell, I even had a couple of recipes in my book and then decided to cut them because I thought a tough PI like Trent wouldn't cook. I worried it would weaken the book."

"I don't think it would have hurt the book. But I think the idea of just writing a cookbook would be great. I'll even help. I can be your official taster."

He threw some bills on the table and stood, helping her up. "I just might do that." He patted her behind as they walked toward the gift shop; he whispered in her ear, "Of course, you helping might be a problem because I'd keep getting distracted."

In the gift shop, Jamie found a hat, sand pail and sunglasses. She modeled the hat and eyewear and had just picked up the pail to show him when her smile fell.

The pail hit the hardwood floor with a metallic clang.

Devon followed her line of stricken vision to see Fred peeping in the plateglass window looking straight at Jamie.

Enough was enough.

Shoving aside his theory of being a lover not a fighter and his general fear of having the snot beaten out of him, he glared back at Fred, who ran.

"Stay here!" he yelled back at Jamie and ran out into the sunshine.

His eyes adjusted. Fred was turning the corner onto Main Street. Devon knew if he cut through the alley, he would come out a little ahead of Fred and maybe be able to stop the stalking once and for all.

The alley was longer than he remembered. He ran faster, his heart pumping in his chest, breath coming in harsh pants while he concentrated on putting one foot in front of the other, running toward the patch of light he knew was Main Street.

He flew out onto the sidewalk, squinting again in the direct sunlight. Bent, his hands on his knees, he sucked in lungfuls of air and searched the street.

Ten or twelve feet to his right, Fred screeched to a stop, did a 180 and took off again.

"Wait!" Devon's voice came out as a raspy croak. He swallowed and straightened. "Come back here, you son of a bitch!"

He'd read somewhere that a hero was someone who was afraid and did it anyway. He'd always maintained he'd rather be a live coward than a dead hero. But today he knew he'd do whatever it took, even risk or sacrifice his life, if it meant keeping Jamie safe. Damn, he sure hoped he didn't end up a dead hero.

Eyes trained on Fred's rapidly retreating back, he picked up his pace.

Jamie came out of the alley. Fred was running at breakneck speed down the street, Devon in hot pursuit. What were they thinking?

Even in flip-flops, Devon was clearly gaining on Fred. And they were both running way too fast for her to have a prayer of catching them. All she could do was stand there and helplessly watch.

As Devon got closer, the door of a black Miata at the curb opened. Before she could begin to yell to warn him, Devon hit the door, flying over it to land in a crumpled heap on the sidewalk.

37

People from the stores surrounding the accident flooded out to the sidewalk, blocking Jamie's progress to her fallen hero.

"Excuse me, pardon me, please, let me through!" She shoved, elbowing her way through the crowd.

Finally they parted to reveal Devon, lying on the pavement, eyes closed. Blood oozed from the scrapes on his knees, elbow and feet, glistening in the sun. He'd lost one of his flip-flops.

Crying, praying he was going to be all right, she fumbled in her shoulder bag for her cell phone.

"I called nine-one-one," said a man standing to one side of the crowd.

"Thank you," she said through her tears, dropping the cell back into her purse.

A very pregnant lady waddled over and awkwardly tried to get down on the pavement on the other side of Devon.

"Oh, my God!" The woman turned horrified eyes to Jamie. "Is he dead?"

Jamie stroked Devon's hair from the lump on his forehead, relieved to hear him moan. "No, thank goodness."

"I'm so sorry!" The woman swiped at the tears streaming down her face. "I told my husband we needed a bigger car! I have a devil of a time getting in and out of that little thing." She waved her hand toward the car Devon had tripped over. "I have to open the door all the way and rock to get out of the seat." She glanced down at Devon again, fresh tears running down her face. "I'm never going to forgive Rocko for being so cheap and refusing to get another car."

An ambulance squealed to a stop, the paramedics jumping out to run over.

"Step back, please!" A rail-thin man in his early twenties, dressed in white, pushed his way through the crowd. His stainless-steel name badge said Eugene Whiting. "Did anyone see what happened?"

Several people began talking at once.

He held up a hand and gave a sharp whistle to quiet them. "You." He pointed at Jamie. "Do you know this man?"

"Yes," she said, glancing down at Devon's still form. "He's my, um, boyfriend."

"Your boyfriend." The paramedic looked dubious.

"My fiancé, actually," she amended.

"And did you see what happened?" He checked Devon's vitals while he talked.

"Well..."

"I didn't see him and opened my door," Miata Girl volunteered. She patted her stomach and pointed at her car, its still open door bent at a weird angle. "I'm pregnant," she said, earning a chorus of snickers from the crowd. "And it takes considerable effort to get out of my car." She sniffed. Someone handed her a tissue to wipe her nose. "So I threw open my door. He was running and hit it and then sort of flipped over and landed on the sidewalk. Is he going to be okay?"

A police car squealed to a stop, two blue uniformed officers jumping out to stride toward the crowd.

"I think so," the medic answered. "Here's the person you need to talk to," he told the officers, gesturing toward Miata Girl. "We have a Caucasian male, late twenties, possible head trauma, multiple contusions. We're taking him to County Hospital to have him checked out, just to be on the safe side."

He put his instruments away and motioned for his partners to wheel the gurney over. They counted and lifted Devon to the white-covered mattress, tucked a pristine cotton blanket around him and then raised the gurney to its full height.

"Wait!" Jamie trotted behind the moving cart. "Is it okay if I ride with him?" At his hesitation, she added, "I don't have a car."

He shrugged. "Sure. You're his fiancée. You count as next of kin."

Strapped into the seat in the ambulance, gripping Devon's hand, she prayed again that he had sustained no serious injuries. Tears streamed down her face all the way to the hospital.

The paramedics jumped out as soon as the ambulance rolled to a stop, leaving Jamie to follow them into the hospital.

The smell of antiseptic stung her nose. Hospitals always seemed stale to her, and she fought the urge to gasp for air.

Devon disappeared behind a curtained area.

"Miss? May I help you?" A nurse approached her, impeding her progress, squeaking shoes and a swishing sound accompanying each step.

"My, uh, boyfriend—I mean, fiancé—was in an accident. I rode here with him in the ambulance." She choked back tears and pointed to the curtained area. "They took him in there, and I just wanted to find out how he's doing."

"What's his name, honey?"

"Devon. Devon McCloud."

"Tell you what. I'll go find out what's going on. You go sit over there, and I'll come get you as soon as I know anything. There's a coffeemaker in the corner. Help yourself." She shoved

Jamie in the general direction of a line of formed plastic chairs that followed the perimeter of the room.

Jamie walked to a deserted area, her flip-flops squeaking on the highly polished, gray tiled floor.

The chair was cold and uncomfortable. She couldn't stop thinking about how comfortable she'd been the night before, warm and secure in Devon's arms. A fresh batch of tears welled to run down her cheeks.

Damn Fred. If she could find him, she'd tear him apart for doing this. Devon was good and kind and decent. He was not only a skilled and imaginative lover, he was a friend. Possibly the best friend she'd ever had, and now he was hurt and it was all her fault for getting him involved in her mess of a life.

"Family of Devon McCloud?" A tall, thin nurse with cocoa skin, her hair pulled back so tightly her eyes tilted up, stood by the desk, a bored expression on her face.

Jamie scrambled to stand and hurried over to the nurses' station. "I'm here! I'm with Devon McCloud."

"Are you family?" The nurse looked down from her considerable height, daring Jamie to tell her a lie.

Jamie straightened to her full height and looked the woman straight in the eye. "Yes. I'm his fiancée." The lie came easier this time, and she was surprised to find how much she wished it were true.

The nurse gave her a once-over, and just when Jamie thought she may not believe her, she sniffed and said, "Follow me."

Panic welled. Didn't hospitals take you to a private place to tell you bad news? Was that why the nurse wanted Devon's family? Maybe he was more seriously injured than the ambulance guy had thought. Maybe he didn't make it.

Fresh tears sprang to her eyes. How would she go on without Devon?

The nurse turned and did an eye roll when she saw Jamie's tears; then she parted the curtain. "He's in there."

"Is he—is he d-dead?"

The nurse's eyes widened. "Dead? Heavens no! Of course not. He just has a nasty bump on his head. The MRI showed no damage; X-rays turned up no broken bones. Other than a few scrapes and some bruised ribs, he should be fine, but the doctor would like to keep him overnight for observation. He did take a pretty good wallop to the head. You can sit with him until they come to take him to his room, if you want. His clothes and personal belongings are in that bag on the foot of the bed. You should take them home with you."

She closed the curtains with a metallic whoosh, cocooning them in a little blue-and-green print cotton cave.

Devon lay still, a big bandage on his forehead, an IV held with tape to the back of his hand, his eyes closed.

Jamie picked up his free hand and gently kissed it and then rubbed the back of his hand against her cheek.

"You're crying." Devon's voice was low and raspy and the most beautiful sound she'd ever heard.

"Of course I'm crying," she said and sniffed. "I thought you were dead."

"Obviously a gross exaggeration." He chuckled and then grabbed his ribs. "Ow."

"Should I call a nurse?" She gripped his hand, willing him to be strong.

"Not unless you plan to keep squeezing my hand until it breaks."

"Oh. Sorry."

"Are you okay?"

"Yes," she said in a watery voice.

"Then stop crying. It worries me. How about Fred?"

"What do you care how Fred is? Fred will be in some serious pain if I get my hands on him, I—"

"I take it he got away."

"Oh. Yes. He ran like the coward he is."

Breath hissed through Devon's teeth.

"Don't sit up!" She shoved on his shoulder, attempting to push him back onto the bed. "What are you doing? You're hurt!"

"Ow! That's the shoulder I fell on. Let go!"

"Sorry, I was just trying to get you to stop moving. Lie down!"

She shoved him back as he leaned forward. The bed rolled away. Devon's weight landed on her, throwing her to the cold tile, where he landed on top of her.

She bit the tip of her tongue when her head bounced off the tile. All around them the sounds of metal crashing to the floor echoed in the little area.

The distinctive sound of rubber soles running on tile got closer. Metal whined on metal as the curtain was thrown back.

"What on earth is going on in here?" White duty shoes and bony white-stocking-clad ankles filled Jamie's vision.

Devon moaned against her neck.

"What are you trying to do, young lady?" The nurse tugged on Jamie's arm and yelled, "I need assistance in thirteen! Stat!"

More running rubber-soled-shoe sounds immediately followed.

Various nurses and technicians lifted Devon off and back onto the gurney, casting dirty looks at Jamie.

She noticed that no one offered to help her up.

Wiping her hand on her dress, she stood and took the plastic bag of Devon's belongings the skinny nurse held out to her.

"Can I still stay until he goes to his room?"

"We're taking him up right now, so you can leave."

"Can't I just go up with him and sit a while? I could help take care of him. I could—"

Devon moaned, and the nurse glared at her. "I think you've done enough for one night. Good night." With that, she turned and squeaked away.

In the lobby, Jamie dug around in Devon's bag until she located his cell phone. It was different from hers, but she figured out how to access the directory and tried to call Francyne. When nothing happened twice, she gave up and read the number off his screen and dialed it on her phone.

"Hi, Francyne, it's Jamie. Devon's friend." She cut a glance at the nurses' station, hoping no one heard her admit to not being his fiancée.

"I know who you are!" Francyne's voice boomed through the earpiece. "Where are you? I have a hot date tonight. At my age, that doesn't happen too often. It takes a long time to get ready. Will you be home soon?"

"That's why I called. There's been an accident. Devon's okay, but he has to spend the night in the hospital, and I need a ride home."

"Bless your heart! What the hell happened?"

"I'll explain when I see you. Can you come pick me up at the County Hospital?"

"I'm on my way."

38

True to her word, Francyne squealed to a stop outside the emergency-room doors a few minutes later. Relieved, Jamie ran out and jumped into the navy Jaguar convertible.

While Francyne navigated traffic, Jamie explained what happened.

"I knew that jerk was up to no good when he came by the office," Francyne muttered, switching lanes amid blaring horns.

"You saw Fred?"

"Um, did I say that?" The old woman's shoulders slumped. "I think I did, honey. He came by while I was watching the leasing office, asking if any pretty girls had rented an apartment lately. Other than the hair, his description fit you to a tee." Francyne glanced over at her. "I take it you're not a natural blonde."

"No. So you told him I lived there?" No wonder Fred had found her so easily.

"Hell, no! Besides the fact I could tell he was up to no good, it's against the rules to give out personal information about tenants. Besides that, it's tacky and wrong, just plain wrong."

Jamie settled back in the soft tan leather seat, the events of the day finally catching up with her. Her eyes drifted shut. The next moment, it seemed, Francyne was tapping her shoulder.

"Wake up. We're here." After they got out of the car, she said, "I put a sign on Dev's door that the office is closed until Monday, due to an emergency. But I'd sure appreciate it if you could dog-sit for me tonight. For Petunia and Killer. I shouldn't be out too late. I'll take them out before I leave. If you limit their liquids, they should be okay until I get home."

Jamie followed Francyne into her apartment, again struck by the difference in the units. It wasn't just the décor—the entire apartment seemed larger. Even the floor plan was different.

"I can't believe how different your apartment is from every other one I've seen," she mused while Francyne bustled around.

Francyne stopped and stared for a moment and then came and sat down next to Jamie on the camelback sofa. "I'm going to tell you something few people know about me." She lowered her voice, leaning close. "I was the architect who designed the complex. I must have been drunk or something when I drew up the plans." She shook her head, a sad look on her tanned face. "I made so many stupid errors. It ended my career. By the time we realized the problems, it was too late. I immediately was on everyone's blacklist. The original owners refused to pay me. Even threatened to sue. I ended up hiring a mad-dog lawyer." She grinned. "You know him. Shirl."

"Shut up! Shirl was a lawyer?"

Francyne nodded. "A damn fine one. He was very successful until his bloodsucking bitch of a wife got hold of him." She took a deep breath. "Anyway, he was able to negotiate for me. I was given part of the complex—my apartment—free and clear, for life. Since it wasn't completed yet, I was able to go back in and reconfigure it to whatever I wanted, at the builder's expense."

"Ah, so that's why you have the only fireplace in the complex." Everything made sense now.

Francyne walked over to the door where the dogs waited patiently and clipped a double lead to their collars. "Yeah, well, don't blab it around, okay? I don't want any sympathy."

"Why would people feel sorry for you? You're obviously doing okay. And you drive a Jag!"

Francyne smiled. "Yeah, my third husband was a dealer. As part of our settlement, I get a new one a year for life."

"That's a pretty great settlement."

"I was a pretty great wife." With that, she left with the dogs, the door clicked shut.

Francyne's ex-husband must have loved her very much to agree to such generous terms, Jamie reflected. Would anyone ever love her as much? She wondered why Francyne had divorced the car dealer.

Quiet surrounded her. She wondered how Devon was resting and if he was in pain. Damn Fred! She would sleep in her apartment tonight and hope Fred made another appearance. And if he did, she was going to have a serious talk with him. It was over. He could not and would not intimidate her anymore. Putting a serious hitch in her relationship with Devon or anyone else was one thing. Endangering Devon because of Fred's stupid, possessive jealousy was crossing the line.

She was mad as hell, and she wasn't going to take it anymore.

Francyne returned a few minutes later, rushing to get ready for her date.

"Jamie, answer the door, would you?" Francyne called from the back of the apartment when a knock sounded. "Tell him I'll be right out."

Dutifully Jamie eased from beneath a sleeping Petunia and Killer and made her way to the door. Her jaw dropped when she saw Francyne's date.

Shirl stood beneath the porchlight; the light reflected from his updo and the rhinestone-studded comb holding it together.

Easily six-foot-eight or better with his stilettos, he strolled past Jamie with a chuckle. "I can see by your face that Fran neglected to tell you who her date was. How you doing, doll?"

Francyne toddled into the room on, Jamie noticed, gold lamé heels that matched the ones worn by her date. She twirled, beaming, while Shirl let out a wolf whistle.

"For an old broad, you clean up good," he said in his distinctive gravelly voice. He looked at Jamie. "We're entering a dance contest at Drag Queen Alley, a bar down the beach."

Too stunned to speak, Jamie nodded.

"There's cold fried chicken in the fridge and sponge cake under the silver dome on the counter, if you get hungry. Also lots of beer and soda, chips and dip. The usual junk food. We won't be late." She paused by the door. "If it would make you feel better, you could call the hospital and see how Dev is doing."

"I don't know the number or what room he's in." If Francyne had a computer, she could go online and get the number, but she hadn't seen one.

"Just a sec," Francyne said to Shirl. She pulled a tiny cell phone from her purse and punched in some numbers. "Hi, this is Dr. Anderson," she said in a low voice. "I'm calling to check on a friend of my wife. Devon McCloud. I understand he was brought in this afternoon." She covered the phone with her hand and whispered, "I'm on hold."

"What are you doing?" Jamie hissed. Francyne was going to get them arrested. "You're not a doctor! Are you?"

"No, but my last husband, Richard, is. He still checks patients into the hospitals around here, so it's not unlikely they would know him and—yes, I'm here. Thank you so much. Yes, I'll relay the message. Good-bye." Her sequined bag swung when the phone dropped back inside. "He's doing great. The nurse said he ate a full dinner, no dietary restrictions, no need for any pain meds. And he's being dismissed at nine tomorrow morning. Want to ride along with me to pick him up?"

Relief swept through Jamie, bringing with it a new batch of tears. Choked up, she could only nod and then wave as Francyne and Shirl left.

By the time Francyne and Shirl got back, Jamie's eyes were itching out of their sockets, her nose totally stuffed and she couldn't stop coughing, all courtesy of Petunia. But the big dog was such a sweetie, it was worth it. She'd just pop an allergy pill and drink lots of water when she got home.

"Do you want to take Petunia or Killer home with you for protection tonight?" Francyne said, closing the door as Shirl left.

Jamie stood and stretched, scratching her neck. "No, I'll be okay. But thanks anyway. How'd the contest go?"

"Great! We won second place. The trophy is smaller than the grand-prize one, but it's still pretty impressive. Shirl's gonna display it in his store."

"Congratulations! I'll try to get down there soon to check it out. I'm glad you had fun."

After giving the older woman a hug good-bye, Jamie cautiously made her way across the deserted courtyard, surprised to find she missed the usual group by the fire pit.

"If I have one more horny woman proposition me, I'm gonna puke," Todd told Rick as they walked through the apartment parking lot. "How do Chris and Drew stand it, you think?" He scratched his chest. "And body waxing is hell."

"Women do it all the time," Rick reminded him. "Just part of the maintenance required to be beautiful." His grin flashed white in the darkness.

"Shut up. Way too much maintenance, if you ask me."

"Kind of gives you a whole new respect for the ladies you date, doesn't it?" Rick halted in the walk-through and motioned to the top of the stairs.

A man stood at Todd's door, clearly picking the lock.

Todd and Rick exchanged looks, drew their service revolvers and crept up the stairs.

Intent on his task, the man didn't notice their approach. The door swung inward. He slipped in, quietly closing it without a backward glance.

"Son of a bitch!" Todd looked back at Rick. "Was that Grant? What the hell does he think he's doing?" He stopped Rick's forward momentum with a hand on his chest. "Wait. What if Grant is somehow mixed up in this? What if he knows where Alexis is, or, worse, what if he's the one who kidnapped her?"

"I thought her boyfriend's name was Ron." Rick edged to the corner of the landing and looked in the window over the table. "I can't see him; he must be in the bedroom."

"We don't know Grant is his real name. For that matter, we don't know for sure Ron Davis was the real name of the asshole who took Al."

"Well," Rick whispered, easing the door open, "we do know one thing for sure. Grant, or whoever he is, is in your apartment. Under Texas law, we could shoot him."

In Todd's opinion, Rick looked way too pleased with that thought. "Hold your horses, Davy Crockett. If we kill him, we may never find Alexis."

"We could just wing him, just enough to inflict maximum pain, to get him to talk."

"Am I going to have to take your gun? I don't want my apartment all shot up. We're not going to shoot him. We're going to arrest him. Let him talk his way out of it at the station." He eased the door shut and motioned for Rick to back him up and then made his way to his bedroom.

Grant stood by Todd's desk, looking through old bills.

Creeping up behind him, Todd used the element of surprise, grabbing Grant with his forearm and pushing hard against his windpipe, gun between his shoulder blades.

"Whatcha lookin' for, asshole?" Todd ground out, emphasizing each word with a contraction of his arm against Grant's throat.

In a move Todd had only seen a few times, Grant twisted and dipped his knees, breaking Todd's grasp. But it didn't do much good. Before he moved more than a couple of feet, Rick was on him, slamming him through the frosted-glass French door and against the living room wall, his pistol at the base of Grant's skull.

"My partner asked you a question, asshole." He jammed the gun deeper into the flesh of Grant's neck. "I suggest you make no sudden moves and answer it."

"FBI," Grant said against the wall. "If you let me move my hand, I can show ID."

"Bullshit!" Rick shoved the gun higher. "Why would FBI be breaking into an apartment?"

"I wasn't breaking in. I have a warrant. Back left pocket."

"Don't move." Rick felt until he pulled out a wad of papers, then tossed them to Todd.

"ID?" Todd dropped the warrant on the desk.

"In my front right pocket."

Rick stuck his hand in and chuckled. "Glad to see me, are you, Grant?"

Grant growled. "It's a flashlight, you fool."

"He's who he says he is," Todd said a few seconds later. "Let him go. You have some explaining to do, Grant."

Devon was ready and waiting when Jamie and Francyne pulled up to the curb the following morning.

Jamie moved to the backseat so he could sit in front. "Are you sure you're all right?"

He twisted to look back at her and winced. "I'm fine. Don't worry. Any more Fred sightings?"

Jamie shook her head, blinking back tears. Fred was lucky

she hadn't seen him. She was still so angry she could strangle him.

Francyne dropped them off by Devon's apartment. "I'll leave you two alone. I need to go grocery shopping anyway. I told Shirl I'd fix dinner for him tonight. Need anything?"

"No, we're good." Devon watched her drive away and then turned a questioning gaze on Jamie. "Shirl? She's having Shirl over for dinner?"

"Don't ask." Jamie unlocked Devon's door and pulled him into the apartment.

Killer trotted up. "Lark!" Rising on his short back legs, he hopped in place, tongue lolling, slinging little droplets of doggy spit in his exuberance.

"Hey, big guy." Devon dropped to his knees to receive doggy kisses. "Did you miss me?"

"We all did," Jamie said quietly, blinking back more tears. "Devon," she choked out. "I'm so sorry this happened!"

"Shhh," he said, rising to pull her into his arms. "It wasn't your fault. Not any of it was your fault. Besides, I'm fine. Stop crying and give me a welcome-home kiss."

She sniffed and looked up into his smiling face, trying to ignore the dark circles remaining from his recent black eyes.

He lowered his mouth to hers, and her eyes drifted shut. It was exactly what she needed.

He deepened the kiss.

She shimmied closer, thrilled to feel the hard ridge already rising beneath his fly. He sure didn't kiss like someone just getting out of the hospital.

She pulled back, her palms cupping his face. "Are you sure it's okay?"

He bucked his hips, nudging her toward the couch. "It's more than all right. It's therapeutic."

"Really?" She grinned, stroking him through his shorts.

He nodded. "And if you help me get these clothes off, we can begin my first therapy session."

"Therapy session?" She tossed his shirt aside and tugged his shorts down.

"Oh, yeah. Welcome-home sex is a very important part of the process. Statistics show ninety-five percent of people who practice welcome-home sex have a faster recovery time."

"You're making that up."

"I guess I'll just have to prove it." He pulled her halter dress over her head and tossed it aside. Lifting her against his chest with his good arm, he feasted on her breasts.

Killer barked and jumped against his leg.

"Not now, dog. Hold it." He grumbled against her nipple and sighed and put her on the sofa. "Let me go lock the scene stealer in his time-out cage." He ran his index finger over her breast, down her abdomen. "Hold that thought."

After taking care of Killer, he returned to find Jamie right where he'd left her. Even better, she'd removed her panties. "I didn't have the heart to lock him up. I bribed him with food instead. In return for a bowlful of soggy doggy treats, he promised to ignore us."

"I missed you," she whispered and swiped a tear from her cheek. "I thought I'd lost you forever when I saw you lying on the sidewalk. I—"

"Shhh, shhh." He crawled onto the couch with her, scooting until they were belly to belly, his erection nestled against her moisture. "Don't cry." He kissed away the tears and then covered her mouth with his, putting everything he couldn't yet say into the kiss.

Beneath him, she shifted, spreading her legs, the smooth satin of her skin moving against his thighs, causing his breath to hitch.

He should stop and get a condom. He opened his eyes to tell

her to wait, but the tears clinging to her lashes like sparkly trapeze artists blocked his words. Next time. Next time they would use a condom.

He flexed his hips, thrusting deeply into her wet, welcoming heat.

Eyes now open, they stared at each other while he moved in and out of her in lazy, seductive strokes.

The heat in Devon's eyes touched her heart. If he didn't love her now, she would keep loving him until he changed his mind.

With a grunt, she pulled him closer, holding him tight while she increased the tempo.

A crash vibrated the walls.

Fred flicked the shards of broken glass from the window frame and stepped in.

39

"I knew you were cops," Grant concluded, his gaze moving from Todd to Rick and back, "but I had to be sure you weren't involved." He glanced over at the mess on the living room floor. "Sorry about the damage. The bureau will pick up the tab."

"I thought you feds always traveled in packs." Rick glanced around. "Where are your buddies?"

"They're around." Grant pointed to his watch. "If I press this red button, they will be on you like white on rice, before you could take a deep breath." He looked at Todd. "I know you're undercover, but I couldn't find anything about the investigation of your sister's disappearance in your file."

"That's because we're here on another case," Rick answered for Todd. "Fraud and possible prostitution. We're working on Alexis on our own time."

"Freeburger, one of my men, thinks he may have a lead. We'll know more tonight when he calls in." Grant held up a hand when Todd advanced on him. "Don't start on me again. I've already told you everything I know. We'll know more, hopefully, tonight."

"She's alive?" Todd squeezed his eyes shut and took a deep breath; then he opened them and pinned Grant with his best intimidating look.

"To our knowledge, yes. Again, I'm not holding out on you."

"Jamie," Devon said, tossing the throw over her and reaching for his pants, never taking his gaze off Fred, "call nine-one-one." He decided to bluff à la one of his favorite movie lines. "Tell them I shot and killed an intruder."

Instead of a look of terror, Fred rolled his eyes. "Nice try. You're naked. Obviously you're not hiding a gun."

Devon yanked up his shorts and put his hand in the pocket. "You don't know that for sure."

"Yes, I do." Fred sighed and held out his hands. "I just want to talk to Jamie. Then, if she still feels the same, we'll leave."

"The same?" Jamie knew she was shrieking, but how could one man be so dense? "Fred, not only do I not love you, I don't even like you! I never want to see you again. How much clearer do I have to make it?"

Fred hung his head and then wiped his eyes before turning a teary gaze on her. "But I love you. I miss you. I know I wasn't good to you, but all that can change."

"Get out. Now," Devon ground out, pointing to the door, one hand pushing on Fred's chest.

Jamie wrapped the throw around her, toga style, and straightened to look at Fred. "I don't want you. I don't love you. I don't need you. What else can I say?"

"But, baby, I've changed! I swear! I went to anger-management sessions after you left. I—"

"Yeah," Devon interrupted. "We can see how beneficial those were by my broken nose. Not to mention the brick you threw through Jamie's window. I'd get a refund, if I were you."

"Shut the fuck up!" Fred bellowed and then turned back to

Jamie, his voice softening. "Baby, please. If you still want to be with that asshole when I'm finished talking—"

"Who are you calling an asshole, asshole?" Devon spun Fred around and punched him.

Fred staggered back, clutching his nose.

Devon hissed a breath and shook his fist, hopping around. "Ow, ow, ow!"

"Damnit!" Fred stood straighter and advanced on them. "I'm trying to say something here, and you all keep interrupting and hitting me. Jamie, I'm a changed man. I'm so sorry for all the pain I caused you! If I could go back and change it, I would." Fists clenched, he advanced, backing Jamie against the sofa. "I know there's not much I can do to make you believe me, so I plan to—"

"Plans change, dipstick!" Francyne yelled as she charged through the front door. "Get him, Petunia!" Francyne promptly jumped on Fred's back, pummeling his head with her fists. Petunia grabbed the fabric of his pant leg and began growling and shaking him.

Killer ran into the room. "Grrr! Lark! Lark! Grrr!" He jumped, bounding off Fred's leg, and then jumped again.

Fred growled and said something, but it was lost amid the noise. He kicked out at Killer.

The little dog yelped and fell against the end table.

Jamie saw red. "You bully! You haven't changed one bit!" Nails poised, she attacked.

Stunned, Devon watched the fracas. Fred flopped around in a vain effort to get away but made no attempt to defend himself. For some insane reason, Devon almost felt sorry for him.

Wading into the fray, Devon pulled Jamie away and plopped her on the couch. "Stay! Let me handle this."

Next he grabbed Francyne around the waist and lifted her, kicking and screaming, off Fred's back.

"Killer! Sit!" Immediately his dog obeyed his command. "Francyne, tell your dog to let go." He wasn't about to touch the crazed rottweiler.

Francyne straightened her muumuu and glared at Devon before ordering, "Petunia! Release!"

The big dog immediately obeyed, sitting on its haunches, eyes trained on Fred, a low growl coming from her throat.

Fred eyed the dog uneasily and then wiped a tear from his eye. "Y'all are crazy."

"*We're* crazy!" Jamie jumped up from the couch, only to be gently shoved down again by Devon. "You're the one whose been stalking me."

Fred heaved a sigh. "I haven't been stalking you. Well, okay, maybe a little bit. But not for the reason you think. I told you, I'm in an anger-management program." He glanced at Devon. "Sorry about the window. I had a setback." He looked back at Jamie. "I've been trying to find you for months so I could apologize and try to make amends for the pain and misery I caused you and give back the stuff I took from you. It's part of my twelve-step program."

"But what about everything you did that can't be changed with an apology? You terrified and bullied me. You killed my cat!"

"That was an accident—"

"Then you chased me all over the country," she continued, "causing me to deplete what little money I had just to stay away from you." She advanced, causing Fred to take a step back. "And what about the spying and throwing the brick and leaving creepy yellow roses at my door and punching Devon? He could have been killed yesterday when he was chasing you!"

"Roses? What roses?" He shook his head and then shrugged. "I didn't say I was cured. It's an ongoing process. And seeing you two going at each other like rabbits didn't help the process, let me tell you." He smoothed his ripped pant leg and straightened. "I tried knocking on your apartment door to try to talk to you. Then I left the stuff I was returning at your door. Now, if you'll just tell me you can forgive and forget, I'll be on my way and not bother you again."

"I'll never forget," Jamie said and then sighed. "But I guess I can forgive you, if you promise to leave me alone from now on."

"I can live with that." He nodded at Francyne and Devon and backed toward the door while Petunia continued to growl. "Have a good life, Jamie."

"Well," Francyne said after the door closed, "if that don't beat all. And here we thought he was a nut job."

Feeling lower than a snake's armpits, Jamie picked up her clothes and headed for the bathroom. She'd panicked and just about ruined a man's life. How stupid. It was past time to pull up her big-girl panties and do the right thing. By the time she'd dressed and returned, Francyne and Petunia had gone.

"Hey," Devon said, standing when she walked into the living room.

"Hey." She stooped to pet Killer and compose herself.

"Jamie, I have something I need to tell you."

Was Devon going to tell her he loved her? And, if so, what would she do? After her confrontation with Fred, everything had changed. What she thought she knew proved not to be the case. What if the love she thought she felt for Devon turned out to be wrong as well? "What is it?"

"Fred didn't leave the yellow rose at your door." He swallowed and looked her in the eye. "I did." He held out his hands, palms up. "I was feeling romantic and thought it would be the romantic thing to do. Then, when you told me how Fred always did that and I saw how shook up you were, I was a coward and didn't tell you it was from me."

"Devon," she said when she stood. "I want to turn in my notice."

"What? Why? Because of the rose?" He walked to her, but she held out her hand, halting him.

"No, but I am disappointed that you didn't feel you could tell the truth. I've caused enough trouble." She gave a watery laugh. "My work here is done."

"But—"

"It's better this way. Trust me. Besides, now that I know Fred isn't skulking in the shadows, I can go back to Denver and possibly get my old teaching job back."

"We have schools right here in Texas that could use a good teacher."

No words of love from Devon. Not even a crumb of hope. Heart breaking, she shook her head.

"It's better this way," she said again. "I'll be gone by tomorrow morning. Good-bye, Devon."

40

"Are you crazy?" Francyne stalked from one end of Devon's kitchen to the other and took another bite of chocolate-chip cookie. "That girl is the best thing to ever happen to you, and you're just going to stand there like a ninny and let her walk out of your life?"

"What else can I do? If I tried to force the issue, I'd be as bad as Fred." He tossed the rest of his cookie into the trash. "I can't keep her here against her will."

"Have you even told her you love her, knucklehead?"

He blinked. "Well, not in so many words. But she should know by the way I act. Words aren't always necessary."

That earned him a whack in the head with the back of Francyne's hand.

"Bullshit!" Francyne stomped into the living room and tugged Petunia off the couch. "I'm going home. When you come to your senses, give me a call. I'll even loan you my lucky vibrator." She paused at the door and gave a sad smile. "And you'd better hope and pray it won't be too late."

* * *

After he cleaned the kitchen and walked Killer, Devon joined Rick and Todd in the courtyard.

"Hey, guys." He flopped into a chair and slumped down, feet sticking toward the cold fire pit. "Todd, aren't you working tonight?"

Rick and Todd looked at each other.

Todd raked a hand through his hair. "Yeah, about that. I guess it's time to fess up. I'm not really a stripper." At Devon's raised brow, he hurried on. "Oh, I really worked as one, but that's not really what I do for a living."

"And that would be . . . ?"

"I'm a cop. From Houston. So is Rick. On special assignment with the Surfside Police Department." He and Rick stood. "Just got word the bust went down without us."

"Does that mean you're both giving notice on your apartments?"

"Just Rick. I plan to make this home base for a while longer. It'll be a drive, but I can commute from Houston."

Jamie scrubbed at her face in an effort to bring her suitcase back into focus. She needed to end this pity party. Grow a backbone.

If Devon had lied to her about the rose, what else might he lie about? Was this what she got for trusting someone again?

Her shoulders slumped. Fresh tears welled. Despite the rose, she still trusted Devon. To be honest, she couldn't even blame him for not revealing he'd left the stupid rose. She'd acted like such a lunatic.

He'd be better off without her. She'd fallen in love with him and in the process almost ruined his life. Even though leaving was the last thing she wanted to do, it was the right thing.

She glanced around the little apartment she'd called home and realized it felt more like a real home than anywhere she'd lived for years.

Walking into the bathroom to check one more time, she stopped, staring at the now familiar face in the mirror.

She was running away. Again.

Fred had never been the real problem. In truth, she could handle the Freds of the world. The real problem was her inability to trust. Because she felt her judgment was flawed, she didn't trust herself, and that trickled down into an inability to trust anyone.

But she knew in her heart, she could trust Devon. Did trust him.

"Devon!" Francyne hurried across the courtyard. "Devon! Have you checked your messages?"

He frowned at her from where he stood with Rick and Todd.

"Not lately, why?"

"Well, I just checked them. There was a message from, well, I forget who, but he wants to buy your book! But I'm confused, he said he wanted to buy your cookbook. When did you write a cookbook?"

He blinked, too stunned to speak for a second. "I sent a proposal by e-mail, but I didn't think anything would happen. At least, not so soon. Are you sure that's what he said?"

"I wrote down the number. You can call him back tomorrow." She clasped her hands, a big smile on her leathery face. "This is so exciting! I—oh!"

The men turned to look at what had caught Francyne's attention.

Grant and a man in a dark suit walked across the courtyard; a tall, thin woman with shoulder-length blond hair and a definite limp walked between them.

Devon squinted. There was something familiar about the woman.

She shrieked and broke away, running toward Todd, who was also running in her direction.

Todd caught her in his arms, swinging her around while they both laughed and talked at the same time.

"I'll be damned," Francyne said softly, watching the display. "It's Alexis!" She tugged on Devon's arm. "Let's go find out what's going on."

"Okay. I didn't even realize Todd knew Alexis." He started across the courtyard but before he could take more than a step Francyne's hand on his shoulder halted his progress.

"I guess now would be a good time to tell you Todd is Alexis's brother." She shifted from foot to foot. "I'd have mentioned it sooner only I was sworn to secrecy."

"He just told me he was a cop." Devon shook his head. "How much more difficult would it have been to just add he and Alexis were brother and sister?"

"Well, that's part of why he was here. He was looking for Alexis in his spare time. I—"

"Hey, Aunt Francyne," Grant ambled up, leaving Alexis and Todd talking quietly by the firepit. "Devon."

"Aunt Francyne?" Devon struggled not to yell. "What else have you been keeping from me, Francyne? Any other relatives or spies I should know about?"

"Oh, stop acting like a drama queen! I couldn't tell you about Todd or Grant. You're a smart boy, if you think about it, you'll figure it out."

He turned to Grant. "Grant? Want to tell me what's going on?"

In response, Grant flipped open an official looking badge. "I've been here investigating the disappearance of Alexis Stewart." He nodded toward Alexis. "My partners and I have been following leads as well as keeping our eyes and ears open around here, the last known address for Ms. Stewart. Seems her brother was correct when he reported possible foul play involving Ms. Stewart and her estranged husband, Vincent Gregory. He held her just a few miles away, out by the fishing shanties. Our break came when one of the fishermen reported hearing screams. Gregory broke her leg when he abducted Ms. Stewart and has had her locked in a fruit cellar in an abandoned house for several months. She was tortured as well as being repeatedly beaten and molested. She'll more than likely have to have her leg surgically repaired."

"Oh, my Lord!" Francyne grasped her chest, her gaze shooting from Grant to Alexis and back. "That poor baby! Is she going to be okay?"

"Yes, Aunt Francyne, according to the doctor who checked her out, she'll recover. At least physically. Gregory wasn't as lucky. She was attempting an escape when our agents closed in. During the ensuing scuffle, Gregory was shot. He died at the scene."

Jamie had just closed her suitcase when a knock sounded. Hurrying to the door, she couldn't help but think about how differently she reacted to a knock now.

A bunch of brightly colored balloons greeted her when she opened the door. They were tied with purple ribbons. Her gaze followed the ribbons down to . . . a purple vibrator, light catching on its embedded sparkles.

A pair of long feet clad in brown leather flip-flops appeared next to the dildo.

On up was a pair of strong legs that disappeared into a pair of khaki cargo shorts. A Hawaiian-print shirt in tan, orange, purple and green completed the ensemble. But it was what she saw above it that took her breath away.

Devon stood looking at her, a smile she could only describe as hopeful on his face.

"Hi. I told Francyne you probably wouldn't be impressed by her lucky vibrator, but she insisted."

Heart expanding, Jamie blinked back tears. In response to his words, she pulled him into the apartment and closed the door. "I'm more impressed with the real thing," she said, pulling him down for a kiss that quickly escalated.

He severed the kiss, pulling back to look at her. "I hope you know I wouldn't share Francyne's wacky ideas with just anybody." He kissed her forehead, then bent to look in her eyes. "I love you."

Choking back tears, she could barely say the words. "I love you, too."

"What's not to love?" He grinned down at her. "Of course, I wouldn't object if you wanted to prove it."

With an answering grin, she tugged his shirt over his head while she backed him toward the bedroom.

Damn, he loved it when a woman—especially this woman—knew what she wanted.

Turn the page for a sizzling preview of
SIMPLY SEXUAL!

On sale from Aphrodisia!

1
_____

Southampton, England 1815

Sara pressed her fingers to her mouth to stop from gasping as she watched the man and woman writhe together on the tangled bedsheets. Daisy's plump thighs were locked around the hips of the man who pushed relentlessly inside her. The violent rhythm of his thrusts made the iron bedstead creak as Daisy moaned and cried out his name.

Sara knew she should move away from the half-opened door. But she couldn't take her gaze away from the frenzied activity on the bed. Her skin prickled, and her heart thumped hard against her breasts.

When Daisy screeched and convulsed as if she were suffering a fit, a small sound escaped Sara's lips. To her horror, the man on top of Daisy reared back as though he'd heard something. He turned his head, and his eyes locked with hers. Sara spun away, gathered her shawl around her shoulders, and stumbled back along the corridor. She had her hand on the landing door when footsteps behind her made her pause.

"Did you enjoy that?"

Lord Valentin Sokorvsky's amused voice halted Sara's hurried retreat. Reluctantly she turned to face him. He strolled toward her, tucking his white shirt into his unfastened breeches. His discarded coat, waistcoat, and cravat hung over his arm. A thin glow of perspiration covered his tanned skin, a testament to his recent exertions.

Sara drew herself up to her full height. "The question of enjoyment did not arise, my lord. I merely confirmed my suspicions that you are not a fit mate for my youngest sister."

Lord Valentin was close enough now for Sara to stare into his violet eyes. He was the most beautiful man she had ever seen. His body was as graceful as a Greek sculpture, and he moved like a trained dancer. Although she mistrusted him, she yearned to reach out and stroke his lush lower lip just to see if he was real. His hair was a rich chestnut brown, held back from his face with a black silk ribbon. An unfashionable style, but it suited him.

He arched one eyebrow. Every movement he made was so polished, she suspected he practiced each one in the mirror until he perfected it. His open-necked shirt revealed half a bronzed coin strung on a strand of leather and hinted at the thickness of the hair on his chest.

"Men have . . . needs, Miss Harrison. I'm sure your sister is aware of that."

As he moved closer, Sara tried to take shallow breaths. His citrus scent was underscored by another more powerful and elusive smell that she realized must be sex. She'd never imagined lovemaking had a particular scent. She'd always thought procreation would be a quiet orderly affair in the privacy of a marriage bed, not the primitive, noisy, exuberant mating she'd just witnessed.

"My sister is a lady, Lord Sokorvsky. What would she know of men's desires?"

"Enough to know that a man looks for heirs and obedience from his wife and pleasure from his mistress."

She felt a rush of anger on her sister's behalf. "Perhaps she deserves more. Personally, I cannot think of anything worse than being trapped in a marriage like that."

His extraordinary eyes sparked with interest as he appeared to notice her nightclothes and bare feet for the first time. Sara edged back toward the door. He angled his body to block her exit.

"Is that why you frequent the servants' wing in the dead of night? Have you decided to risk all for the love of a common man?"

Sara blushed and clutched her shawl tightly to her breasts. "I came to see if what my maid told me was true."

"Ah." He glanced back down the corridor. "Daisy is your maid?" He swept her an elegant bow. "Consider me well and truly compromised. What do you intend to do? Insist I marry her? Go and tell tales to your father?"

She glared at him. How could she tell her father that the man he regarded as a protégé was a licentious rake? And then there was the matter of Lord Sokorvsky's immense wealth. Her father's seafaring enterprises had not faired well in recent years.

She licked her lips. His interested gaze followed the movement of her tongue. "My father thinks very highly of you. He was delighted when you offered to marry one of his daughters."

He leaned his shoulder against the wall and considered her, his expression serious. "I owe your father my life. I would marry all three of you if such a thing were allowed in this country."

"Fortunately for you, it is not," Sara snapped. His face resumed the lazy, taunting expression she had come to dread. "As to my purpose, I thought to appeal to your better nature. I wanted to ask you not to dishonor my sister by taking a mistress after you wed and to remain true to your vows."

He stared at her for a long moment and then began to laugh. "You expect me to remain faithful to your sister forever?" His eyes darkened to reveal a hint of steel. "In return for what?"

"I won't tell my father about your dishonorable behavior tonight. He would be so disappointed in you."

His smile disappeared. He stepped so close his booted feet nudged Sara's bare toes. "That's blackmail. And there's no way in hell you would ever know whether I kept my word or not."

Sara managed a small triumphant smile. "You do not keep your promises then? You are a man without honor?"

He put his fingers under her chin and jerked her head up to meet his gaze. She found it difficult to breathe as she gazed into his amazing eyes. Why hadn't she realized that beneath his exquisite exterior lay a deadly iron will?

"I can assure you, I keep my promises."

Sara found her voice. "Charlotte is only seventeen. She knows little of the world. I am only trying to protect her."

He released her chin and slid his fingers down the side of her throat to her shoulder. To her relief, his air of contained violence dissipated.

"Why didn't your parents put you forward to marry me? You are the oldest, are you not?"

She glanced pointedly at his hand, which still rested on her shoulder. "I'm twenty-six. I had my chance to catch a husband. I had a Season in London and failed to capitalize on it."

He curled a lock of her black hair around his finger. She shivered. His rapt expression intensified.

"Charlotte is the most beautiful and biddable of my sisters. She deserves a chance to become a rich man's wife."

His soft laugh startled her, and his warm breath fanned her neck. "Like me, you mean?"

Sara stared boldly into his eyes. "Yes, although . . ." She

frowned, distracted by his nearness. "Emily might be a better match for you. She is more impressed by wealth and status than Charlotte."

"You possess something neither of your sisters has."

Sara bit her lip. "You don't need to remind me. Apparently I am impulsive and too direct for most men's taste."

He tugged lightly on the curl of her hair. "Not all men. I have been known to admire a woman with drive and determination."

She lifted her gaze and met his eyes. Something urgent sparked between them. She fought a desire to lean closer and rub her cheek against his muscular chest. "I think I will make a far better spinster aunt than a wife. At least I will be able to be myself."

His lazy smile was as intimate as a caress. "But what about the joys of the marriage bed? Might you regret not sampling those?"

She gave a disdainful sniff. "If what I have just seen is an example of those 'joys,' perhaps I am well rid of them."

His fingers tightened in her hair. "You didn't enjoy watching me fuck your maid?"

Sara gaped at him.

His smile widened. He extended his index finger and gently closed her mouth. "Not only are you a prude, Miss Harrison, but you are also a liar."

Heat flooded her cheeks. Sara wanted to cross her arms over her breasts. She trembled when he stepped back and studied her.

"Your skin is flushed, and I can see your nipples through your nightgown. If I slid my hand between your legs, I wager you'd be wet and ready for me."

Sara's fingers twitched in an instinctive impulse to slap his handsome face. She waited for a rush of anger to fuel her courage, but nothing happened. Only a strange sense of waiting, of tension, of need—as if her body knew something her mind hadn't yet understood. She let him look at her, tempted to take his hand and press it to her breast. Somehow she knew he would assuage the pulsing ache that flooded her senses.

As if he'd read her thoughts, he reached out and circled the tight bud of her nipple. Sara closed her eyes as a pang of need shot straight to her womb.

"Sara. . . ."

His low voice broke the spell. She covered herself with her shawl and backed away. As soon as she managed to wrench the door open, she ran. His laughter pursued her down the stairwell.

Valentin stared after Sara Harrison as his shaft thickened and grew against his unbuttoned breeches. He absentmindedly set himself to rights and considered her reaction to him. She needed a man inside her whether she realized it or not. Perhaps he should reconsider his plan to marry the young and oh-so-biddable Charlotte.

His smile faded as he followed Sara down the stairs. John Harrison had a special bond with his eldest daughter. Knowing Valentin's sordid history, would John allow him to marry his favorite child? It was interesting that she hadn't been offered to him as a potential bride to begin with.

He strolled down one flight of stairs and made his way back along the darkened corridor to his bedroom. There was no sign of Sara.

Valentin surveyed his empty bed and imagined Sara lying naked in the center, her long black hair spread on the pillows, her arms open wide to welcome him. He frowned as his cock throbbed with need. Sara Harrison would not be a complacent wife. To lay the ghosts of his past, he needed to settle down with a conventional woman who would present him with children and leave him to his own devices.

Before leaving town, he'd spent an uproarious evening with his friends and current mistress, composing a list of the qualities a man required in a society wife. One of her sisters would definitely be a better choice. He suspected Sara would be a challenge.

Her frank curiosity stirred his senses. He'd wanted to part her lips and take her mouth to see how she tasted. He'd forgotten how erotic a first kiss could be, having moved onto more interesting territory a long time ago. Her innocence and underlying sensuality deserved to be explored. Wasn't that what he truly craved?

He stripped off his clothes and let them drop to the floor. The meager fire had gone out, and coldness crept through the ill-fitting windows and door. At least he had a few days' grace before he needed to make his decision. John Harrison was not due to return to his family until Friday night. Valentin climbed into bed. His brief, interrupted tryst with the enthusiastic Daisy had done little to slake his desire.

Valentin tried to ignore the unpleasant smell of damp and mildewed sheets as he closed his fist around his erection and stroked himself toward a climax. Imagining it was Sara who touched him made him want to come quickly. He didn't allow her image to destroy the sensual buildup of sexual anticipation that burned through his aroused body.

He pictured her startled face as she'd watched him fuck Daisy. Had she wanted to touch him herself? The thought made him shudder. His body jerked as he climaxed. He closed his eyes, and a vision of Sara's passionate face flooded his senses.

His last thought as sleep claimed him was of her coming under him as he took his release deep inside her again and again.